THEY EAT THEIR OWN

Praise for *They Eat Their Own: A Thung Toh Jig 2*

"Complex card game rules fold in naturally amid ominous gifts, mysterious conspiracies, and carefully placed reminders of the unresolved problems from the first book. ...a well developed, satisfying, character-driven story... Fans of elaborate worldbuilding will be swept up by the combination of heist action and games of chance..."

— ***BookLife***

"This series continues to surprise me. ...The book is filled with non-stop action, and a lot of suspense. There is even a romance angle which I actually like. (Don't remember that happening in quite some time). I think it is because the love between Sylandair and Aliara seems real. ...an intriguing plot, vivid imagery, complex characters, and excellent writing combine to give the reader an entertaining read."

— ***Kat Dietrich, Kat Loves Books Blog***

"The world building is such a strength of this series. Dockhaven, in my opinion, is one of the best settings in fantasy/sci-fi, on par with the great ones such as Lankhmar, Ankh-Morpork and Sanctuary. It is so well described, you can practically smell the sea salt and feel the wind blowing the stink from the slums. The dichotomy of high tech and low fantasy really shines through, and creates such a unique setting."

— ***Steve Caldwell, The Bookwyrm Speaks***

"This novel continues to deliver complex characters, but its true strength lies in the world-building. Readers are presented with a world that manages to feel both familiar and alien. You will never feel displaced in Dockhaven; rather you'll find yourself consistently intrigued to learn more about its inhabitants."

— ***Sam Cooke, Bookstagrammer @ReadNext***

Praise for *Things They Buried: A Thung Toh Jig 1*

Named to *Kirkus Reviews'* Best Books of 2019
Imadjinn Award Winner Best Fantasy Novel, Imaginarium 2020
Independent Book Publishers Award Gold Medalist, Fantasy
New Apple Literary Official Selection, Action/Adventure
Kindle Book Review Finalist, Sci-Fi/Fantasy

◯ ◯ ◯

"The worldbuilding is nearly flawless in its execution, which will entice readers to immerse themselves in the story and acclimate themselves to its strangeness as they go. … The intriguing plot makes excellent use of its primary characters, resulting in a breathtaking, harmonious read... An empathetic, complex, and offbeat tale."

—*Kirkus Reviews* (starred review)

"Readers who appreciate dense worldbuilding will be gratified by the complexity of King and Swanson's work... The creepy threats and fierce fights in this densely imagined novel will gratify fans of dark fantasy, especially those who want real depth in between thrills."

—*BookLife*

"This is how you write a dark fantasy world! This is how you deliver diverse and complex characters to your readers. This novel was excellent and a breath of fresh air."

—*Sam Cooke, Bookstagrammer @ReadNext*

"*Things They Buried* is one of those books that combines creative world building with fantastically drawn out characters.... sci-fi and steampunk elements intermixed with the lowest of fantasy elements in such a way they just fit, even when they shouldn't. It is definitely up there with some of the great fantasy settings."

—*Steve Caldwell, The Bookwyrm Speaks*

Novels by King & Swanson

Things They Buried: A Thung Toh Jig 1

They Eat Their Own: A Thung Toh Jig 2

A Good Thief: A Thung Toh Jig Prequel

THEY EAT THEIR OWN

a Thung Toh jig

AMANDA K. KING
&
MICHAEL R. SWANSON

ISBN 978-1-7335783-2-5 (paperback edition)
Library of Congress Control Number: 2020936534

Edited by Glen Hollow, Ink.
Cover design by Amanda K. King with Euan Monaghan
Cover painting, *Bettel Hand,* by Michael B. Fee
All photographs by Michael R. Swanson, unless otherwise credited

Printed and bound in the United States of America
First printing May 19, 2020

Published by Ismae Books
contact@ismae.com
Indianapolis, IN 46219

ismae.com

For Josh Dalton,
who never had the chance.

Ismae: The Known World

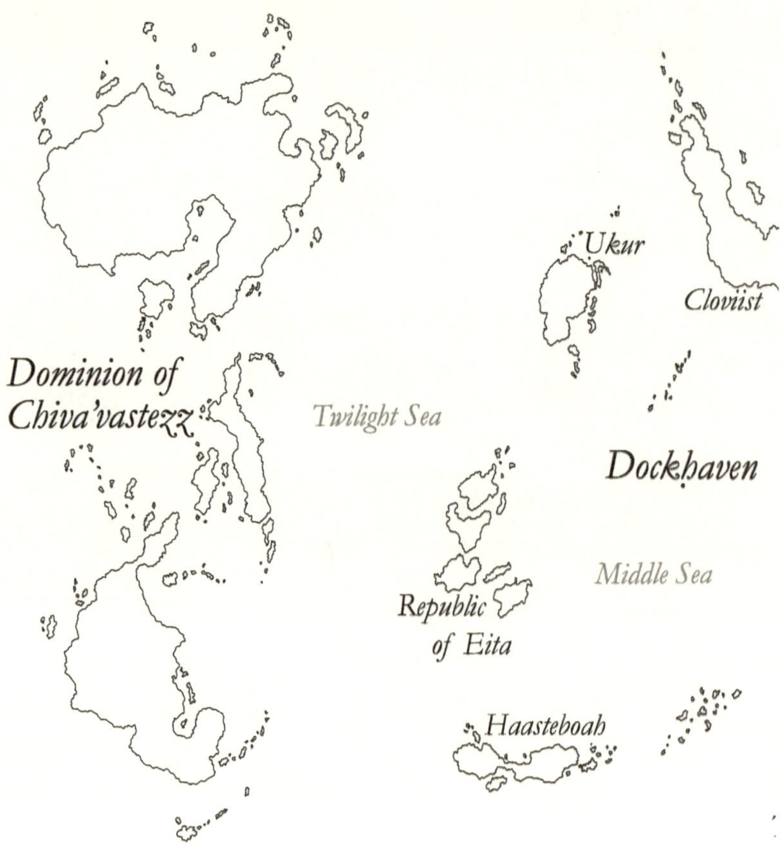

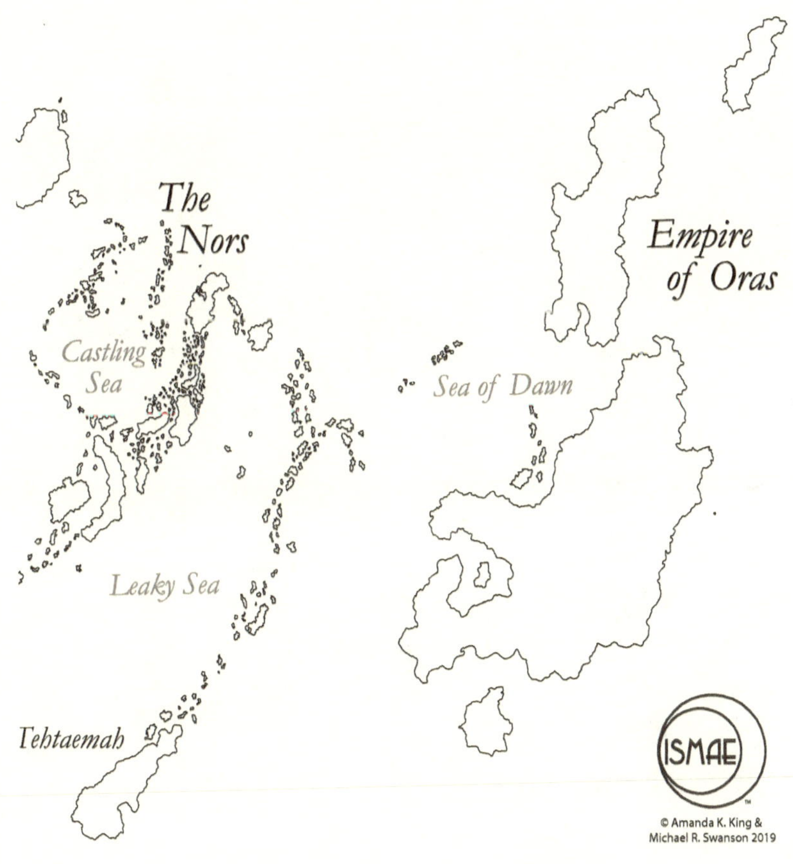

The
Nors
Empire
of Oras
Castling
Sea
Sea of Dawn
Leaky Sea
Tehtaemah
ISMAE
© Amanda K. King &
Michael R. Swanson 2019

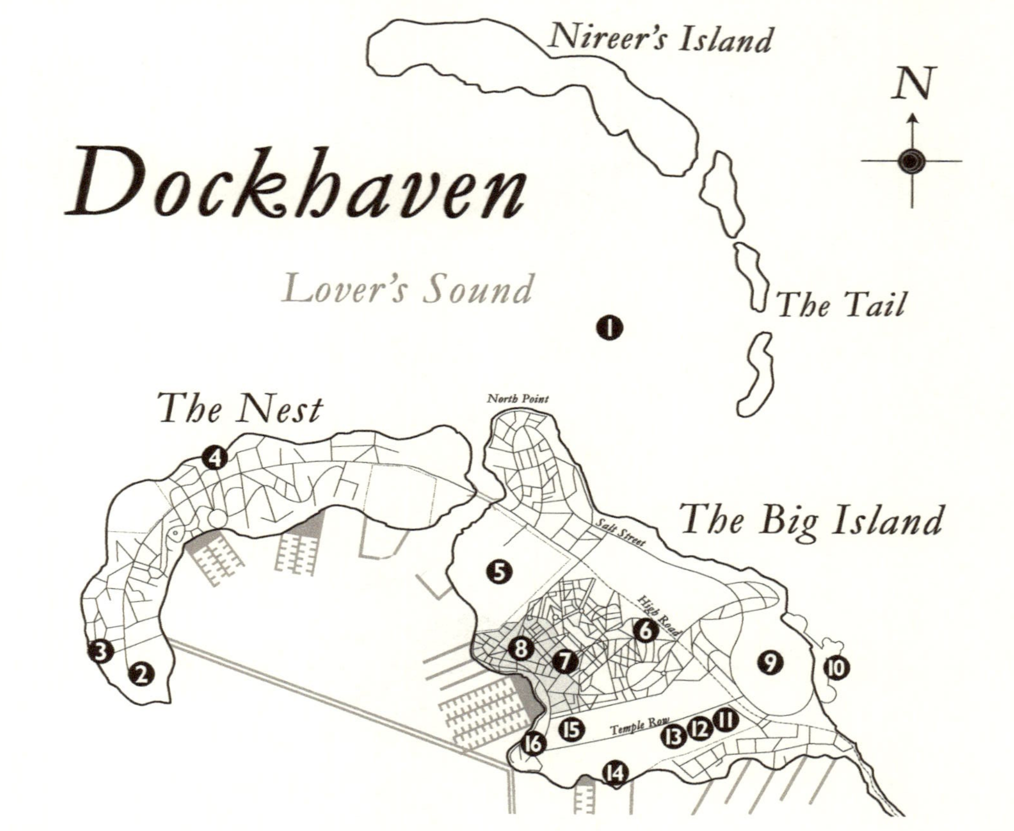

Dockhaven
Nireer's Island
The Tail
N
Lover's Sound
The Nest
North Point
The Big Island
Salt Street
High Road
Temple Row

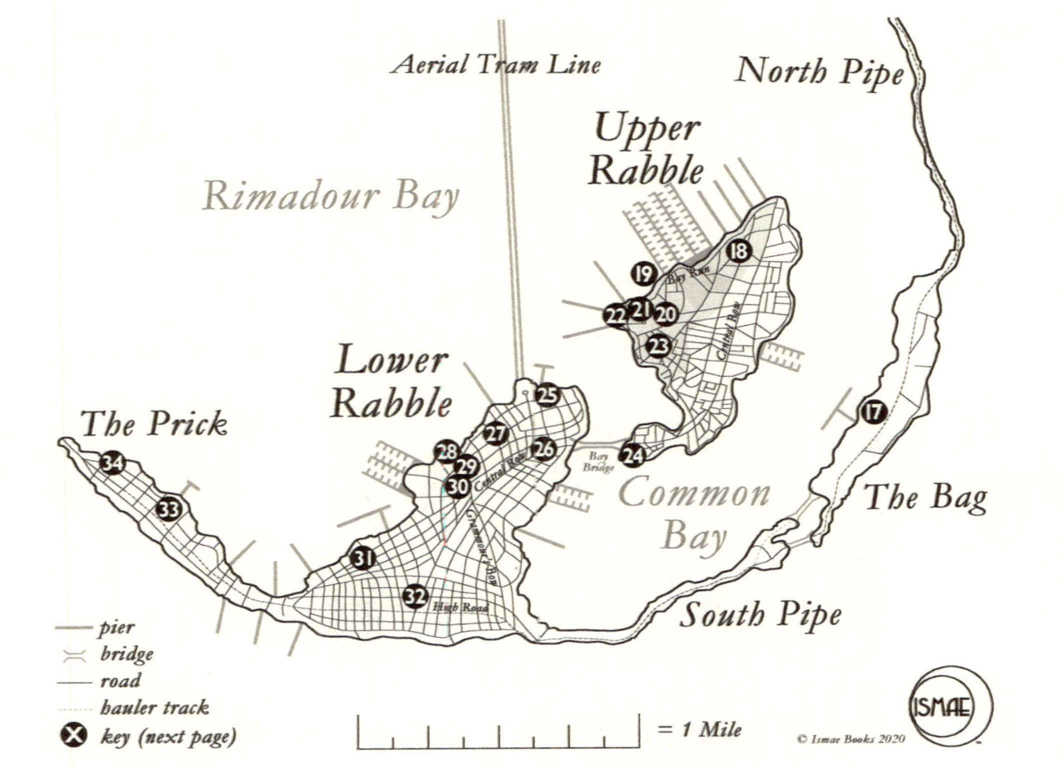

Aerial Tram Line
North Pipe
Upper Rabble
Rimadour Bay
Bay Row
Central Row
Lower Rabble
The Prick
Central Row
Bay Bridge
Grammour's Bow
The Bag
Common Bay
Herb Road
South Pipe
pier
bridge
road
hauler track
key (next page)
= 1 Mile
ISMAE
© Ismae Books 2020

Dockhaven Map Key

1. The *Ipesia*
2. Rimadour Park/City Hall
3. Carsuure estate
4. Dobencourt estate
5. Bank of Dockhaven
6. Abog Union
7. The Critter Pit
8. Wharf market
9. Desalinization plant
10. The Promenade
11. Imythedralin Estate (formerly Orono Estate)
12. Mucha Hall
13. Estoan Lodge
14. Our Lady of Artfulness
15. Seers of Dream & Waking
16. Caba Club
17. City Corps' jail
18. Slaughteryards
19. The Runoff
20. Fohmsquah's building
21. Yinago Tower
22. Bung Building
23. Pukatown
24. Domestic Consignment
25. The Bitter Barnacle
26. Order of Omatha
27. Mardo's
28. The Heap
29. Yartair's Food Counter
30. Belvedor Inn
31. Pinchknuckle Bakery
32. The Triangle
33. Spriggan Temple
34. Thung Toh contract house

The Calendar

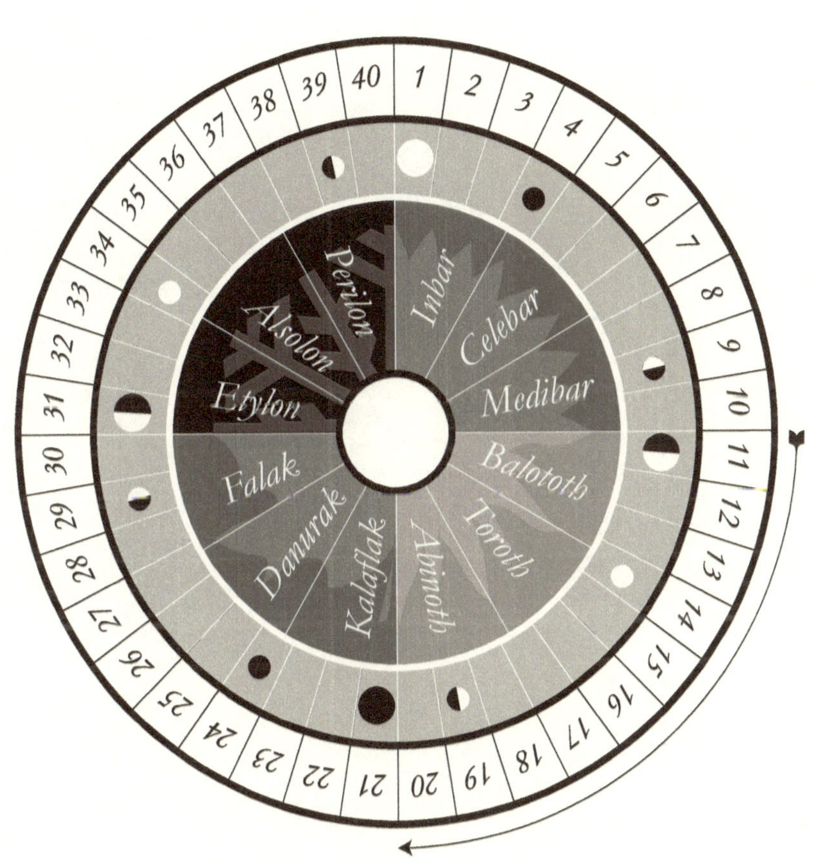

PROLOGUE: **VINDYL**

2085 PERILON 29

"I hope they resist." Baaraja opened her mouth, tongue touching the roof, and dropped in a tablet of akka, powdery pink. Like creeping frost on a window, her rosy lips faded to sickly green as the drug dissolved. "I've got an itch."

Vindyl snorted. It had been more than a quartern since the raid on the freighter *Fayrill*. That vessel had offered the boarding party no resistance, and now the *Nimomyne's* escort had fallen with only one shell; no relief for Baaraja's itch.

The sea slapped lightly at the bow of the launch as Fatrick eased them toward their quarry, his sun-ruddied mitt on the throttle ready to bring the impeller drive to full when Vindyl gave the cue.

Like Baaraja, the rest of the squad was itchy, ready for a bit of violence and some silver in their purses. They were a good group who'd follow her orders without hesitation—despite the series of feck raids the Harir had handed Captain Bikhark.

For nearly two days now, their ship, the *Twilight's Blight,* had been anchored a few miles beyond the horizon from Dockhaven waiting for their next target, the *Nimomyne,* putting them dangerously close to one of the Middle Sea's busiest shipping lanes. The location made Vindyl twitchy. Though they'd handily taken the *Fayrill* in these waters, she didn't like fishing with the same net twice.

When the spotter ship's farspeaker had reported their target a half-day out, Bikhark had sent a detachment to adjust the warning buoys used to guide vessels through the narrow channel of Dockhaven's southern barrier reef. No land could be seen in this stretch of sea. Excepting those buoys, all navigation was compass and stars. The *Nimomyne* would sail into their captain's snare just as the *Fayrill* had. The target's navigator would notice the disparity, but not before the cargo ship was trapped, notoriously treacherous reef before them, menacing raider ship behind.

When the *Blight*'s lookout reported the *Nimomyne* inbound, Bikhark had moved them close to a fork in the spread of buoys and gave the order to raise the yawl and scimitar. He intended to intimidate, to herd their target into the altered course through the reef, and the *Nimomyne*'s captain did not disappoint, veering east upon spotting the raider ship. The *Blight* pursued. The *Nimomyne* picked up speed. Bikhark called for the *Blight* to heave to, allowing the *Nimomyne*'s crew a moment of reprieve, certain they'd outrun a Yenderot raider ship, before their keel cut into the reef's first ridge.

"They're caught now!" Baaraja shouted as the *Nimomyne* dragged across the coral.

Vindyl waved the signal flag and braced as the launch lurched to full speed.

From behind, the clatter of the *Blight*'s guns being brought round carried across the waves, muted but not lost.

"Prepare to be boarded," Bikhark called through the loudhailer, his baritone made meager by the tin. "Resistance will be met with lethal force."

The *Nimomyne* came to rest canted to port, its starboard side splashed playfully by foam-tipped waves well below the waterline.

With a *crack* and whine, a shell from the *Blight*'s long nine cut the air above the launch, terminating with a sharp *clang* as it ripped a hole high in the stack of their target's fore aspirator sail. Bikhark expressing his earnestness.

The bright contrast of the reef line came into view just before

Fatrick cut the drive, letting their momentum carry them the final distance.

"Guns out and ready," Vindyl told her squad, and for a moment, the boat was filled with the soft *ba-rum* of mag-weapons powering up.

When the launch bumped quietly against *Nimomyne*'s freeboard, Marit lashed it to the pilot ladder.

"My turn." Baaraja grinned, revealing her drug-greened gums, and stood with the practiced grace of one accustomed to balancing against the sea's roll. As the squad's second-in-command, she held the unenviable position of first boarding.

Baaraja jerked a steel helmet over her web of long braids, *hupped* three times—the squad answered in kind—and scaled the freeboard ladder while Fatrik kept his rifle trained on the *Nimomyne*'s rail. She paused just below the gunnel and lobbed over a stunner that went off like a ball of lightning. She followed it by a moment and hollered, "Clear!"

The rest of the squad scrambled up behind her, leaving only Vindyl and Fatrick in the launch.

After a surprisingly short time, someone started yelling. "You Yenderot know that this is a Marthoth Air & Sea vessel! This is in violation of our agreement!"

Vindyl tugged on her Ebb Weave cap, checked her weapons, and climbed the ladder. As boarding commander, recalcitrant captains were hers to handle. She climbed aboard the dull freighter, its rust-streaked bulk painted grey, Marthoth's red logo wrapped around the aft aspirator sail. Nondescript crates and equipment were lashed to the deck. The air smelled faintly of ozone and piss.

Big or small, the stunner had knocked the crew on their asses. Faces flush with winter chill, a half-dozen karju and twice as many of their diminutive puka crewmates were sprawled about this section of deck. The group appeared to have been standing in rows until the burst went off, some dropping where they stood, others in mid-dash. All were now either unconscious or visibly dazed, groaning and weeping as Vindyl's squad checked for weapons before anyone made it to their feet.

Near the open door of the bridge castle, a tight-faced chivori woman in red-and-grey overalls—assumedly the ship's captain—was wagging a finger in Baaraja's face. The raider laughed at the effort, her karju bulk eclipsing the yapping slip of a chivori. The captain was either stupid or far too confident in the Yenderot's unwritten agreement with Marthoth.

"Bring your captain over here and my farspeaker will contact Mister Marthoth." The *Nimomyne*'s captain shoved an aging puka forward. "Or my farspeaker can contact your leader—what is it you call him?"

"Harir," Vindyl answered, walking up on the pair.

The woman spun, finger still wagging like an irritated schoolteacher's. "Yes, you can tell your Harir to—"

"Shut her up," Vindyl told her second.

Baaraja shoved the admonishing finger in her mouth and snapped her teeth closed, slicing smartly through the chivori's grey flesh. She'd probably hit bone. The captain shrieked, a sound so piercing it could have alerted ships miles away if the wind had been right.

"You're the captain?" Vindyl asked when the screaming tapered off into gulping moans.

The woman tugged tentatively to free her finger. Baaraja held tight.

"Are you the captain?" Vindyl asked slowly, her voice dark.

"Y-y-yes."

At Vindyl's nod, Baaraja pushed the mangled finger free with her tongue. Blue-black gore smeared her akka-greened lips and dribbled down her chin.

The captain slumped to the deck, finger extended before her like a repulsive insect. "What are you fecks waiting for?" she screeched at the sky, tears spilling from her long eyes. "Get out here before this crazy quim eats any more of me!"

The words made no sense.

Then Vindyl realized the trap.

Behind Baaraja, a hooded figure emerged from the doorway, boarding gun shouldered.

Baaraja laughed on, unaware.

Vindyl watched the moment play out in the slow smoothness of underwater movement. "Get down!" she yelled.

Baaraja's expression went quizzical. She turned, saw her opponent, and raised her pistol. Little more than an arm's length away, the hooded figure fired. Scatter shot sprayed Baaraja, blowing through her head, little dimples bursting from the back of her steel helmet. Baaraja crumpled.

Marthoth had hired a protection detail. This was the price to be paid for the Harir's arrogance.

From behind Vindyl, Marit yelled, "Eyes to fore!" The crack of his pistol followed.

Vindyl fired her scatter gun on the hooded karju who'd ended Baaraja. He went down, blood gushing from the side of his neck. A second mercenary took aim and fired as he exited the bridge castle. Vindyl sidestepped, catching a few pellets in her arm. She dropped her spent gun. Knife in his offhand, the merc closed fast. No time to draw her own blade. Vindyl swung, her fist popping him in the temple. He wobbled, eyes rolling, arms drooping. Vindyl caught the sagging man, pivoted, and tossed him overboard. Before he struck water, bright pain burst in Vindyl's haunch. She'd been stabbed.

Vindyl spun—the ache in her ass ignored—and wrenched the knife from her attacker's hand. A lithe chivori woman with purple hair glared at her, metal glinting on her raised fists. She swung awkwardly upward, aiming for Vindyl's chin. Vindyl leaned back, the mercenary's knuckle-dusters barely brushing her ribs, and kneed the woman in the gut. Air whoofed out, and the chivori stumbled but kept her feet. Tougher than expected. Vindyl drew the knife from her haunch as she closed. The chivori raised a hand to block. Vindyl drove the blade down, through the merc's palm, pushing until it was buried in the woman's throat.

When she shoved the body away to scan for her next adversary, Vindyl found the skirmish had ended almost as quickly as it had begun. Her squad had either killed or were busy killing the rest of the mercenaries—eight including the one she'd thrown overboard, each one wearing a baldric buckle that marked them as Abog Union. Marthoth would double, probably triple that number on his next ship making the run from Tehtaemah.

She saw one of her men with his guts spilled laying among the dead. Vindyl bit back the order to execute the *Nimomyne*'s crew immediately. She still needed them to find what she came for.

"Marit," she called, "you're my new second."

The rangy old chivori nodded.

"How many of ours are down?"

"Two wounded, three dead, counting Baaraja." His reply trailed into a grumble.

Baaraja would be missed. She'd been a good compa to most of the *Blight*'s crew for quite a few cruises. Vindyl would sort out her own feelings about the loss later in her bunk.

"Now…Captain." Vindyl limped over to where the bitten woman cringed, wounded hand cradled in her lap. She hoisted the aging chivori by the collar, dangling her with toes barely touching the deck. Lips to the lower lug of the captain's ear, Vindyl whispered, "If you have any other surprises prepared, you best tell me now or I'll add your blood to the mix."

Unable to produce coherent words, the Captain shook her head.

"Right," Vindyl said. "Me and my compas—the ones your Abog gang didn't leave on the deck—are going to take a look around this manky vessel of yours. If we see something we like, we're scaling it. Understood?"

"The—" The captain breathed in short gasps. "The cargo's all industrial…nothing but building materials."

Vindyl chuckled. "Oh, we know about the cargo."

"I-I-I don't understand…" The words tapered off into hysterical gibbering.

Vindyl dropped the woman before she passed out or pissed herself and addressed her second. "You know what comes next?" she asked.

"Send a pair to make sure the ship is clear," Marit said, "the rest round up crew, then we pick the boodle."

"Move fast. These whinging gobies wasted our time. The others will have reset the buoys and have a crew ready to offload the loot before we've searched a single hold." Vindyl pointed to a slice across Marit's forearm. "And wrap something around that. I don't need you bleeding out."

She turned to the *Nimomyne*'s dazed crew and let her gaze roll slowly over them. "Which one of you is the cargomaster?"

No one spoke.

Vindyl strode up to the biggest one, a karju with a pot belly and a chinstrap of a beard, and pressed the bloody knife into the soft flesh beneath his chin. "Is it you?"

"Cargomaster's dead," he whispered and pointed to the body of a woman with a fist-sized hole in her chest.

With the tiniest pop, the tip of the blade punctured his flesh. The man made a terrible face and whined like a rutting cat.

"Who can take me to the owner's hold then?" Vindyl asked, voice raised. Blood trickled over her hand.

"I can show you," said a nasal voice down the line. A peat-green puka stepped forward, middle-aged for her species and showing every moment.

Vindyl returned to the whimpering karju. "Is this true?"

"Y-yes," he said, attempting to speak without driving the blade deeper.

Vindyl withdrew the knife and followed the puka down into a hold filled with massive ceramic building components stacked inside one another like bowls in a pantry and enormous panes of thick glass piled high and strapped to the hull. At the far end was a bulkhead decorated with lewd scenes painted by bored sailors. At karju-height hung a hygrometer, its dial the size of Vindyl's face.

"Lift me up," the puka said.

Vindyl tapped the blade against her thigh dubiously, wary of another ruse.

"I need to reach that." The puka stood on tiptoe and swiped vainly at the hygrometer.

"Why?"

"I need to pull the trigger. It's in an opening behind the casing." She put hands on hips and frowned. "Or *you* can reach into the mystery hole and see if anything bites."

A stashed weapon was more likely than a door trigger. Vindyl moved the device to one side. A dark opening loomed behind. Eyes narrowed, she studied the puka, who crossed her arms.

"Is this gonna slice my hand off?" Vindyl asked.

"*Pfft.* Let me do it if you're too scared," the puka said.

Vindyl reached wrist-deep into the darkness. At the back was a handle. She pulled, yanking her hand free at the end of its travel. Gears creaked and a large section of the bulkhead popped back.

With a grunt of effort, the puka slid the panel to one side and pointed. "Is this what you're after?"

Inside were two crates large enough to require a pair of rhochrots with a pallet jack to haul. Both bore the Marthoth Air & Sea logo and Tehtaemah inspection stamps. One also sported a Dockhaven inspection stamp; curious since the package hadn't yet arrived in that city.

"Open this one," she told the puka, pointing to the crate with the Dockhaven stamp.

"Tritic. My name is Tritic."

"Fine. Open it, Tritic."

"I need to use a prisebar." She rubbed at the fin of a nose that sprouted from the top of her skull, where a hairline should be. "Can I get one or will you…?"

"You can grab one but," Vindyl crouched, eye-to-eye with the puka, "you use it for anything other than opening crates, I'll slit your throat and leave you in this hole to die staring at all this dross."

The puka scampered to a nearby locker, returning with two bars, and offered one to Vindyl. While she pried free the lower nails, Vindyl popped the uppers. Inside they found dozens of smaller crates and boxes, the largest as big as a karju's torso, the smallest the size of Vindyl's palm.

"You know what's in these?" Vindyl asked.

The puka spent a moment scanning the contents. "I don't see any packing lists."

Vindyl's nostrils flared. She was beginning to wish she'd dragged chinstrap down here instead. She grabbed a tall, narrow crate and worked it open. Inside was a painting of a rock formation set against a desert sunset. The work was nice enough, but not what she was after.

Someone on deck fired a pistol. The puka yipped. A few people screamed, a few others cheered. Marit was doing fine as second.

"Get busy." Vindyl opened a square crate of various geegaws. She retrieved a delicate bronze bowl, studying the four-legged creatures running circles around its belly. Though she recognized the style of markings from the *Blight*'s stopovers in Reilemynia, this wasn't what the Harir expected.

"Any crate smaller than this," Vindyl demonstrated the dimensions with her hands, "move out into the main hold."

The puka nodded and sorted parcels while Vindyl picked through the rest.

The intermittent shots from the deck continued.

"I'm gonna die here, aren't I?" The puka stood in the main hold, staring blankly at her collection of sorted crates. "You'll kill me if I stay here. They'll kill me if I go up."

Another shot from above. The puka cringed.

"Yep," Vindyl said.

The puka produced an almost musical string of curses.

Vindyl chuckled. She tossed a beaded belt back into the crate and started on another's lid.

Tritic yelped at the next shot. "I have an awful husband and six awful children," she said.

"Keep sorting."

"Well, five awful ones and one my husband hasn't ruined yet." Her voice caught and Vindyl could almost hear the tears falling. "I guess now he'll have his chance."

Vindyl fished a bare-chested, four-legged icon from a crate and tossed it back.

"I always heard raiders gave crewmembers a chance to join up instead of dying," the puka ventured. "I'd like to join."

"Usually we do but not this jig."

"Wh-why?"

Vindyl shook her head. She didn't know the reason, just that the Harir had specified they were to leave no witnesses.

"I'm a farspeaker," Tritic said, hopeful tone in her voice.

Vindyl stopped digging through a particularly thin crate and scrutinized the puka. "Have you already sent a distress call?"

The puka flushed and nodded. "The captain ordered it as soon as she saw the Yenderot flag."

Vindyl adjusted her grip on the prisebar and stepped toward Tritic.

"Wait, wait!" the puka raised her hands protectively. "I can send another message and tell them it was a false alarm."

"Do it."

The puka closed her eyes, flinching with each pistol report. Her lips moved with silent conversation. After a moment, her dinnerplate eyes popped open. "Done. They said Marthoth sent an Abog skiff out to escort us in. They're not calling it back. It's about halfway here."

A short succession of shots rang from above.

"Sax's tit!" Tritic yelped. "I don't want to die in this hole!"

Vindyl pried the lid off a long, thin crate, tugged out hunks of stuffing, and withdrew a shadowbox framed in dark wood. Settled in the velvet-lined interior was a grotesque platinum face unlike any species she'd ever met. *This* was what the Harir wanted.

Vindyl smiled.

The face smiled back.

PART ONE
IPESIA

SYLANDAIR

The sun, low in the east, glinted off the rippled surface of Lover's Sound, its sleepy light cutting through the *Ipesia*'s panoramic glass walls and sending glowfly flares dancing over the gaming deck's polished appointments. A glint flitted across the dry eye of Duke Sylandair Imythedralin, bringing him around to morning after yet another night spent trading barb and wager at the lyntyyl table. He rubbed his eyes with thumb and forefinger for a moment then slid on wire-rimmed sunshades—a meager guard against the crouching dawn.

Through two sunrises and more than thirty rounds, Syl had attempted to defeat Flark, owner of myriad buildings across Dockhaven's Upper and Lower Rabbles, including the Heap, the cockeyed structure Syl and Aliara called home. After a winter of annoying and double-crossing Syl, Flark had attacked again days before the Sowers Festival began. The nasty old bung had petitioned the City Council to raze the Heap, attempting to force Syl, the building's last holdout, to accept his latest bid. Rather than capitulate, Syl had determined to put Flark so deeply in his debt that forfeiting the Heap's deed would be preferable. Thus far, neither had made much progress toward their respective goals.

As he was in business, Flark was an inscrutable and adept lyntyyl strategist—though he seemed to possess almost no discernable skill in reading the subtleties of his fellow players. Despite this shortcoming, the pile of silver bars and assorted coins in front of the surly land baron totaled marginally less than Syl's own. With three days of the Festival already behind him, Syl needed to change his strategy or face the eventuality of losing his and Aliara's home.

He scanned the barge's gaming deck in search of her, wondering what his mate might be doing to amuse herself at this carnival of hedonistic delights while he sat here treading water. Aliara was not fond of social events, and after her near death at a fete last autumn, he had been pleasantly surprised when she'd assented to join him aboard the *Ipesia* for Mintryl Marthoth's annual new-year's celebration. While Syl had attended more often than not since becoming Duke of Isay, this was only the second time Aliara had joined him.

"Shall we take a break after this round?" Syl asked the other players at the table, their faces homely with too much drink and too little sleep. "I believe we all could do with a meal and a wash."

No one spoke, though one or two heads nodded.

Syl flicked lacquered fingertips at the aged and bespectacled dealer, Darvin, indicating the game should continue. Darvin dropped the master die in its cup and, with a sigh, shook it as though it held the weight of a thousand dice.

Darvin gave the players a slow blink and muttered, "Lyntyyl table one. Round thirty-four. Hand six."

He flipped the cup on end. The die clattered briefly before quieting, its result hidden beneath the cup pinned in place by the dealer's frail nut-brown hand. With a long hooked stick, Darvin shifted the small silver statuette of a foppish badger into position in front of Syl, quickly followed by the player's dice.

Syl rattled the trio of tens in his leather cup and tossed them onto the red felt. He selected the two and nine and collected eleven cards from Darvin. It was a good hand. With the remainder from the last, he held enough cards to work with but not so many as to be unwieldy.

Syl slid the dice to Daisy, a portly female puka and Flark's one-time wife, who wore a dress so green it almost made her skin seem blue in comparison. She rattled the dice a single time in her cup, dashed them onto the table and stood on her chair for a better view of the result.

"Imt's eyes," she cursed under her breath before calling for her cards.

Flark chuckled with bitter amusement—as he did each time Daisy botched her efforts. She repaid in kind when he failed. Their marriage had been divested long enough past that the pair could endure being in the same room, but not so long that they had given up nattering at one another.

"I'll take seven," she told Darvin.

"You never were good at lyntyyl," Flark muttered.

Daisy made a face as though she might attempt to spit across the table at him.

"It's not a game for women," the old puka said, raising his voice. "Am I right, Duke?"

Syl's brows shot up. He had not expected to be enlisted as arbiter in their acerbic banter. "I hold no such belief, Mister Flark. Lyntyyl relies so heavily on luck that I fear personal attributes have little to do with the outcome."

Flark snorted and chewed absently on something, possibly his own tongue.

With a firm nod at Flark and a pat on the arm for Syl, Daisy settled back into her seat and studied her new cards, fiddling with the namesake sateen flower paradoxically affixed to her hairless scalp. Though the adornment made her no more appealing, Syl had found its presence useful; she fidgeted with the piece when displeased with her draw.

Tired of waiting for Daisy to cede the dice, Idra Carsuure, Dockhaven's mayor and a chivori like Syl, snatched the tens and dribbled them into her monogrammed cup.

"Terrible, this rash of raids on inbound freighters of late, would you all agree?" Syl asked.

Idra gave him a brief, dark glance as she shook the cup roundly. Syl held his tongue until she was about to loose the dice.

"Perhaps one day we will see that picket fleet of yours, Idra," he said, hint of venom in his voice.

She flinched, the cup tumbling from her hand, the dice rolling limply away. The cup banged into the polished oak box at table's center, the game's hold and home to all the silver and platinum players supplied as wagers.

"Surely, with such a fleet you could prevent ships being lost just over the horizon," Syl added, smiling pleasantly.

"The picket ships have been delayed due to a shortfall on the funding." Idra's angry gaze pinned Syl. "I'm fairly certain you know that, Imythedralin."

"That is unfortunate. I suppose you will need to employ a mathematician to assist in learning where the city's loss was incurred," Syl said, relishing the jab.

The nostrils of her round-tipped nose flared in a way only she could make lovely. "Why don't *you* assist, Imythedralin? I'm sure you can afford to make a donation for the good of our city. After all, you do have the resources lying about." Idra's voice was as cold as the water in the Sound. Her eyes flicked to the dice, jaw muscles clenching and releasing beneath her fog-grey skin.

She had been at the table almost as long as Flark. Syl had fed her a steady stream of caba and themot—down then up again—the combination keeping her on edge as intended.

"I should be glad to demonstrate my civic pride in such a way," Syl said. "However, most of my resources—as you put it—are currently committed to improving the desalinization plant."

"*Pfft*. The city's water costs are twice what they were before you took control."

Syl lay his cards face-down on the table and stared at her soberly. "Really, Idra, you cannot expect me to uphold the rates in a contract signed more than two decades ago by people who now are dead." He paused to sip his caba and resume his cards. "Besides, the additional monies go toward removal of the ruined portions of the plant…and restoration of the Promenade."

The effect was satisfactory. Idra's eyes went wide. Her jaw clenched. This was the first Syl had mentioned the project, which would restore the long-neglected boardwalk and public green. As mayor, Idra believed herself privy to everything going on in the city.

"Mayor," the dealer said, "It's your draw."

"I'll take four," she snapped.

Too few cards to play a decent hand. A corner of Syl's mouth quirked. Her stake had dwindled to the point where he could either force her to pass or drive her out of the game this hand.

Idra leaned back in her chair, pawed her cards with samite-gloved hands, and heaved a sigh. Flark's reaction was nearly instantaneous. His glistening eyes shifted to her augmented bosom and he unconsciously reached for his belly. After a moment's massage, the puka came abruptly out of his trance.

"Vesven!" Flark prodded his karju bodyguard with the polished walking stick he kept hanging from the table's edge. "Dice!"

Vesven Dobencourt pushed himself away from the pillar he'd reclined on for hours and placed the dice in front of Flark. It was a humiliating role for someone from such a highly placed family.

The dour puka patted the bedraggled suede charm bag lying on the table beside his mound of silver and ran the three dice between his palms like a baker forming stick-bread.

"What Idra suggests may be a good opportunity for you, Mister Flark, given your interest in joining the shipping trade," Syl said, watching for reaction from behind his dark lenses. Flark offered none. "Being the one to bring a picket fleet to Dockhaven would most definitely win you the admiration of the Council and your new peers in the shippers association."

Flark had shared this aspiration during one of their impromptu kisselball games at Syl's penthouse. It was a pursuit Syl had supported earnestly and had assisted in planning. It was a pity the puka had not honored their agreement—one more insult stacked between them.

"I've reconsidered, Duke. An opportunity to negotiate better fees for my material imports will come along soon enough." Flark rolled the dice and pointed a stubby finger at the dealer. "Gimme twelve."

Marthoth's fleet administrator, Javit, huffed like a kartah bull about to charge. "You're overestimating Karna's value."

Javit was half-again Syl's height and easily three times his weight. With four legs and thick skin like living stone, Javit took up a great deal of space and required an entirely different set of furniture when visiting Syl's penthouse. A species of prodigious size and strength, the rhochrot had only one gender and a rather humdrum reproductive process, something Syl found both intriguing and pitiable. When they'd appeared on Ismae during the War of Whispers two millennia ago, the rhochrot had been hailed as saviors, turning the war in the Duin's favor. After the campaigns had ended, the other species were not entirely sure how to assimilate or even properly address them. When the morphology of adapting the rhochrot's complex collection of pronouns to Plainspeak proved too much for most, the species was deemed unilaterally female, owing to their ability to bear children.

"You both should consider sponsoring the picket fleet. Were you to do so, I'd be sure you received special consideration from my employer." As she rolled the dice, Javit's dark eyes flicked to Syl before locking on Flark. "You may find yourselves needing it."

"A fine suggestion, Javit," Syl said. "I will discuss it with Mintryl when we dine later."

From orbits settled so far apart they were almost on the sides of his head, Flark's enormous brown eyes rolled toward Syl. His compost-colored lips turned down in a frown.

"Perhaps," Syl continued, "we can form a combine of interested parties to make up Idra's shortfall."

Idra's face pinched, an unflattering aspect on such a lovely façade. Syl offered her a smile.

Darvin dragged the forgotten dice to the sharp-faced chivori man seated between Flark and Javit. Syl could only recall that one's surname: Menelow. The appellation was as common as cats among phao, those chivori not hailing from Chiva'vastezz or Eita. Other than dark purple eyes—bloodshot and ringed sickly blue from the extended play—and an ability to slouch stiffly as though relaxing in the slightest would cause him to unravel, Menelow was unremarkable. He had joined the game after sundown the night before and was now down to a pittance. Every hand as badger, he bet two silver bars and ended with a few cards. Only fourteen cards now remained in his draw deck. Soon his chair would be empty, and Syl would have one less distraction.

Menelow snatched the trio of player dice from the felt and rattled them slowly in his own cup, vinegar gaze passing over his opponents. He cast them, the dealer read the roll, and Menelow called for his draw. He snatched his cards from the table and held them strangely close to his face as if smelling them, a behavior he indulged in when displeased.

Play passed to Javit, Syl's attention with it.

"I read the *Nimomyne* was the most recent victim of these raiders," Syl said. "A fine ship, I'm told. Or at least it was."

"It still may be if we can get it off the reef." Javit accepted her draw from the dealer with a nod. "It's Tokimer's grace that the wreckers have no interest. It's too big and the raiders didn't leave anything on board that doesn't require a crane to offload. I scheduled Ruutana Salvage to start on the work after the Festival. Meanwhile, we're paying a half-dozen Abog to live aboard…for all those mercs are worth."

"Do it quick," Flark said. "I need those materials by the beginning of Celebar at latest. I'm losing a pile of silver waiting on you."

Syl snorted at the bung's audacity.

"He should have had more than one escort." Flark smirked at Javit. "If he wanted the raider clans to take him seriously, Marthoth should join the Billidoc Coalition of Traders."

"And lose half his coin to dues?" Javit snorted.

"My clerk at the packet office said the *Nimomyne* was also carrying artifacts out of Tehtaemah," Syl said, "ones from the dig site most recently purported to be Vosharilim. I cannot help but imagine the value of the antiquities aboard. A pity they should be lost to the undermarket…assuming that is where they landed, of course." Behind his dark lenses, Syl's long eyes slid toward Idra, who looked anywhere but at him. "Regardless, I am certain it will be a boon to *someone's* collection."

The dealer lifted the cup, revealing the master die's roll. "Value is seven," Darvin said. "Badger sets blind post."

Syl pushed a stack of silver toward the hold.

"The badger bets twenty bars," the dealer said without enthusiasm.

Idra and Menelow shared a groan. He passed while she met Syl's wager—barely. Daisy, Flark, and Javit matched the amount without hesitation.

"Your stacks," Darvin said.

In turn, the players laid out their stacks, groups of cards whose combined value equaled the master die's, whether by addition or subtraction. Syl played his stacks, leaving two uncooperative cards for the next hand, and eyed the other players. Idra sorted and re-sorted her cards in a way that signaled dissatisfaction. Daisy, fiddling with her flower, appeared equally annoyed. Menelow waved a steward over. Javit crouched on her hassock in calm readiness, all four legs tucked beneath her. Flark was a mask of blandness. He didn't twitch. He didn't sniffle. He barely seemed to breathe.

When their stacks were laid, each held a remainder; play would advance to another hand. Without a winner, the round continued, the burgeoning hold's prize unclaimed.

Everyone stretched and yawned while Darvin prepared for the next hand. Syl drew an amethyst glass vial from his waistcoat pocket, tapped themot onto the side of his hand and snorted the pale-yellow dust. His head buzzed for a moment like the hives behind Bretad's Sweet Shop before the stimulant settled in. Puka farspeakers used the drug to extend the range of their telepathic skills; karju and chivori used it recreationally.

The group rolled for badger. Menelow won. It would be a dull hand with that one at the helm.

"Lyntyyl table one. Round thirty-four. Hand seven," the dealer called. With his customary sluggishness, Darvin tumbled the master die in the cup and turned it over, value hidden.

Syl waited until the draw dice reached Idra before continuing his campaign of annoyance. "Idra, I was told you were recently gifted with a new piece of art for your collection."

This time she held onto the cup, though the dice scattered. "What are you babbling about, Imythedralin?"

"Perhaps I was misinformed," Syl said, frowning elegantly. "Councilor Pitta Dobencourt sent one of her husbands over last quartern—I can't remember his name, the brutish one."

"Ugh, you mean Grehv."

"Yes, I believe that was his name. He said you were the recipient of a genuine Jetsam."

Her eyes snapped from the dice to Syl. "You call that art? Ha! That hack vandalized city property!"

Flark snorted. Menelow cleared his throat. Daisy watched with silent amusement while Javit made a conspicuous effort to ignore the conversation.

"Ah, yes, Grehv said it was found at the bank. What did it do?" Syl asked, tapping his lower lip in a pantomime of concentration.

"Jetsam's works always do…something. Remember that sinister, palsied herd of windup kartah outside Splar's Meat Market a few years back?"

"Hers was hanging off the bank's gate," Flark said. He paused, spiteful chuckle threatening to become a coughing fit. "When the wind blew, our darling mayor moved up and down on the gate. Looked like she was sneaking out, bag'a Calla's over her shoulder."

Menelow threw his pointy head back and laughed. It was the most animated he'd been. The others joined in, unable to maintain the illusion of ignorance any longer.

"It was atrocious." Idra flipped her hair and pretended to study her cards. "Looked nothing like me."

"Mayor Carsuure," Darvin said softly, "it's your draw."

"Nine," Idra snapped. "Give me nine."

Draws complete, Menelow set the wager at two silver bars, as expected. His eyebrows, as pointy as his nose and chin, jittered with anxiety while Flark moved so little he might have been dead. Daisy rocked in her seat, humming a nonsensical melody. Javit counted and re-counted the loops dangling from her septum. Idra toyed with a large firestar pendant at her neck, eyes flitting from Syl's amethyst vial to her pile of coins, which had diminished to near nothing.

"A lovely necklace, Idra." Syl slid the themot across the felt toward her.

The skin tightened around Idra's eyes. She gave him her most politic smile before tapping the drug onto the bare skin of her wrist and inhaling. She passed the vial to Flark, as had become the table's custom, a little jab at Syl's expense shared between them. Unless taken by a farspeaker, themot had almost no effect on pukas. By nature, their species could go sleepless for days before succumbing to exhaustion. Flark was simply enjoying wasting what was Syl's.

Syl flicked a pair of bars into the hold and elbowed Daisy. "The jewel is stunning around her delicate neck, do you agree?"

Daisy tossed her bars in the hold and glanced at the firestar pendant. "If you're desperate for everyone to stare at your bubs, then sure, it's pretty."

Idra released an offended huff.

Syl chuckled. "You are a delight. Daisy, I cannot fathom why Mister Flark released you from his grasp."

Daisy giggled. Flark muttered an oath and spat on the floor.

As the wager moved to Idra, she flagged the closest floor manager, who hurried over. The pair whispered heatedly for a moment then Idra removed her necklace and laid it in his palm.

Syl caught the floor manager's wrist as he passed. "Allow me to purchase the lady's marker."

"Of course, Duke Imythedralin." He bent toward Syl's ear and lowered his voice discreetly. "The piece is not particularly valuable. We offered twenty Callas."

"A single silver bar? Pitiful," Syl said. He slipped the necklace into his pocket and passed five bars of his boodle to Idra, far more than the jewel was worth. The silver would be his again soon enough.

She took the bars without comment.

Somewhere in her flighty mind, Idra believed Syl's inheritance should have remained in her keeping. He'd surprised her last year when he had finally claimed the funds held in trust by the city since the purported death of his one-time master and tormentor, Orono. Idra had spent a substantial portion—some on the city's picket ship project, but much on her personal whims—and repaying him had left her deeply and dangerously in debt. Taunting her with that knowledge was a pleasure Syl could not forgo.

Play moved on and Syl lost himself in strategy and calculation, startled when Aliara materialized from the milling crowd and slipped onto his knee.

"I'm bored," she announced.

Syl held his focus for another beat before he closed the fan of cards and shifted his attention to his mate. "A lovely surprise to see you, Pet."

She sighed theatrically. "It's dull this year."

Syl could not stop the bark of amusement. Marthoth offered his guests every entertainment they might desire: the finest collection of gaming tables in the Middle Seas, live performances both musical and theatrical, restaurants manned by Dockhaven's finest chefs, and a space in which all manner of sexual dalliances could be enjoyed. Guests were even treated to a nightly fireworks display, viewed from the barge's panoramic glass windows or atop the open-air upper deck, where a band played, revelers danced, and liquor poured like the coming spring rains.

That Aliara found it difficult to stay entertained here had once mystified Syl. He now understood her restlessness would not be cured by a frolic such as this; her vocation provided far more gratification.

"There is much to do here." He slid fingers beneath his sunshades to rub his sore, gritty eyes. Even with the protective lenses, the growing morning agitated them. "I believe I heard something about an impending performance in the lounge."

"Ended. Pretentious. That puppet show at your salon was better."

Flark snorted, and Aliara's gaze flitted over to him. She didn't care for the bung, often vanishing during his visits instead of enduring the old puka's leers.

Most pukas Syl had known were fabulously modest and blushed deep pine when confronted with anything remotely sexual. In a species that tended to seek out strong leadership, those rare pukas who fit that role rose quickly and often discarded such working-class trappings. Like Flark and Daisy, they wore bejeweled rings, had mouths worse than any karju bilge rat, and enjoyed activities more perverse than an inbred chivori. Wealth and influence, Syl had decided, negated a puka's natural prudery.

Aliara's lip twitched in a way Syl recognized as a calculating smile. She leaned into him and crossed her long legs, giving Flark a better view—and significant distraction from the game. Eyes pegged on her, the old puka relaxed back into his chair and rubbed his dome-like belly.

"Good to know. I shall invite the troupe to return another time." Syl played along with Aliara's diversion, palming one of her petite breasts, reconstructed by Master Enan Ranaran only months ago, following the tussle with the thing Orono had become. The surgeon had done magnificent work here and on the organs beneath. The filmy periwinkle piece Aliara wore barely veiled the regrown bub and its mate. "Perhaps engage someone interesting in conversation?"

Flark shifted. The rubbing turned briefly to patting.

"Nobody here is interesting," Aliara said.

Idra made a sound somewhere between cough and growl.

Syl ran fingers across Aliara's cropped, black hair. Though it had grown while she was bed-ridden, the back and sides were again rigidly short. Only the extra length on top evinced the long winter in bed.

"Why don't you play a game?" Syl gestured toward the cordoned-off area near the band. "You would do well at darts."

Aliara shrugged, lower lip jutting out in a mockery of a pout. Syl bit back a laugh. Her attempts at coquettishness were rare and delightful, though they reminded him more of Aliara as a child than as a lover. When being coy had no effect on Syl, she twirled the dark tail of his hair with one hand and slid the other between them into his lap.

"Let's leave," she whispered, fingers making her intention clear, "and visit the southern Nors."

Flark's cards sagged so low that the table at large could read their values. His free hand continued its slow, unsavory massage of his belly while his rheumy eyes crawled over Aliara. Syl usually enjoyed others' appreciation of his mate, but this left even him queasy.

"I am in the middle of a round, Pet. I doubt these lovely people would appreciate my leaving with so many of their Callas." Syl gestured around the table. "After the Festival I will book us passage to Elnor. Sea or air, your choice."

Aliara made a sound of disappointed indignation.

"Badger's stack," the dealer announced.

Menelow stopped sniffing his cards and busied himself with stacking.

"Very well," Syl said. "Perhaps you should do something you've been talking about since you rose from your sick bed?"

Aliara rolled her sloe eyes and groaned. "I visited *that* room."

Flark jerked forward as though struck.

Syl chuckled. "No, not that, Pet."

The dealer cleared his throat. "Duke Imythedralin, it's your stack."

"Yes, of course. Apologies."

Syl stretched past Aliara and stacked his cards, one remaining in his hand. Daisy barely allowed him to finish before building her own stacks.

"Perhaps you could go back to work," Syl told Aliara.

She cocked her head and stared into the space over his shoulder for a long moment. Her hand withdrew from his lap and she slid away, fading into the crowd. With regret, Syl watched the sway of her slim hips as she disappeared amongst the merrymakers.

Flark's braying, nasal laugh disturbed Syl's musings. "See, you old goat, just like I told you, you can't play lyntyyl worth a plop."

Daisy grabbed Idra's half-full cocktail and hurled it at her former spouse. The glass sailed past Flark's ear and bounced off Vesven's stomach, splashing his white shirt with dark red caba.

Flark's laugh built. "Can't even aim."

"For our children's sake," Daisy flopped back into her seat, her enormous eyes narrowed to slits, "I hope you die before you squirt an heir into your new trull's belly."

Aliara navigated the bodies blocking her path, the need to leave like a wind at her back. As she squeezed through a cluster of chattering douses, one of them greeted her as "Duchess." She hurried away without reply. Her anonymity was lost in this ridiculous place. Everyone knew she was Duke Imythedralin's companion. They made assumptions. Syl had wanted the status and the influence that came with a Vazztain title, but Aliara would sooner jam her bane needle into her own neck than be fettered by such a thing.

The friendly partygoer called to her again. She ground her teeth and sped up. Watching the crowds had been entertaining for a day or two but now they smothered her. She felt lost and alone and more than a little greasy.

She'd woken in their cabin in the grip of a nightmare, a muddle of memory and illusion she'd experienced repeatedly since the incident last autumn. As with every time before, it had left her uncomfortable, uncertain, needing the reassurance of familiarity and refuge. When she'd reached for Syl this time, she'd groped only empty sheets.

Aliara had shaken off the half-remembered dream, dressed as the event prescribed, and descended the *Ipesia*'s succession of lurid staircases—all lacquered garra wood and polished brass rails—to find Syl still at the lyntyyl table. How he could stay conscious and engaged with such a group of twits baffled her. Many had been the months they'd paid their way thanks to his talents at the gaming table, but it was unnecessary now. She couldn't grasp why he kept at it.

She climbed those same staircases, half wishing he'd joined her when she asked. While she'd hoped her distraction would help him crush Flark in her absence, she'd been serious about abandoning the party. This was their first foray away from the penthouse since her recovery began. Leaving him felt off-beam. Staying felt worse. After a full winter penned up together, Aliara couldn't fault Syl for wanting some distance. At least he'd understood her need to decamp, and his suggested alternative was as entertaining as the one she'd proposed.

The smell of warm bodies, floral incense, and uurost tickled her nose as she slipped past the mingling room and its revelers, anxiety fluttering in her chest. Thoughts of returning to work with the Thung Toh had swum through her brain like an agitated school of plati fish for quarterns. She'd been sedentary for too long. She needed to return to herself, to test her body. She needed to be more than set dressing in whatever drama Syl had embroiled himself in. Work would resolve that, but it was possible her skills had grown barnacles during her down time.

The disquiet in her chest kicked.

She slipped into their stateroom and closed the door against the clamor beyond. Innumerable Aliaras, each smaller than the last, looked back at her from the entryway's mirrored bulkheads. In this ridiculous costume, she looked like some Waking Night gift waiting to be unwrapped. She laid a hand over her left breast, where the twisted version of Orono had driven a hole through her at the fete last autumn. She closed her eyes and saw her former owner's mutated weapon of a tail spiking down, felt the crack as her ribs shattered, the warmth of her spilled blood. She would have drowned in her own viscera, Master Ranaran had told Aliara, if Orono had not taken that lung years before.

She didn't realize she'd gasped until she let the breath out again.

It was also possible the replacements and augmentations the surgeon installed in her would fail. Their newness was another risk to be considered as she returned to work.

The fingers of her right hand absently teased the black nut of the bane gland in its palm. That zoet had been an enhancement of choice, a tool of her profession, a weapon for when her other skills failed and killing became necessary. But Master Ranaran's recent work had been a compromise. She'd agreed to the essentials, organs grown to replace those Orono destroyed, but Syl had insisted on replacing or upgrading others, ones that had been damaged during the old pervert's experiments on her young body. Syl was right— she'd live longer thanks to her internal renovations—but the new bits still felt wrong, as though she'd cheated.

Her fingertip tracked an old scar running collarbone to nipple, its puckered darkness barely visible beneath the pale blouse. There'd been no arguments over the scars. Syl had understood her need to keep those childhood mutilations stippling her body. He hadn't so much as suggested Ranaran remove them.

Aliara left her reflected duplicates to their own musings and slid the mirrored closet door aside. Nothing hanging there was appropriate for where she was headed, but she didn't much feel like stopping home first. She traded her sandals for the familiar black, soft-soled boots laced to her knees. They made her feel a little like herself.

Over the scant party costume, she threw on a high-collared coat, one of too many gifts Syl had showered on her over the winter. While she was bedridden, he'd gone a bit mad with his long-eschewed inheritance, purchasing rafts of clothing and furniture, even buying and renovating the penthouse that abutted theirs at the top of the Heap, making them sole proprietors of the uppermost levels—much to the displeasure of Flark, owner of the rest. Syl had outbid and outmaneuvered him, sending their former neighbor on a holiday to the Ritora Doublet resort in northern Chiva'vastezz before the old puka bung had a chance to counter.

Despite that victory, he'd been melancholy over the winter, locked away with her. He'd seemed as caged as she had in spite of the many visitors to his salon and the hours spent entertaining and beguiling guests. When his business was done and she needed no nursing, he'd retreated into his own thoughts. Given their last year, that was a dangerous pastime, and pensiveness did not suit him. So, when he suggested they attend Marthoth's floating fete, she'd agreed without complaint.

Satisfied the coat and boots would conceal her impractical shirt and skirt from her fellow Toh, Aliara snatched one of Syl's hats, domed with a narrow brim, slipped on her round sunshades, and dove back into the sparkle and flash of the party outside. Finished with any pretense of civility, she tugged the grey flannel hat toward her nose and threaded her way silently through rooms filled with tinkling music, overbearing merriment, and the exacting glare of the *Ipesia*'s sentinels. She didn't breathe until she stepped into the new spring's poured-glass sunlight.

Aliara slid into a seat at the launch's prow. A few others settled in behind her, happily jabbering about their antics aboard Marthoth's barge. As the launch bobbed gaily across Lovers' Sound, chilly sea spray peppered her face, stirring her from the illusory world of the mogul's celebration. Behind her, the captain babbled at the other passengers. She let his words drift away, instead focusing on the roll of the hull over the morning waves and the guttural rhythm of the craft's adolescent propulsor as the zoetic creature drove the craft forward.

For a few moments, the cliffs flanking the gap between the Big Island and Nest swallowed the little boat in shadow and chill, quieting the chatting passengers. They sat silently as the antique captain neatly maneuvered them through the channel into dawn's explosion over Rimadour Bay. Conversation resumed.

When they came to rest at the wharf market docks, Aliara

allowed the others to disembark first. The old sailor offered her a hand as she climbed ashore, and she slipped a Calla into the wrinkled palm, vanishing into the city before he could voice his gratitude.

The smell of baking bread roused her stomach. She couldn't remember the last time she'd eaten. Passing a bakery cooling the day's assortment in the serving-window racks, she snatched a bun, tossing it from hand to hand until it was cool enough to eat. It was soft and rich and just a little sweet. Aliara looked over her shoulder. Stenciled above a painted array of children gobbling breads and pastries was "Nothing But Crumbs." She'd remember it for Sviroosa's days off.

Neither of the two pedicab drivers Aliara tried would venture into the warehouse-bordered slum known as the Prick, even when enticed with a full Calla, more than they'd make in three days. So she walked. No one noticed her, no heads looked her way. It was perfect.

The bun was gone by the time she reached the tram station and managed to net an empty gondola for the ride across the bay. It was a clear morning, rare and pleasant at this time of year. She could make out the whole of the crescent-moon island-city, from the high cliffs of the Nest and Big Island, sloping down along the Pipe into the filth of the Lower and Upper Rabbles, the whole thing terminating with the nasty little bit of land called the Prick—her destination.

Dockhaven was a city built by a self-proclaimed kook. After the Cataclysm, only the highest tips of the ancient volcano's caldera still peeked above sea level, but that had been enough for Rimadour to build his "city in the center of the world." When he put out the word of his plans, venturesome speculators had flocked here and stayed, business and trade flourished, and—as unlikely as it had seemed— the smallest populated landmass in all of Ismae became its hub of trade.

As her tram carriage neared the Lower Rabble station, a low rumble echoed across Rimadour Bay. Aliara scanned the skyline. A cloud of dust rose from the Upper Rabble where a building had once been. She'd seen enough implosions in this city to recognize the effect. Some bung was wasting no time starting the new year.

Her tram carriage creaked to a stop and Aliara exited into the white, sterile-looking concourse that somehow still smelled like piss. She dodged the early morning smattering of riders and bypassed the lift, opting instead for the ten-flight descent to street level. Her anxiety faded further with the welcome exercise, more still as she entered the noisome morning hubbub of the Lower Rabble. The stink and warble of the shouting vendors and passers-by wrapped her in comfortable concealment.

Here she was not the Duchess. She was just Rift.

Down the still-shadowed street, a pair of tippled karju fought sloppily, the glow from the Bitter Barnacle spotlighting their comical brawl. A few other patrons stood nearby, betting and hooting. Aliara slipped into the group, sliding a short blade from an onlooker's belt sheath. She'd be a fool to go into the Prick unarmed.

Coat tickling her ankles in spring's chill breeze, Aliara left the drunken competitors and wound her way down Central Row until it met High Road, which ran like a scoliotic spine through Dockhaven, from northern affluence to southern slum. A distant racket hit her lower lugs first, resonating in her jawbone with a gentle tickle. She'd lived here long enough to know the sound of the Hauler, the Haven's cargo train. It traveled slowly, maybe twice the pace of a brisk walk.

The Hauler chugged down the Pipe's slope, the drive wheels clattering like a brigade of rolling tabors as they locked into the center track. The bullet-nosed engine clattered past, steam puffing from a chain of pipes along the top of its boiler. When the first open-bedded freight wagon passed, Aliara grabbed an edge and hopped on, crouching behind a stack of boxes. If caught hitching a ride, she would be rudely poked with a conductor's stick, but it was still better than wandering through the Prick on foot.

BRIZZA

"Pass me the eggs, Brizza," her father said. He was big for a puka and smiled a lot. She'd seen him when he was alone enough to know he saved his smiles for the family. When he was by himself, he looked like her aapa after her oocha died and went to the sea.

Eyes focused on the front door, Brizza handed him the bowl of eggs and shifted her rucksack to her lap. She'd readied it this morning as she always did, but today she'd packed everything she really cared about, leaving her lesson book and writing gear in the bedroom she shared with her parents and three younger siblings.

"Aren't you hungry?" her father asked.

Brizza could hear the voices of the evacuating pukas outside. Sometimes, someone would bang against the wall, making her flinch. Their neighbors were trying to move as much as they could out of the building before the landlord's deadline. Not her family. Not so much as a tea towel had moved in this cuddy since Flark's rent collector had notified them of the building's demolition.

"No, Taapa. I…" Brizza glanced at the counter where her mother was plating griddle cakes. She lowered her voice. "I want to leave like we're 'sposed to."

Her taapa's smile wavered as he watched her mother.

"I don't want to blow up," Brizza whispered.

After her moocha and some of the other families had decided to stay, a boy down the hall had told Brizza she'd more likely be killed by falling debris than actually being blown to bits. She'd cried all that night and every night since, muffling her sobs in her pillow so the others wouldn't hear.

"No, your moocha knows best," Taapa whispered and put an olive-skinned hand on her knee. "We're safe, sweet girl."

"But I'm scared."

His face went stern. "You're a big girl now, and I expect—"

"Here we are." Moocha deposited cakes on everyone's plates.

Taapa straightened, removing his hand.

Moocha frowned at Brizza's untouched eggs. "What's the matter? Did I make them too salty again? Your sister and brothers seem to like them just fine." She swept her arm to indicate Brizza's younger siblings, all of them engrossed in breakfast like it was the beginning of just another day.

Someone outside started yelling and there was a sound like furniture falling down a stairwell. Brizza gasped.

"No, no darling," Taapa said. "It's just her nerves."

"Oh," Moocha flicked a dismissive hand, "we'll be fine. They won't dare detonate with people still in the building. The Corps won't let them. Besides, only a fool would kill paying tenants." She chewed a forkful of eggs. "Eat up."

Brizza's stomach protested, but she picked up her fork. It was loaded with cake and halfway to her mouth when someone knocked at the door.

Moocha wiped her mouth and gave Taapa a puckered frown. He nodded, they both rose, and she opened the door.

A dour-looking, muscular puka stood there in a bright green carapace chest plate and helmet. He leaned in and looked over their cuddy. "What? You haven't done anything?"

Moocha crossed her arms. "No need, we're not leaving."

"You people have been told. The demo is to proceed today. No matter what." He glowered at her parents.

Her moocha smiled in that way she did when she spoke to fools.

"Would you like to join us for breakfast?"

The man took off his helmet and ran a hand over his hairless head. "We're already late thanks to the protesters. This is the final check. I won't be back. The charges are wired and once we get people moved away from the building, we're going to detonate. This isn't a bluff, you gotta get out now. Grab these children and any valuables you can carry and go."

Brizza bit her lip and hugged her rucksack a little tighter.

"You need to leave." The man resumed his helmet. "Now!"

When neither of her parents made any indications of budging, he threw up his hands and stomped away.

Moocha harrumphed and slammed the door. "It's perfectly safe, children," she said as she settled back into her place at the table.

Brizza watched her family eat and listened to the ruckus in the hallway slowly dribble into nothing. By the time breakfast was over, the whole building was quiet outside of the clank of Moocha doing dishes.

Before she realized what she was doing, Brizza pushed back her chair and stood. Her moocha turned away from the sink. Taapa slowly lowered his teacup.

Brizza looked at her sister. "Fahnta, take the boys and get your rucks. I'm going to walk you to the Order. Hurry or we'll be late for lessons."

Moocha scowled and reached for the grease strainer.

Taapa stepped between them and blocked her mother as she readied a swat. "Now Slina," he said in his sternest voice, "maybe it's best that the children go just like any other day. It'll show Flark how little we think of his threats."

Moocha's face softened slightly. "Fine, but you'll miss it when they come to interview us. By tonight the news callers will be saying your father and I and any of the other families that stayed are heroes." Then she giggled as though the situation was funny, like she did whenever she thought people were being stupid, and went back to washing dishes, whistling *Under the Boughs of The Denurd.*

Fahnta and the boys rushed into the room. The youngest, Joot, asked, "Can we stop at the sweet shop on the way?"

Brizza nodded. "As long as you're good and don't make a fuss."

Joot clapped and ran out the door, Krach close at his heels, leaving a flustered Fahnta to chase.

Moocha kept whistling and washing, ignoring them all.

"Come with us, Taapa," Brizza whispered.

He looked at Moocha and back to her, "We'll be fine, Kitten. You go keep an eye on the youngsters. Tonight, we'll have a great laugh about all of this."

Brizza kissed his cheek and hugged him so hard he probably couldn't breathe, then turned and ran after the little ones. She caught up with them on the fifth-floor landing, in a circle and playing clapping games.

"Up, up, up," she chided.

Old enough to have some idea of what was happening, Fahnta jumped up and moved, but Krach and Joot complained and dawdled near a lump of clay on the wall, coiled wire connecting it to its twins down the corridor. Brizza grabbed them both by their ruck straps and herded them down the dim stairwell.

"Stop shoving," Joot complained. "We won't be late for lessons."

But Brizza kept moving, almost dragging them from the stairwell onto the first floor. Someone outside was shouting through a loudhailer, their bellow tinny and thin. The gathered gawkers hollered and pointed as Brizza and her siblings burst out the front door. A helmeted man frantically waved them away from the building.

Fahnta asked something, but Brizza didn't answer. She scooped Joot up onto her back, grabbed the others' hands and ran, not stopping after ducking under the cordon. She'd take the children to lessons at the Order of Omatha like usual, then visit her Aunt Kittul, Taapa's sister in the Lower Rabble. She'd know what to do.

Brizza and her siblings were nearly over the Bay Bridge when she heard what could have been a trio of bangers followed by a rumbling *whuump*. She looked back toward their neighborhood as a column of dust climbed into the sky. Echoes fading across the harbor, she squeezed back tears. She'd miss her taapa.

SCHMALCH

Three bright bands flashed in succession behind the windows of the Yinago Tower from bottom to top. They blew out into the air like shimmering swarms of insects fleeing from their nest before raining down on the street below. Schmalch felt the vibration crawling up his legs a heartbeat after. The tall, dark tenement swayed like a tippler as cracks shot up its dirty-black walls. It collapsed in a tight heap with a *whuump*, dust billowing at its base. The cloud of debris raced down the street toward where Schmalch watched from the safety of Fohmsquah's sixth-floor walk-up above Phyyll's Bread Basket.

Chivori all over the Lower Rabble were probably rubbing their jaws and complaining. Maybe Flark imploded the thing during the Sowers Festival party so he didn't gam off any of Dockhaven's rich ones.

Schmalch turned away from the window. There was nothing to see there besides slowly settling dirt. Framed by the pass-through, Fohmsquah was still in the kitchen. She'd been there near-constantly since Flark made his announcement to the Yinago's tenants. Her son Chisev had been running Domestic Consignment *and* taking care of the twins. And Schmalch had been spending his holiday moving two apartments-worth of belongings from that building into this one.

Everything and everyone were packed into this one-bedroom cuddy, which was already pretty small for Fohmsquah and her kids.

Bedrolls were littered between the furniture of the common room. The bedroom was packed with everything Fohmsquah's bound-family could manage to rescue before their building went down, leaving only the front room for all three families to sleep in. Only after two days of helping them move was Schmalch finally able to keep all their names straight.

Fohmsquah's brood was gone, Chisev out buying perishables, Worch and Ilit in classes, but the other two families were settled in. A baby girl slept in a bassinet at the end of the sofa, her mother slowly rocking with one hand while she held the nursing twin with the other. Beside her, the babies' father was in a heated argument with his own father about what anyone could have done to prevent Flark from kicking everyone out of their homes. That was one household.

Curled up on the other side of the room was a sleeping old man, beside him a girl just shy of adulthood like Chisev. She sat holding her knees curled up to her chest, looking like a boil about to pop. That was the second. It was a lot to fit in one place.

When he'd learned about Fohmsquah's predicament, Schmalch's first thought was that the strays could camp out in the big apartment above Domestic Consignment, but the windows there were busted and the roof leaked. Not a good spot for old people or babies at this time of year. He hadn't shared that idea with Fohmsquah. He had suggested they contact the Duke and ask to stay in the guest rooms, but Fohmsquah insisted he say nothing.

"Duke Imythedralin has already done so much for us," she'd said. "Sending strangers to live in his house while he's away…it seems like too much of an imposition."

Schmalch still would have tried to send the Duke a message if she hadn't made him promise not to. Something about Fohmsquah made him want to do what he said he would. He'd tried to tell Chisev once how lucky he was to have a moocha like her, but the words hadn't come out right, and Schmalch had changed the subject. He wasn't sure how to tell the boy that every kid who ever lived in the Spriggan Temple's orphanage dreamed about mothers like Fohmsquah.

"The City Council will do nothing, you know that," said Dibrin, the babies' father. He threw up his hands and rose, attempting to pace in the cluttered space. "The Dobencourt woman could not care less about either one of the Rabbles. She barely worries herself about the Big Island."

"That's why we have the Mayor," said his father, Khark. "That's why we keep Carsuure. She may not be perfect, but she's—"

"One of us? The Mayor may have come from the Rabble, but that was two lifetimes ago. Now she's just like the rest of the toffs on the north side. She gave Flark leave to kick us out with only two-days' notice, barely waiting for us to clear the evacuation zone before his drudge hit the trigger!" Dibrin leaned on the dining table and growled. "Now the two of them are off on Marthoth's barge doing whatever it is you do when you're richer than Nys, and we're all crammed into Cousin Glech's cuddy." He paused and glanced at Fohmsquah.

The family was still tentative about using her late husband's name in her hearing. She didn't appear to notice, or if she did, she didn't stop her flurry of cooking.

"We have to do something," the young father said. "We could organize a picket of the Bung Building, be there and waiting when Flark gets back from his swish party. Stop *him* from getting into his home."

"Just let the Mayor and the Council have a crack at it first, Dibrin." Khark patted the cushion beside him. "Sit down, Son. Relax. There's nothing you can do right now."

Dibrin released a bark of irritation, spun on his heels, and stomped out of the apartment, slamming the door.

The sleeping old man, Piprich, started. When he saw nothing had changed, he returned to his nap.

Schmalch had never voted. When he asked the Duke what he

thought of the upcoming election, the chivori had smiled the way he did when he was being sneaky.

"Opinions make enemies," the Duke told Schmalch. "If you want the advantage, listen to theirs and keep yours to yourself. They will assume you agree."

"He'll be back," Khark told the room. "Dibrin'll cool down, curse the Nest with some friends, and by morning he'll be back to his old self. We'll find another place to live and be out of here in no time. Right, Blumlech?"

The nursing young woman nodded as she pried one infant off her breast, exchanging it for the other.

Across the room, the adolescent girl, Glevit, pulled her knees up tighter and began to cry.

Schmalch went over to her and gently rubbed her smooth head. "I'll help you all find new cuddys. Don't worry. This is just temporary."

She nodded and drug her sleeve across her nose.

"It's not that," Glevit said, big brown eyes still dribbling. "I'm afraid for my friend. Her mother said she wasn't going to leave. They're protesting, just like Dibrin says we should."

Schmalch plucked his handkerchief from a pocket and handed it to her. Keeping it on hand had been one of the Duke's simplest lessons, but one of the most useful. "I'm sure her taapa will get them out before—"

The apartment door banged open and Chisev hurried in, laden with shopping bags and wide-eyed. "Brizza's family was still in there," he said, "and Miss Marhig says there might've been more."

Glevit turned her face against Schmalch's shoulder and sobbed.

ALIARA

The Prick resolved into increasingly dilapidated neighborhoods, past buildings that should have been abandoned and businesses that had been long ago. The Hauler stopped just clear of the Temple of Spriggan to unload. Aliara slid off the wagon and ducked past Mud's Bar. Down the long alley, past trash bins and the stray cats that had survived the winter, she found the familiar coiled stair. She descended, pressed the trigger brick, and when the low door opened, she rolled handily into the tiny red-lighted room. Facing the bulky steel door, she closed her eyes and recalled the entry sequence, half-wondering if it had changed in her absence. She pressed the series of rivets circling the door until the familiar gears ground within. Dial, crank, and keyhole emerged.

Something in her stirred in anticipation. With damp fingers, she rubbed the braided key hidden in her coat collar's seam—the key she was never without. She'd not been this jittery, this uncertain since the first time she'd faced this door. Then, there'd been no key, and divining the many catches had taken hours. But that was the fundament of the Thung Toh—you had to *want* to belong so badly you would devote yourself to the idea of belonging, even without being certain the Toh was real.

From the first instant Aliara had learned of the organization's existence, she intended to count herself among them. She'd lurked in bars and dark byways for months, eavesdropping on conversations in search of any hint of the Toh's location. One night in a quiet corner of the Bottlescrew, she'd come across an elegant chivori and a grubby puka huddled together at a close-by table. The puka blended, dirty skin and mucky brown clothes complementing most other patrons and employees. His companion's suitcoat and fitted pants were conspicuous in the shabby Lower Rabble bar, but the thumb-sized ruby pinned on his jacket seemed flagrant, almost a taunt to the gutter babies who frequented the place. Carved into the shape of a feather, its sale could have fed and housed Syl and Aliara for a year, a pleasant upgrade from the cleft between buildings they'd called home after Syl had denied Orono's bequest and the local bootlickers had thrown them into the streets.

She glanced around the barroom. No one else seemed to have noticed the ornament. Odd. She'd expected far more interest in such a valuable piece.

Aliara leaned over the fly-specked bread on her plate and focused on the duo's conversation.

"…extraction *and* two eliminations?" the puka asked. "Busy day."

"Yes, it was." The chivori slid a wriggling velvet bag across the table. "Now scurry back to the Toh house. Luugrar's expecting those chits."

Aliara's plans to filch the ruby evaporated.

"Right." The puka dropped the bag and its annoyed contents into a pocket and looked around uncomfortably before clearing his throat. "Uh, anything, uh, else you got for me, Traus?"

The well-dressed man's tight, grey mouth stretched wide across his face. He withdrew another bag from his coat and shook it. Silver tinkled inside. "Waiting on this?"

The puka licked his olive lips and held out a hand.

"No stops. Straight to Luugrar."

"Yeah, Traus, I got it." The puka wiggled fingers and the bag dropped into his palm.

The chivori rose and strolled to the exit with a casual confidence that said this was not his first trip to the seedier regions of the Haven. Aliara let him go. Her quarry lingered a few minutes, slurping his dinner and beer. After a fine belch and a feeble pass at a barmaid, the puka tossed coppers on the table and scampered outside.

Aliara allowed three breaths before becoming his shadow.

Oblivious to her presence, the puka led her through the knotted seaside neighborhood along the now-familiar path. Within sight of the Prick's lighthouse, he turned abruptly down an inhospitable alley. She followed on cat's paws, passing trash bins, scavenging animals, and the peeling paint of long-forgotten advertisements. The puka vanished down a winding staircase at the alley's end. She followed slowly, hanging as far behind as she dared. When his steps halted, Aliara was certain she'd been spotted. Then a scrape, a thud, another scrape, and all went quiet below. She waited hundreds of heartbeats in the thick silence before continuing down the steps to a puzzling dead end.

She'd groped the walls until her fingers were raw before locating the loose brick high on the underside of the stairs. She wiggled it and a passage, low and wide, slid open. She darted in without thought of what might lie on the other side and found herself trapped in a little room filled with the nauseating undulation of red lumia light. She spent what felt like hours working the rivets ringing the door, sussing the dial, and finally cracking the lock, constantly afraid someone would arrive or depart and interrupt her, undoing the opportunity. She understood the meaning of the many dents that pitted the door's surface, tempted to add some of her own.

As she'd worked, her mind conjured images of what she might find inside—a challenge to fight, a group of wealthy villains, a cabal of black-robed adherents of Fext—yet when the final pin snicked into place and the quarrelsome door swung open, she could do little more than gape. The studious karju in wire-rimmed spectacles seated before her, head bowed toward his desk, was far from anything she'd imagined. He was short for his species but strong, wooly once-brown hair gone nearly white, coffee-colored skin etched with a web of wrinkles. At the creak of the door, he looked up from the pile of papers. She braced for a jump or a shout or even a physical challenge. Instead, he merely nodded politely and picked up his marking stick.

"Welcome to the Thung Toh. Your name and specialty?" he asked.

"Rift," Aliara had said, surprising herself with the spontaneous byname. "Theft."

Her repertoire had developed tremendously since that day. Kneeling before the well-worn combination lock, the wool of her coat itchy against her naked knees, the dance of nerves quieted. She turned the dial and listened, ear against the cold metal. In only a few clinks, she was inside, staring at the same old face, as well-worn as the lock. This time, however, Luugrar *did* jolt with shock at the sight of her.

"Rift!" He hopped up and hurried around the table, arms spread, baggy cardigan flapping around him.

For a moment, Aliara thought the contract house manager intended to hug her. She wasn't sure how to react. Instead Luugrar took her hands in his and held them as he beamed at her like he had a very impressive secret. Staring into that reassuring face, it was difficult to believe he'd once been the Toh's top dripper, a specialist in elimination by poison.

When he realized her discomfort, Luugrar released Aliara, patted one shoulder, and returned to his perch behind the desk. "We heard horrible things about what happened to you—you died, you were an invalid, you lost all your limbs…" He waved his hands to indicate a continuing list.

She relaxed, allowed a small smile. "Just a hole in my chest."

Luugrar's fuzzy white brows rose as his eyes drifted to her coat front. "Since you're breathing, I assume it's been filled."

"Yes."

"Excellent. Fist told me very little when he came to inform me of his jig in the Nors, only that you'd been gravely wounded, but weren't quite dead."

"Accurate."

"Tell me," he leaned forward, elbows on his ever-present mound of papers, and motioned her closer. "Was this part of the hubbub back in Danurak? The nonsense on the Big Island that had the Mucha all het up?"

She held his eyes.

He smirked and returned to a conversational volume. "I see, I see. Back to work then?"

Aliara nodded.

Luugrar moved his spectacles into place and feathered through the litter of his desk, muttering "yes, yes" as though someone were contradicting him until at last he looked up, expression straddling weariness and irritation.

He clicked his tongue. "I just assigned Dreg a jig I would have held for you had I known." He smiled and winked. "Traus sent the gen over by chit late last night. It's a quick turnaround; deadline's the end of the Festival. I had to get someone on it. 'Spose I should have waited just a bit longer." He shifted his spectacles to the top of his head. "Would you be willing to partner with our youngest operative?"

Aliara bit her lip as she considered. She'd worked with the boy once or twice over the handful of years he'd been among the Toh. He'd originally gone by Dread, but a joke built around the contract house and he quickly became Dreg, despite attempts to maintain his more dignified moniker. He had talent but poor impulse control and took unnecessary risks—and, as with all chivori his age, he often had difficulty keeping his thinking above the waistline.

Luugrar lowered his voice. "I'm worried he'll be in over his head."

"What's the jig?"

"Two eliminations and a bit of retrieval, complicated by the targets' locations and potential for inviting the City Corps' attention."

She gestured for him to continue.

"Marthoth Air & Sea has lost a valuable asset—Karna, the lead bookkeeper—to a newer rival." Luugrar offered her a wry grin. "The Lord of Pukatown has apparently crossed the bounds of acceptable business practices. Flark lured Marthoth's bookkeeper away along with some of Marthoth's ledgers and information on his business contacts."

"Those are the retrieval items?" Aliara asked.

"They are. Two ledgers and a journal." Luugrar tapped a chewed-on fingernail against his desk. "Plus, one other item."

Aliara raised her brows.

"A Voshar death mask."

One brow lowered. Syl had mentioned one was bound for Dockhaven.

"I know," Luugrar said, "but the client assured Traus it was no joke. It's something they found at the newest Tehtaemah dig."

"The one they say is Vosharilim?"

"Aren't they all?" He smiled, a wicked look that reminded her he'd once been far less grandfatherly. "Until they're not. The Mucha are involved in this one. Could be real."

Aliara frowned. Syl had mentioned the project at breakfast a couple quarterns ago. She hadn't thought much of it. Every year someone declared themselves to be the true locator of the ruins of Vosharilim, capital of an empire lost to the Cataclysm. At the end of the First Epoch, it was a city of extreme wealth and cultural center of the now-extinct voshari species. That made Vosharilim Ismae's most sought-after archaeological site. Most of those convinced they knew where to look wound up destitute laughing stocks or buried beneath the Great Desert's sands. Only a few were lucky enough to find cities—albeit ones that were not Vosharilim.

"I'm told Flark's on the *Ipesia*." Luugrar returned his cheaters to the top of his head and leaned back in the chair, arms crossed. "Unless I'm mistaken, you have access."

She nodded.

"That should simplify things. Dreg has the social graces of a rutting walrus. I wasn't sure how he'd manage to get inside. The bookkeeper was last seen at Flark's penthouse. The records are assumed to be there as well. The challenge will be getting Flark off the barge." He grumbled and flipped absently at his paperwork. "The contract stipulates there is to be no bloodshed or disturbance onboard the *Ipesia*. I trust you'll find an opportunity to remove the target from that environment."

She smirked.

"Had I known you were available…" He raised a hand and shook his head. "No matter. The fee is fifty silver bars for elimination of Flark, twenty-five for the bookkeeper, and twenty-five more for the retrievals. The boy claims to need the coin."

Aliara snorted. Dreg always needed silver.

"Don't know what he does with it," Luugrar said, shaking his head. "I don't think he's changed clothes in two years. He won't like splitting the boodle, but I suspect he'd like dying even less. Are you interested?"

"Without him, yes. With him…" She pulled a face.

"What?"

"See if he's amenable."

On slippered feet, Luugrar shuffled deeper into the room where a few operatives waiting on contracts sat at shabby wooden tables. He stopped briefly at one where a puka and a rhochrot known as Dire and Prime were softly chatting with a sultry karju named Bruclydian, all of them drinking spirits they'd brought with them. They laughed uproariously at whatever Luugrar said then pointed him to Dreg, who stood at one of the lockers, cursing and fumbling with something. The contract house manager intercepted him and the two spoke in low tones with frequent gestures and dramatic sighs, Dreg's eyes repeatedly flicking to Aliara. The conversation ended with a sharp word from Luugrar. The pair walked toward her.

Luugrar slid into position at his desk as Dreg arranged himself aggressively close, eyeing off with Aliara like alley cats behind a fish market.

Dreg's narrow face tapered to the smooth point of his chin. His nose was a bit too long and his eyes seemed perpetually sad, though his smirking mouth told a different tale. Mildly shorter than her, he was almost a cinereal, one of their species whose skin, hair, and eyes were matching shades of grey. He'd enhanced his natural coloring by coordinating every scrap of clothing. It would have been good camouflage had he not varied the generally unremarkable style with hair in a swirl of constantly shifting colors, a zoetic enhancement that must have cost him dearly. For work, he pulled the panoply into a stubby tail and hid it beneath a hood. He could not, however, hide the changing shades of his eyebrows or the fuzzy nib below his bottom lip.

"Luugrar tells me you want my jig," Dreg said.

"Tells me you need the help," she replied.

Luugrar studiously ignored them, busying himself with his many papers.

"I want that whole commission. I need every one of those ladies."

Her gaze slid to the pointless and costly affectation sprouting from his scalp. "Adding a tail?"

He hissed. "Look, there'll be loads to filch. The target's rich. His cuddy has to be ripe for a scaling. We'll split it. Scrape your Callas that way."

Money didn't mean much to Aliara. It was transitory, and she'd done fine without when necessary. There was no way, however, she would let this reckless puff of hair take it all.

"Commission was yours first. I'll take a quarter share." She held his eyes for a beat. "This time. And *all* antiquities of my choosing."

Dreg frowned and examined his scuffed boots. He returned to her with a smirk. "Right. Anything older than you, you can have."

Aliara stared until his grey eyes shifted away. "I lead," she said.

"It was my jig first, Rift," he said, voice holding its rasp despite the whine. "I'm binnacle on this one. I know what I'm doing. I don't need some older-than-the-floods razee leading me around."

She shrugged one shoulder and watched his face twist from petulance to surrender.

"Sink it," Dreg growled. "Deal."

Their fingers slid over one another's palms, cementing the agreement.

"Details," she said and held her hand out.

Dreg withdrew a chit from the breast pocket of his coat and tossed it to her. She pinched the ugly little creature gently between her thumb and forefinger, stroked its lumpy pink back, and stared into its lone eye, blacker even than her own. The chit went limp, focused only on her. In her mind, Aliara saw the catalogue photo of a Voshar death mask, heard Traus' voice recounting the same information Luugrar had delivered in far fewer words. He'd left out only one item: The recovered mask was to be left in a drop box at the Bank of Dockhaven. Aliara returned the chit to Dreg, who zipped it back into his pocket.

"You have the drop box key?" Aliara asked.

Dreg dug into another pocket and produced a small steel key. He gave her a nasty look and returned it to the pocket.

"Flark was on the barge," Aliara said. "Unlikely he'll leave soon."

"*You* were there?" Dreg's color-shifting brows went up.

"Yes."

"Can you get back in?"

Aliara took the invitation marker from her pocket and rolled it across her knuckles.

Dreg gaped. "Maybe you'll be worth the silver after all."

DREG

"Cellarette's in there." Rift jerked her chin toward an expensively furnished room. "One only. I don't need a tippled partner."

Dreg nodded, his face composed in an expression of indifference. As she started down the long hall dividing the apartment, he lingered in the foyer, enjoying her strut, imagining what she'd hidden under the bulky coat. He reached down and adjusted his roused critter to a more comfortable position.

When Rift disappeared up the winding iron stairs, Dreg let out a long breath, ran a palm over the stubby tail of his hair, and headed toward a drink. Across the parlor, an open drop-front cabinet twinkled with liquor bottles that invited him to sample. Hate it though he might, Rift was right—he needed his head straight for this jig. A good tipple was pleasant in the right setting. It was a shackle while scaling the side of a building or dodging some kartah of a guard.

Dreg opened a bottle of blackberry mead from Blisus of Imtnor—better than anything he'd find around town—and looked over the parlor. The furniture was an odd collection of antiques from around the isles. In front of the folkstone-tiled, slate-hearthed fireplace, a pair of dark-leather Pre-Occupation Hestal reclining chairs flanked an Orasian humidor table from a couple of emperors' lifetimes ago. All of them sat atop a Norian rug that cost as much as a few years rent in Dreg's building.

He dropped into one of the chairs, resting his glass on the broad moga-wood arm. Inside the humidor Dreg found a mishmash of exotic smokables: uurost, kosa, and paash. The smell was too tempting. He pocketed a tarry ball of kosa; later he may want to ignore the wear and tear of this job and enjoy a really swish dream. Sitting back, he took another swig of the mead, letting it roll slowly over his tongue while he looked out the picture window onto the bay.

After a few moments, he grew bored with the midday sun's glinting off the sea and explored the room. Over the fireplace was a painting he'd seen years ago in a textbook, an artist's imagining of some mythical battle between the Akkorak and one of the Duin, Aessatal. She was painted as a mostly nude white-skinned woman with silver wings. The beast was a scaly red sphere bursting from the sea in a torrent of waves. Dreg had really liked that textbook. He rose and moved over to the painting, brushing fingertips over the rough canvas, the hard nubs of the old oils nipping his skin. Had it hung in any other apartment, he would have returned later and filched the thing.

Dreg took the last swallow of the mead and turned a slow circle. He wanted this—the painting, the room, the wealth it represented. *This* was what he worked for, why he took any twitching job Luugrar offered, why he lived in a bilge well and squirreled away coin while he ate scraps. It chaffed him that Rift had all of this and still wanted a cut of his jig.

His parents had worried every day about how they would survive the next. They never changed, never tried to do anything more than that. The biggest gamble they would take was their monthly trek to the Lower Rabble for Tenta's Fish Fry. Not once had he seen either of them risk the crumbs they had for a chance at the whole loaf.

That wasn't him. If it was, he had enough coin saved now to start his own meadery in the rural Nors…if he wanted to be bored. Dreg wanted more. His father had been a deputy dockmaster, always, always, the underling. When Dreg wasn't attending classes, he lurked there at the docks, watching the ships, eavesdropping on the people, and—much to his displeasure—learning the ropes of bureaucracy.

On the night he snuck onboard *The Spriggish Bym*, the most swish ship he'd ever seen, Dreg's true ambition finally came clear. He was a couple years into his saypa, not quite a child, not quite an adult, stupid and clumsy. The ship's watch caught him, of course, and he was lucky the captain, Ruutad, didn't slit his throat. Dreg understood now that the man was a raider, possibly a smuggler or lord of the undermarket, but back then, all he knew was Ruutad was surrounded by gloss things, swank women, and a crew who jumped any time he sneezed.

While onboard *The Bym*, Dreg had stolen a little quena bird carved from streaky ochre stone, one of a set of zoo animals he'd spied during his explorations. The creature's hollow, pinpoint eyes had called to him, and it was in his pocket in a heartbeat. When Ruutad had retrieved the statue from its hiding place, he'd smiled at young Dreg in a way that still sent the boy's blood cold.

Against his better judgment, Dreg returned to Rift's cellarette and refilled his glass with the violet liquor as he replayed the scene.

"You don't want to steal from me, you sooty little twitch." Ruutad hadn't so much as touched him, but the menace had been unmistakable.

The boy who would become Dreg nodded and swallowed his tears.

"Why'd you take it?"

"It-it was so pretty," Dreg stammered.

The big karju had snorted at his honesty, his snoot jiggling, its silvery cosmetic glinting in the moonlight. "Nothing else *pretty* you wanted?" Ruutad growled.

Dreg shook his head then nodded. He wasn't sure of the correct response. He *wanted* everything he'd seen, but he hadn't been fool enough to take more than the bird.

"It's all pretty," he said. "I just wanted to see the ship, mister."

"Just wanted to see…?"

Dreg wiped the sleeve of his pajama top across his dripping nose. "It's a-all so swish. Not like the other dross around the Haven."

Ruutad had stared at him for long moments, but Dreg held those hard, brown eyes despite wanting to dive from the rail and swim under the dock. Finally, the man threw his big, tanned head back and laughed. It was badger's luck when he not only let Dreg keep the bird, but also allowed him to stay the night aboard the ship, eating and drinking and being doted on by women who thought the little chivori boy cute.

He'd come back the next day after classes. *The Spriggish Bym* was gone, but its promise lingered.

Dreg still had the carved quena, a fixture on the dresser in his cuddy, a reminder he saw every day.

"Enjoying yourself?" Rift's voice broke the memory.

Dreg flinched, slopping mead onto the cabinet. He righted himself and resumed his customary sneer, downing the rest of his glass with a shrug.

Rift dropped her rucksack on the kisselball table and leaned against its edge, studying him, those long, black eyes boring through his well-honed cockiness. She was geared up in a black catsuit, ever-present black boots, and holstered stilettos strapped at each of her hips. He'd bricked himself the first time he worked with her, only flubbed his part once or twice. She didn't mention the errors, but he was sure she remembered them—was probably tallying them now. His stomach flopped like a suffocating fish, and he wished for another drink.

"We'll stand out," she said abruptly.

"What?"

"In Pukatown."

"*Pfft.* I can blend."

Her unpainted mouth quirked at one corner. "We're tall for that neighborhood."

"So? I don't worry about being remembered," Dreg said. "The Corps aren't exactly honed."

"You've been fortunate."

He grunted. "Fine. What do you suggest? You *are* binnacle."

"Use someone who blends," she said.

"Huh?"

"Someone who can move around the building."

"Oh." Puka tenements had low ceilings. They'd be conspicuous slouching through the hallways while they cased the place. The picture in his head was ridiculous. "Yeah, we better get someone for interior recon."

"We'll visit the Barnacle."

"The Bitter Barnacle?" He snickered. "Doesn't seem like you'd dirty your toff boots there."

She shrugged.

He snatched the bottle he'd been draining. "You want a pop?"

She put her hand over his glass.

Dreg yanked it away and poured. She wanted to do the planning, fine, but she wasn't his mother. He gulped, coughing as the mead stuck in his throat. Rift waited, her face pointedly bland.

Maybe this would be her last jig. Maybe he'd be back to her penthouse for that painting and anything else he pleased.

"So, after your compa scopes the place," Dreg asked, "then what?"

Rift's shoulders bobbed. "Depends on what he finds. We'll survey outside."

"Not much of a plan."

"Not much to go on." She lightly patted his pocket where the chit napped.

Dreg belched into his fist. A bit of blackberry splashed into the back of his throat. His head swam more than intended, and he cursed himself.

Rift straightened and jerked her chin toward the exit. "Let's go."

SYLANDAIR

Syl lost count of how many revelers stopped him between gaming floor and cabin. By the time he arrived, the need to relieve himself was nearly overwhelming. He slid key into lock and had cracked his cabin door when a tall chivori man with zoet-green eyes leaned against the bulkhead beside him. He was muscular and well-dressed, his char-colored hair short and sharp.

"Sylandair, I've been looking for you," he said. "I thought to find you in the mingling room, but you've been conspicuously absent this year."

"My interests have lain elsewhere, Isnarin. Apologies if you have been left unsatisfied."

Isnarin laughed. "Surprisingly, that is not my reason for wanting to see you." He leaned closer and took a conspiratorial tone. "Last night at the Onpuur's reception I was approached by Chella Stond with an elimination contract on you."

Most who knew Isnarin believed him nothing more than a harmless gossip and socialite, but his well-crafted persona was a blind. For those he liked—and those who paid well—Isnarin offered more covert services.

Syl closed the cabin door, hand drifting toward his concealed dagger. "And did you take it?"

"Of course not," Isnarin said, faux offense flitting across his features. "I told her I'd consider it and give her my answer after the

Festival.”

“Should I expect an illness in my near future?” Syl asked.

Isnarin favored a slow-acting Vazztain poison. The symptoms would appear as nothing more than a common virus, counting on the target’s lack of immediate action to do its work.

“None brought by me. I am much too fond of you. Besides, I know you’ll pay me better to find out who Chella’s customer is.” Isnarin leaned in and kissed him. “What say we discuss it in your cabin?”

Syl resisted the themot-fueled urge to murder him here in the passageway. Instead, he retrieved a silver bar from his pocket and passed it to Isnarin, “Consider this a deposit. Apologies, but I am due back at the lyntyyl table soon and I need to wash up.”

Isnarin slipped the bar into the folds of his shirt, “I’ll find you later…when we have something more to discuss.”

“Gratitude.”

“Until then.” Isnarin kissed him again and swaggered away.

Syl ducked inside his cabin, sure to shut and lock the door, and hurried toward the lavatory. He wheeled around the corner into the main room and froze, need to urinate forgotten. Positioned precisely in the center of the breakfast table was a miniature house, one that was all too familiar.

Its base on one side was a solarium, two stories and a peaked roof stacked on top. The other side was a broader box, sloped roof angling toward the house’s center. A turret divided them, its bulbous top swirled with bands of rainbow colors.

It was the house he’d grown up in, the house in which Orono had savaged Aliara and Syl daily, the house he had dismantled and sent to the depths last autumn after Victuur Haus finally ended the mutated zoeticist.

The idea that he would never have to see a single brick of the thing again had brought Syl unimaginable pleasure. Finding it sitting here—even in miniature—left him nauseous and cold, violated yet again by the horrible place. He wished he'd not yet suggested Aliara leave the *Ipesia*.

Syl crept toward the model and touched it. It was solid, not a hallucination caused by the inebriants and narcotics he'd been consuming. He carefully dragged the table it squatted on away from the window wall and walked a slow circle around it. The sculpture was painfully accurate, though some of the original building's details, worn away over the years, were absent. It was as if the artist had seen the Orono Estate as the wreck it had become yet tried to represent it in all its garish glory.

Syl stopped half-way round the table. A crooked handle stuck out of the back, set between Orono's balcony and the stone terrace, the spot where one of the inventor's zoetic creations had died. Stamped on the patio in block letters was "Jetsam." The activist-cum-artist had turned their baleful eye on Syl. Had Chella's client, the one who had purchased the contract on Syl's life, commissioned the piece? If the piece was not a commission, and her client was, in fact, the artist, Syl was uncertain why Jetsam would want him dead. Perhaps an indictment of his role in last autumn's fete incident? Many people had died, and some still blamed Syl for driving Orono from his underground lair.

It could instead be a protest against Orono himself. Much about the zoeticist's untoward activities had come out since his death, though Syl had managed to keep his and Aliara's details largely private.

If this was a Jetsam piece, it *did* something, and the handle was the most obvious component. Syl turned it slowly. Something inside made a light clatter that sped up the faster he cranked. He closed his eyes and focused on the sound, the smooth shear of metal over metal, sharp and bright. It took him back to aftermids spent in the kitchen with Aliara and Flibuul. Orono's old puka attendant had been a marvelous cook, who insisted on making everything from scratch. Syl easily recalled watching him teach Aliara to make bleuurin, the raw ingredients slowly transforming into a steaming, crispy treat.

Syl stopped cranking. They had ground meat to make that pie. Flibuul's grinder had made the same noise.

Syl pushed the striped turret gently with one finger. It wobbled. He lifted it off. Inside were the knives and augur of a grinder, thick, shiny, and sharp. Syl returned the spire to its place and checked the building in search of a door or window from which its product would issue. Unsurprisingly, the front door swung out, a smooth steel tube leading up and into the structure. Jetsam had accurately depicted both the appearance and the nature of the building's character.

Syl leaned back, crossed his arms, and stared at the miniature, half expecting it to hop up and scurry away.

Though there was an unspoken injunction against killing one another on Marthoth's pleasure barge, Syl was unconvinced all in attendance would honor old forms. This intrusion into his private cabin was clue enough.

Isnarin could easily have made the delivery. He clearly knew where Syl was staying, but then most everyone knew Syl and Aliara occupied the deck-six luxury cabin, and at least two dozen other people had been in the corridor when Isnarin had said vrasaj.

Syl's bladder disturbed his contemplation, urging him to a different room. He showered, donned fresh clothes, and threw a blanket over the diminutive Orono mansion. Before returning to the lyntyyl table, he stopped at a concierge desk and arranged for a runner to collect the atrocious thing and deliver it to Sviroosa.

As he walked through the clotted collections of the wealthy and those who served them, the lingering questions of who had deposited the piece in his room, who was hiring for his death, and whether the two were related changed Syl's perception of the celebration and its attendees. Syl had kept the details of Orono's brutality secret after his death. Only a handful of people knew the old zoeticists' true nature well enough to equate his old home with a meat grinder. Nonetheless, he could imagine none of them leaving the unsettling sculpture in his cabin.

Syl settled at the lyntyyl table. From behind dark lenses, he scanned his opponents' faces, attempting to divine if one of them had gone so far as to commission his demise. While Idra could dissemble with the best of politicians, her expressions—however fleeting or subtle—always gave away her ploy. At the table, her face showed only concern for her next wager.

Flark's countenance was as impassive as it always was, though a vitriolic outburst might present itself at any moment. The bung had the most to gain from such an act. He wanted Syl's property, and the two of them had frustrated one another's machinations on more than one occasion. Though the latest reversal in their ongoing rivalry had gone in the puka's favor, Syl required little effort to imagine Flark would be so petty and conspicuous as to hire Jetsam, let alone fund Syl's murder.

Daisy was anxious, but her eyes were flicking to Flark, not Syl. A comforting indication that she, unlike her divested mate, knew the price of betrayal. Javit's attention, when not on the game, drifted to the old puka as well. She had more reason to hate Flark than Syl— unless she and Marthoth had learned something new. The card-sniffer showed no interest beyond his game. Unless Menelow was offended by Syl's inability to remember his given name, the bland man had nothing to gain.

Syl closed his eyes, drew a deep breath, and returned focus to the game.

While Javit, the hand's badger, built her stacks, Syl took the vial of themot from his pocket and twirled it between thumb and forefinger. "Care for a snuff, Idra?"

The Mayor extended her hand and Syl tossed it to her. She inhaled a small yellow mountain from her bare wrist and rolled the vial to Flark. The rotund, rickety puka tapped a bit on his thumb knuckle and snorted.

"Have you decided what to do with your property on Temple

Row yet, Imythedralin?" Idra asked.

Syl winced. The subject was too close to his thoughts. Perhaps he had underestimated the Mayor.

"Not as yet," he said. "Why do you ask?"

He studied her pretty face as he arranged his cards. Perhaps she had improved dramatically at this craft. Or it could be simple happenstance; the estate had been a popular subject of conversation for the aristocracy since Orono's mansion had come down.

"It's been a point of discussion at nearly every Council meeting since you took possession. Many of our citizens would like to see it born to a new form sooner rather than later."

Syl shrugged, counting out his fourth stack. "It is mine to do with as I like. I cannot fathom why an empty, walled property should cause such a fuss."

"That may be, but your neighbors—and others—would like to see the memories supplanted."

Lone card in Syl's hand, he ceded to Daisy, who quickly played her stacks.

"The structure has been razed," Syl said. "Would they like me to salt the earth as well?"

Idra made a face like a child told to eat squash. "If you don't present a plan soon, the Council does have options available. Rimadour did love his bylaws." She showed teeth with her smile.

"Seems to me you'll be homeless before long if you don't take one of my offers on the Heap's penthouse," Flark said, touch of glee in his dinner-plate eyes as he laid down his stacks.

Idra laughed. "Tell me, Flark, what would you do with that property if you and Imythedralin did reach an agreement?"

Menelow played his stacks with three remaining. Another hand ended without a winner. The round moved on.

"It's on Temple Row, the end close to the desal plant, right?" Flark asked.

The puka's false ignorance rankled Syl.

Idra nodded.

"I'd put up a tall building, luxury flats," Flark said. "Price them high. Rooms for the help go underground with some sort of swish food served on the main level. Name it something short and mysterious, maybe The Coil." He raised his bejeweled hands, framing an imaginary sign in midair, nodded, and slumped back into position. "People'd kill to live on Temple Row. Too bad Master Emat's dead. Maybe I can get one of his journeymen to design it."

They rolled for badger and Darvin shifted the silver statuette to Syl, who turned to Daisy, "You, too, are a well-regarded developer. What do you think of the plan?"

Flark snorted. "Don't bother asking *her.*"

"Ah, but Mister Flark, I often find the successful among us are supported—if not propped up entirely—by brilliant mates."

"Divested," Flark muttered.

Daisy scowled at him.

"Your opinion, Madame Daisy?" Syl asked.

The woman, equally as round as her former mate though many times more pleasant, wrinkled her nose. "It sounds like another eyesore, like all his new builds," Daisy said. "It rankles me to say, but he'd probably make a success of it. He knows the Haven's land game. Of course, he knows nothing about anything else, certainly not about women, but that's his little trull's problem now, not mine." She popped a morsel from the plate at her elbow.

Flark grabbed his walking stick and viciously poked a steward unfortunate enough to be within reach. In the blurred hours they had been playing, he'd used the stick against waitstaff, his guards, and random passers-by in attempts to obtain service. Given Flark's advanced years, Syl could hardly blame him for the lethargy. The same decades were far harder on a puka than on other species.

"Bring me a brew, a shot of khuit, and two scorillion patties," Flark commanded. The woman nodded and hurried out of poking distance. Flark passed one withering look over Daisy and returned to Syl. "The land game, like any, Duke, is a matter of giving your customers what they want. Of course, then you have to adjust your agreement once they have it." He chuckled. "And if they can't pay the rent, well, you have new employees, ones you don't need to pay. At least ten of the cuddies in my building at—"

Flark was cut off by a loud crash from the nearby table. A pair of men, rather saggy, if well-dressed, rolled on the floor, shouting abuses and clawing at one another like children. They separated and struggled to their feet, both snarling through their flaccid jowls.

Lyntyyl play stopped as the table gawked at the impromptu entertainment. Flark's guard, a dark woman who traded shifts with the burly ginger Vesven, positioned herself between her employer and the melee. Flark poked her with his stick until she moved enough to offer a good view.

Daisy elbowed Syl. "Two bars says the one in black's still standing when it's over."

"No," Syl said.

"I'll take that," Menelow called.

The taller combatant, blonde in a green-striped suit, wheeled and bumbled into a cordoned-off area, screeching as a dart sunk into his shoulder. The other—pink shirt, black suit, and dark hair— tackled his wounded opponent. A few bystanders wandered up, cheering the combatants on. Together the pair tumbled into the nearby string quartet, toppling a minikin and sending her velarin flying. The instrument crashed to the floor, its strings popping with bright twangs and pings as the pegbox snapped from the neck.

Marthoth's guards separated the pair, ejecting the blonde immediately. The dark-haired man in black was smoothed and returned to the gaming table by a floor manager, who mumbled a string of apologies. Menelow grumbled and slid two bars across the table to Daisy.

"That man," Javit nodded toward the gentleman in black, "is the owner of a farm that supplies propulsors to our fleet. He could stand on the kisselball table and piss into the crowd without being removed, so long as no one more important to Marthoth was splashed."

"You could've told me." Menelow's scowl made his face even sharper.

"Where," Javit asked, turning back to the table with a disconcerting grin, "is the fun in that?"

A puka in the uniform of the Farspeakers Combine wound through the dispersing gawkers and skittered up to Idra. On tiptoes she muttered into the Mayor's ear.

Idra sat forward, her expression storm-cloud dark. "What in the depths have you done, Flark?"

The old puka looked up at her with dull, unconcerned eyes. "When?"

"This morning you scug! Tenants were still inside that building!"

Flark shrugged and returned to his cards. "They were warned."

SCHMALCH

Thanks to a winter of coaching by the Duke, Schmalch had become a gloss sleebach player. He'd already won more than five Callas this aftermid and was certain he'd score the current round's boodle too. The hold was up to one Calla and thirty-eight coppers, and from the eager looks on his opponents' faces, it might creep up a bit more. As Schmalch considered his next move, his challengers across the marble-strewn board shifted and grumbled.

Anxiety was good, the Duke had told Schmalch. The more edgy and impatient the other players were, the more mistakes they'd make. The tactic seemed so obvious. Schmalch couldn't believe how many years he'd wasted being the nervous loser.

He moved two orange marbles into green spaces then tossed ten coppers in the pot.

"Raise," he said.

Frabo, the watery-looking minikin settled across the table, chuckled. "Dumb move, puka."

Schmalch shrugged one shoulder—a gesture he'd picked up from the Duke—and took a slow sip of his brew.

"Always appear confident, even if you are not," the Duke had told him during one of their many games. "Allow your opponents to believe you know something they do not."

Schmalch watched the worry behind Frabo's hazel eyes as they scraped the sleebach board. The minikin's hand jerked toward a grey marble then lurched away.

"Hurry it up, Frabo," Yemenie hissed through pink-stained lips. She shifted on the bench and adjusted her bulging bubs beneath her leotard. "I'm on next, and I'd like to have this wrapped up by then."

Frabo showed her his palm. "Stow it. I'm thinking here. I need another drink." He lifted his mug and waved it in the direction of Garl and the bar.

Yemenie sighed and turned to the stage, where a pair of bony, barely dressed chivori men writhed in what was intended to be a synchronized dance. To Schmalch, it looked more like a bunch of spasms matched up with the thudding beat of the melody engine that flanked the stage.

A puffy-eyed waitress walked by, her nose rubbed dark-pine from the hanky she'd been using to blow it.

Yemenie leaned in, displaying her cleavage, and whispered, "Did you hear about Hizzi's family? Lost her mother, a brother, and four cousins when the Yinago came down this morning."

Schmalch nodded soberly.

"Hizzi would've been there too if she hadn't had to work." Yemenie leaned back in her chair. "Has nothing now."

Frabo snatched a single yellow marble in his brown hand and shifted it to a red spot. He leaned back and grinned. "How about that?"

Schmalch opened his mouth, witty reply freezing in his throat as a slim, charcoal-grey hand dropped onto his shoulder. He followed the black-clad arm up to where Rift loomed over him, face shadowed by her hood, eyes hidden behind round lenses. She was dressed for work. He relaxed, but only a little.

"Rift," he said, "what're you doing here? I thought you and the Duke were at the big party?"

"Follow," she said.

"But I'm winning. The Duke says, 'never leave the table when you are winning.'"

"He says a lot of things. You're done here."

A man, roughly Rift's height with the same stretched-out features of their species, drifted up next to her. He, too, had concealed himself behind a hood and dark shades. His lips were set in a hard line across his bony face. The fuzzy blob of hair below his mouth was some incomprehensible color or series of colors, brilliant against his dishwater skin. His hands were thrust into the pockets of a long, grey oilcloth coat that bled into the matching shirt, pants, and boots as if he were made of nothing but dust.

Schmalch's eyes flicked back to Rift. "The Duke gave me the quartern off," he whined. "Come on, Rift. Let me finish the round."

She leaned over, breath warm on his ear. "I have work. Fifty Callas."

"You two finish up the game," Schmalch told Yemenie and Frabo. "I'm out."

He swung his legs over the bench and left the others bickering about how to split the hold.

Rift led him to a table as far from the stage and other patrons as possible and slid into a chair, angling her back to the wall. The dusty man followed, waiting until Schmalch climbed into his seat before settling in.

"Who's he?" Schmalch asked with a jerk of his head toward the stranger.

The man grunted.

"Dreg," Rift said.

It was a weird name, but Schmalch had heard weirder. He smiled at Dreg, who nodded a little.

"We need reconnaissance," she continued, slipping the shades down her nose to reveal hard, black eyes.

Schmalch felt his heart pick up speed. The last time he'd done that sort of stuff for her, things had gotten progressively worse until he woke up surrounded by a pod of big scaly draas.

The fear must have shown on his face because Rift raised a

hand, the one with that creepy bane zoet in it. With that poison thing pointed at him, the gesture wasn't as calming as she'd probably intended it to be.

"Nothing like the underground," she said. "This location's open, public."

"So why do you need me?"

"It's Pukatown."

"Rift thinks we'd be conspicuous snooping around," Dreg said in a voice that sounded like he needed to clear his throat.

Schmalch chuckled. "You would. Where is it? Anyplace I know?"

"Number eighty-two, Bay Run," Rift said.

Schmalch pinched the bridge of his nose, just above his eyes, and squinted in thought. "You mean the Bung Building?"

Schmalch knew the building, though he'd never had reason to go inside. He could see the showy thing from the window of Fohmsquah's apartment. Chisev, who'd taken up painting during the winter, found the tall boxy high-rise irritating, complaining that "it cuts out the sky and obstructs any decent view of the bay." Worch and Ilit had begun calling it the "toy tower" because they could build one like it with the blocks Schmalch gave them for Waking Night.

Rift nodded. "We need a quiet way in."

"And you want me to check it out for you?" Schmalch asked.

"Yes."

"For fifty Callas, sure. I'm in."

Dreg pointed a slim grey finger at Rift. "That's coming out of your coin."

Her eyes transferred slowly to him and held. Schmalch was glad he wasn't on the receiving end.

"Get my friend a drink," she said.

"What?" Dreg asked, more disbelief than question in his tone.

Rift jerked her head toward the bar. Dreg looked as though he might protest, changed his mind, and stood. Behind the sharp line of his sunshades, Schmalch was sure the chivori was rolling his eyes.

When he'd gone, Rift returned to Schmalch. "Talented but impetuous. Proficient someday. If he lives."

Schmalch understood enough of her words to hear the warning. "You think he'll get us in trouble?"

"There's a chance."

"What if I get pinched?" Schmalch asked. His heart danced in his chest again. "You'll come and get me? I won't have to stay in the Bag, right?"

"You won't be doing anything you can't get yourself out of."

"But what if they see me with you while you're doing… whatever it is you're doing? I don't want to go to jail. I've been there before and…" He shuddered. Each time it had been a painful and humiliating experience. Schmalch would do pretty much anything to avoid another stint in the Bag.

Rift raised the hand again. "Sylandair or I will retrieve you."

"Right away? Not days after or anything?"

"Right away."

"What if you're busy?"

"We'll send Sviroosa."

It sounded reasonable. And unlike the Duke, Rift usually said exactly what she meant.

"Promise?" he asked.

"Yes." Her eyes flicked to Dreg at the bar. "Trouble won't come from the Corps. If anything feels off, run." She returned to Schmalch. "Still want to do this?"

Schmalch sucked on his lips and considered, feet swinging a staccato beat against the table legs below. Fifty Callas would take care of his ante for a year. He might even buy Sviroosa a new plant to thank her for the gloss jacket she'd made him.

"Right," he said. "Yeah."

Dreg sloshed a brew down on the table. "Your drink, Lord Puka."

Schmalch took a sip from the thick head. It was the worst of the swill Garl sold, the stuff Schmalch hadn't drunk since becoming the Duke's assistant.

"Um, gratitude," he said, uncertainly.

Rift rose and nodded toward the exit. Schmalch slid from the chair and straightened his coat just like the Duke had instructed. When he walked away from the table and his barely touched drink, he was pretty sure he heard Dreg growl.

SYLANDAIR

"And…that…is…me," Daisy said as she lay down her final stack of cards. She raised her empty hands, stubby fingers fluttering, a move punctuated with a nasal cackle. She had won. With only eight hands in the round, the hold was light.

Syl had won the round immediately following Aliara's departure. Since then, he had been unable to empty his hands of cards.

"The hold is yours, Madame Daisy," the dealer said.

Stacking her coins and bars, Daisy chortled like a freshly fed animal. Syl supposed she had once been attractive for a puka, but age and aggravation had done their worst. He wondered how many years she would enjoy after Flark went back to the sea.

Syl slipped off his sunshades, withdrew the polished watch from his vest pocket, flipped it open, and frowned. "I have an appointment approaching quickly. What say we adjourn for a few hours, stretch our legs, and see to all other necessities?"

The others nodded or murmured agreement. Idra stood and stretched with an audible crackle of joints while Daisy dropped off her chair, still busy tallying the silver liberated from the hold. The others followed with grim faces. Only Flark remained, chomping at the remnants of his meal.

Syl slid a few Callas to the dealer and rose, his own joints protesting. He straightened the pleats of his pants, slung his suitcoat over one arm, and perused the room. Though faces had changed, activity on the gaming deck seemed much the same as it had the last time he'd left the table. No one appeared to be paying particular attention as he made his way toward the ironically named Pedestrian, a cozy, yet painfully chic restaurant.

With the round of lyntyyl wrapped earlier than expected, Syl was glad for the chance to arrive at the restaurant first. This meeting with Mintryl Marthoth was integral to his plans for his duchy, Isay. He could use the spare moments to compose his ragged nerves.

Syl wound his way past the other gaming tables, debating whether or not to stop for a cocktail. His mind was a muddle of agendas competing for his attention. The Festival had allowed him to focus on Flark, whose broken agreement had left Syl without the death mask, a necessary possession if he intended to thwart Nihal Savesti before she could replicate Orono's horrific experiment. Flark's attempts to swindle Syl and Aliara out of their home had compounded his nuisance. Add to that Aliara's return to work, Syl's failing duchy, as well as his investigation of the records he'd found in Club Perpetual last autumn, and the elimination contract on his head seemed almost too much to juggle.

He paused to gaze out the panoramic window at the waves of the Sound, centering himself. If only he could send all his concerns to the depths as easily as he had consigned the bricks of Orono's mansion to Ruru's embrace. Syl closed his eyes, took a deep breath, and focused on the immediate: Marthoth and his potential regarding the Duchy of Isay.

A poor harvest and shipping delays the previous year had left Isay's annual revenue woefully short of the crown's expectations. Had Syl not covered the shortfall with his personal funds, the duchy would be in arrears, a convenient justification to remove its duke should the Empress wish. Given his history with Her Majesty Dotij Tefif'Cazuul, Syl had little doubt his removal would equal death.

Determined to avoid any recurrence this year, Syl had commissioned a spark-enhanced seed from Rilvmor Agrizoets to guarantee a boon crop. In addition, he had evaluated a number of alternative revenue streams available to his duchy. Many of the potentials represented new commodities for Isay, sale of the rest had been expressly forbidden by the crown. It was for all this that Syl required Marthoth; the shipper's dependability and discretion were renowned.

A hand gripped his arm. Syl jerked free and turned—ready to break the offender's wrist—and found Idra smiling up at him, the copper-gilt tips of her silvery-white hair glinting in the lumia lights.

Syl had not noticed her following him. The implication was unnerving.

"Your message last quartern…" Idra said with a quick bat of her lashes, tipped to match the hair.

"Hm?"

"You said you acquired something I might find interesting, but," she gave him a pouty frown, "you weren't specific. I've been curious, Sylandair."

"Ah yes. The item—items, actually—came to me mid-winter."

"Similar to what you've procured for me in the past?"

"A nearly unique find."

Her smile spread, revealing little cracks in her too-thick lip tint. "Did you bring them with you?"

Syl nodded.

"Show me."

"Later. As I mentioned at the table, I have an appointment."

The pleasant flirtatiousness vanished. "Given the situation with your building, who's more important than your mayor?"

Syl let a scoff slip.

A glower tickled the corners of Idra's pale blue eyes, but she kept her best fake smile in place.

"I made arrangements to enjoy a repast with our host," Syl said.

"The hulking git will wait."

"Next recess perhaps?"

Idra's forehead wrinkled and her mouth drooped to a childish frown. "You plan to spend the whole break with that scug? What could you two possibly have to discuss that could take that long?"

"I'm afraid, Idra dear, this concerns neither you nor Dockhaven."

Her eyes narrowed.

"If I have time afterward, I would be pleased to show you the acquisition and discuss my terms," Syl said. "For now, the concerns of Isay take precedent."

"Ugh. That puddle of a duchy?"

He sneered. "Do you really think it wise to antagonize me at this time?"

"Fine, Imythedralin. I'll be waiting in the mingling room. Find me when you're done with your appointment."

She wheeled and flitted toward the central staircase, ember gown eddying behind as though her body dribbled lava. Syl watched Idra for a moment, checked his watch, and strolled to one of the *Ipesia*'s many courtesy bars, mind roiling once more. Fresh drink in hand, he leaned against the bar and allowed his tangled thoughts to unravel. He'd learned long ago the best way to get a song out of one's head was to sing it through.

Over the past months he had pondered this next phase of his life. When he had first stood over the mangled and mutated carcass that was once Orono, Syl had experienced an almost bewildering sense of emptiness. Haus had done thorough work; there was no doubt the old pervert was finally dead. For the first time in memory, no shadow lurked over him and Aliara, silently affecting their decisions. The absence had been glorious at first. Now, the world seemed too open.

Syl had distracted himself by conceiving new objectives and tending to Aliara in her convalescence. He had spent those first days doing nothing but lying in bed, watching her breathe, feeling as though he, too, had a hole in his chest. It was his fault she had been injured, his fault she had nearly died. She had not really needed him, though. Her recovery could be credited to Sviroosa, Ranaran, and her own uncompromising resilience, but Syl had found succor in pretending that his ministrations had some meaningful effect.

When he was certain Aliara would live, the old discontent had returned to fill the void.

Having stayed with them after the fete incident, Haus then kept Syl occupied making plans. Though their motives differed, both wanted to locate Nihal Savesti and frustrate her attempts to recreate the experiment that had left Orono so horribly mutated. Should Nihal manage to grant herself unending life, the horrors she could perpetrate on all the isles would dwarf those Orono had heaped upon Dockhaven. Syl had levelled his old keeper's mansion and its contents, filled in the underground chamber, and was razing the ruined areas of the desal plant. He wanted every vestige of Orono gone, and that included the research documents Nihal had absconded with—after committing fratricide in his parlor.

Nihal's brother, the late Master Hergis Savesti, had left Syl and Haus with only two clues about The Book of Omatha. First, he had said that successfully making its promised transformation would require spark from a voshari, a species vanished from Ismae some two millennia past. Second, was spark from one of the B'hintal Dadeyah termini, zoetic creatures scattered across Ismae and connected to the green moon's hub. Planted in the soil like unchanging flora, the termini were the physical interfaces with the Egress, Ismae's ancient system of near-instantaneous transport, whose only fault was the traveler's sickness that followed use. The Cataclysm had left all Dadeyah's termini beneath the seas, lost and unusable.

The plan had seemed simple: Haus would track Nihal. Syl would hire agents to locate, surveil, and if necessary, acquire any artifact known or even purported to contain any remaining tissues from a voshari. No one had spark from a Dadeyah terminus. None had been found. It was of no concern.

Then word of the Castling Sea dive reached them. Having finally cooperated, Queen's College and the Mucha Colleges believed they had together located the city of Gasole, home to one of the lost termini. Plans changed. After calling in a few markers, Syl ensured that when the Gasole dive's crew set out, Haus was on it, ready to thwart Hergis' sister should she attempt to scale any samples recovered by the thoroughly unaware researchers.

By the time the month of Etylon came, Haus was gone to the dive and workers were busily expanding Syl and Aliara's penthouse into the neighboring unit. Directing their efforts, surrounded by noise and chaos, gave Syl an outlet for his restlessness, though the efficiency of the construction firm left him aimless once again within a few quarterns.

The next motivation came on a grim Alsolon morning when the sky spat rain so cold it froze midair and clattered against the windows. A runner from the farspeech office knocked on the door before dawn, message tin in her shivering palm. Astonished the girl had managed to scale the precarious stairs to the penthouse, Syl tipped her liberally and sent her to the kitchen for the breakfast Sviroosa was preparing. He plucked the wriggling chit from its tin and gazed into the glassy black eye. The familiar nasal drone of the Lower Rabble's farspeaker supplanted Syl's morning ennui.

"Message for Duke Imythedralin from the Dominion of Chiva'vastezz," the voice said. "Message is as follows: 'Raiders have attacked the port of Isay. Sixteen dead, most are of the house guard. Majority of new blalal berry seed stolen, main docks and loading cranes destroyed, harbor flag taken. The crown has deployed a frigate to the area. No other response or assistance is expected. We await your instruction, Proxy Yyere.' End message."

His duchy was a more-than-odd target for a raider clan. It was deep in the Dominion's waters and did not possess much of value. All significant holdings would be found in Faisa, the duchy's seat, located miles inland from the port. Pausing their rampage long enough to abscond with his harbor flag made it obvious the move was a missive.

Syl would have, under normal circumstances, chartered a baluut for Chiva'vastezz upon receiving the news. Yet, with Aliara growing more active each day—despite her surgeon's admonitions—he was loathe to leave, and she could not travel in her state. Inaction, however, was unsupportable, so he'd done what he could from the Haven, trusting Yyere to manage the rest. Obtaining reliable and discreet transportation from Marthoth would be another sizable step toward Isay's recovery.

Syl rattled the ice in his drink, took a last sip, and climbed to deck two, where Pedestrian waited. As the bistro's door came into in sight, he was intercepted once more.

"Duke Imythedralin?" a pleasantly remembered dulcet voice inquired.

"Lady Orilausko," Syl replied before turning. It seemed a petite chivori woman would again hamper his progress toward Marthoth. At least Orilausko's raillery would be more enjoyable than Idra's disappointing attempts at repartee.

Years away from Dockhaven had not dulled Orilausko's elegance—yellow-green silk set off simple silver accessories, her jet hair piled and looped like unassuming art. Intricate black tattoos ran down her neck and spine, over her shoulders and down both arms, sinister vines, sprouting not fruit but icons that illustrated the accomplishments of a Seer of Dream and Waking who had once sat at the Vazztain Empress' left.

More than a decade past, Orilausko had been exiled from the Dominion, days after Syl's first attendance at court, the rumored causes profligate. Believed dead, she reappeared months later in Dockhaven, where she'd built a new life and fortune as proprietor of the Caba Club, before disappearing once again years later, this time into the backwaters of Locnor.

Yet she always returned to the Haven for Marthoth's semiannual galas.

Syl took her hands and they brushed ears, wondering as he'd done with everyone since Isnarin's revelation, whether or not Orilausko was here to kill him.

"A welcome pleasure, Your Ladyship." He released the one-time Seer's hands.

"It's hardly necessary to call me Lady anymore, Duke Imythedralin."

"The same could be said for addressing an old friend by his title."

"Old friends are the most dangerous and often the quickest to take offense," Orilausko countered with a wink.

Syl laughed. She was a lovely, funny, intelligent woman—and unnerving. He had several times considered inviting her into one of his intrigues, but always found himself unable to do so. Orilausko's pleasant gaze, vapid when coming from another, made Syl feel as though she could see into him so deeply that she would leave him without secrets.

"I was terribly sorry to hear of your mate's injury." Orilausko's voice was sweet and mellow. "She has recuperated?"

"Indeed, Aliara is well. Gratitude," Syl said.

She pressed her lips together, looked to either side, and stood on tiptoe. "Have you been to court recently?" she asked in a melodramatic whisper.

"No. Why?"

Her furtiveness disappeared into a frown. "I was hoping you'd have some gossip. I love the Festival, and plenty of chinwagging goes on here, but sometimes I miss the drama of court. You give people enough money and they'll show you just how wicked they can be." She laughed, a girlish giggle. "And hearing about all that wickedness is so entertaining."

"I will pay you a visit after I next attend court, and tell you every gory, ghastly, and vulgar story I hear." He took the watch from his pocket. "But for now, I fear I must leave you or I will be late to dine with our host."

Orilausko stepped aside to let him pass. "Ask for their *sklintara e cono*. No." She waved her suggestion away. "You won't need to. Mintryl will already have some waiting."

As he always did when speaking with her, Syl wondered if Orilausko spoke of a mere assumption based on her knowledge of and experience with Marthoth or if a legitimate vision of the impending meal had manifested for her. Someday when he was less concerned with propriety, he might ask.

SCHMALCH

Outside, aftermid had shifted to early evening, and people were going from workday to Festival time—laborers, shoppers, entertainers, and revelers. Rift cut a line through them, Schmalch and Dreg riding her wake. The news callers shouted about the Mayor trying to attract more Mucha graduates to the city and her new project with the Norians before launching into how her election odds were dropping thanks to death count from the Yinago's implosion this morning. Their voices mixed with vendors hocking everything from pretty scarves to live ducks. Schmalch couldn't make out details from any of the pitchmen.

He scurried along after Rift and her buddy, dodging taller bodies. A street seller offering re-soled shoes leapt in front of him, thrust a pair of scuffed lace-ups in his face and started shouting about how wearing these shoes would result in a wage increase. Schmalch ducked under the man's legs and hurried away. With the fifty Callas he was about to make, he could buy all that guy's used shoes. Not that he wanted to.

As they reached Bay Run, the Bung Building emerged from the fog, as ugly and squat as its owner, its dirty bricks black with the early evening mists. The place was nearly twice the size of the Heap, where Schmalch lived with the Duke and Rift and Sviroosa. The top two stories of this one were set in from the edge and taller than the other levels, like a baby's hat on a fat man's head. That part was all glass and lights you could see for blocks, not like the lower levels with their flat walls, narrow windows, and slide-up doors. The only trimmings were lively painted advertisements and scattered graffiti.

Rift had been right. She and Dreg stood out against the pukas who roamed the streets, though not as much as the nearby pair of rhochrots dickering with a vendor over a bag of red byk fruits. As Rift drifted past the vendor's cart, a yellow-rinded piminee bigger than Schmalch's fist disappeared from the pile. The vendor was too busy arguing with her enormous, four-legged customers to notice.

Rift stopped a block away, sinking into surrounding shadows in a way Schmalch could never quite master.

"What is that?" she asked, nodding toward the Bung Building.

"You mean the building? That's the one you wanted, right?" Schmalch asked.

"No." Rift pointed down the street to where a platoon of agitated pukas crowded the front door of the Bung. A few members of the City Corps lingered nearby, looking angrier than the protestors. "Them."

"Oh yeah!" Schmalch said. "I guess you've been out in the Sound since Waking Night. Flark imploded a building this morning."

"Didn't you hear about it at the fancy party?" Dreg asked.

Rift's brows drew together. "He razed it. So?"

"He evicted everyone who lives, uh, lived there on Planting Day, just threw 'em out," Schmalch said. "Fohmsquah's bound-family's living with her and the kids right now. Her cuddy is *full*. They're saying a few families were still inside when it came down. Everybody's pretty gammed off at Flark, so they're hanging around his building and yelling."

Dreg laughed. "And he's not even here to see them."

"Huh?" Schmalch looked from one grey face to the other but found no answer.

Rift led them past the angry crowd to the darkening lee of the Bung and squatted, eyes at Schmalch's level. "Go in. Look for an inconspicuous route to the penthouse."

Schmalch nodded, glad to have recognized the big word. "You'll be here when I get back?"

"Here or close." She looked up at the building.

"What if you're not?"

"Leave. Go home."

"Right."

Rift stood and scanned the shore-side dock while Dreg studied the building's wall like he might find gems buried there. Schmalch scampered away, squeezing between the angry protestors until he popped into the building like soap from wet fingers.

Shields and shock batons at the ready, a couple of karju Abog were eyeing anyone entering the spacious lobby, probably one of the building's few levels sized for the comfort anyone other than pukas. Schmalch did his best to smile, offering the pair a casual wave as he hustled past. Beyond, tenants came and went through stairwells on both sides of the lobby, none of them showing any interest in Schmalch. In the center of the room sat a lift framed with wrought iron curlicues, the only pretty thing in sight. A pair of unusually muscular pukas stood on one side of the door chatting. When Schmalch entered the lift and reached for the control lever, one of them followed.

"Uh-uh. Nope." The muscleman shook his head. He was about Schmalch's height, but darker green, almost brown, what their people called a barker. His arms were as thick as a karju's.

Schmalch swallowed the urge to run. "Just going up." Thinking about what the Duke might say he added, "I have business up there." He fished one of his newly won Callas from of the pocket of his suitcoat and held it out. "Can you take me up?"

Both of them laughed.

The first one leaned back and studied Schmalch. "You might look the part," he poked Schmalch's coat with a dirty finger, "but this lift's not for you, not for nobody but Flark unless he says they're all right. It goes to the boss' place, that's it, and he sure didn't leave me your name."

"But you don't know my name."

"Don't need to. He didn't leave no names at all."

"He didn't leave no names," the second one said. "He's not here, ya tetchy douse."

Schmalch returned the Calla to his pocket and gave the pair his best fake smile. "Right. Apologies. I've never visited the Bun-, um, him before. I'll try the stairs."

"You do that," the first one said.

Schmalch hurried away, feeling their eyes on his back, and rushed upstairs. The stairwell ended at the twelfth floor. A corridor ran a rigid rectangle around the building, doorways on both sides of the hall. With the penthouse on top, that meant no air well; the interior apartments had no windows. Everything was designed to puka-height. "Shorter buildings mean cheaper ones," Flark had explained one day when he and the Duke were playing cards.

Schmalch read off apartment numbers quietly to himself, watching for any specially marked doors or another stairwell.

He'd made it half-way around the building when he spied a lighted sign sticking out from the wall that announced another exit, probably the one from the other side of the lobby. Still, he'd need to check it out. The place was quiet except for a group of young pukas casting coppers. Schmalch started down the hall and they looked up. For a moment, all he saw was the horrible slack faces of the kids who'd attacked him and the Duke and Rift a few months ago. He closed his eyes, swallowed, and looked again. Fohmsquah had taught him that one.

These kids were big, close to being out on their own. Two boys who looked like twins squatted in front of a tall, angry-looking boy and a round girl, possibly pregnant. Almost as one, they smiled.

"Who're you?" the tallest one asked. He took a toothpick from between his teeth.

The twins stood up, coppers forgotten on the floor. The girl hung on the leader's arm like clumsy jewelry.

"Nobody," Schmalch said, strolling forward as casually as he could manage. "I'm just visiting my…my aunt."

"Oh, are you?" the tall boy asked.

The girl giggled.

"Which cuddy's she in?" the boy asked, smile growing. "We might know her."

Schmalch glanced at the doors flanking him. He stood between 1212 and 1211. He'd started at apartment 1236. He went with his best guess. "She's in 1204."

All three lackies giggled.

"Is she new?" the boy asked, moving to block passage when Schmalch was almost on him. "Cause last I looked, Spizl and his pap were the only tenants there."

Schmalch made a show of frowning. "Maybe I wrote it down wrong. How about 204? Does an old lady live there?"

The boy, now within arm's reach, grinned. "Feck if I know. Two's not my floor."

"That's a swish jacket," the giggling girl said, pointing to Schmalch's brown corduroy coat.

"Yeah, it sure is." The boy snatched a bit of fabric and rubbed it between his fingers. He reached into his pocket and pulled out a sharp, double-edged sticker. "Give it up, toff. While you're at it, leave all your dosh in the pockets."

Schmalch gulped and did the only thing that came to mind. He waved at the empty space behind the group "Vrasaj, Auntie!"

The quartet looked over their shoulders.

Schmalch spun and ran.

The group caught on and followed.

He was half-way to the stairwell door when he felt the first tug on his coat. Then a yank. The coat threatened to slide off his shoulders, but Schmalch clung on. It was his first dress coat. Sviroosa made it.

There was no way these twitches would have it.

Only two strides in front of him, an apartment door creaked open. An old woman and some shaggy pet on a leash came blundering out. Schmalch dove to the side. Stitching popped and the grip on his coat released. He raced forward, bouncing off the stairwell exit's door frame before rushing down the steps, the hooligans' patter mixing with shouts and the angry yips of the little animal.

Schmalch vaulted the handrail, landing with a *whoof!* on the steps below, barely on keel. One of the twins tried to follow but yelped and bounced down the stairs. He swiped at Schmalch as he passed, only brushing a pantleg before his skull cracked against a tread. His eyes rolled back, and he slid limply onto the landing. Schmalch hopped over him and ducked into the seventh floor, curses at his back.

He rushed down the corridor toward the other exit, nearly tripping as he came around a corner and caught his foot on a bit of worn carpet. A man carrying a basket of laundry down the hall leaped to one side. As he passed, Schmalch grabbed the basket and hurled it behind him, catching the tall boy in the chest. The thug swore and stumbled while the laundry man chastised him.

The other twin still gave chase.

Schmalch raced into the second stairwell, kicked the stop out of place, and slammed the door, the goon only heartbeats away. Schmalch leaned on the door, legs braced against the newel post. He lurched painfully as his pursuer slammed against the steel surface hard enough to crack bone.

Schmalch took off. He heard no more footsteps, still he ran— down the stairs, through the busy lobby, between the Abog guards, and into the chanting protesters.

Crouched in the crowd and carefully avoiding the Corps, Schmalch worked his way to the side of the building where Rift waited. The instant he was out of sight, he stopped and took off his coat. The back seam was ripped almost halfway up, some weird ribbony thing dangling out like a thirsty cat's tongue. Worse yet, the lift man had left a greasy blot on the lapel when he'd poked Schmalch.

Something between panic and grief ran through him. He hoped it wasn't ruined, hoped Sviroosa wouldn't be upset. Maybe he could buy her something *really* nice with the fifty ladies Rift was paying him. That might soften her unhappiness when he showed her the stain and tear.

Schmalch drew a deep breath and slunk around the corner of the building.

Both chivori were gone. His eyes weren't as good as theirs in the dusk, and they had been dressed in gloomy colors. Maybe he just couldn't see them. Schmalch crept toward the seawall, watching for any movement, seeing none. He was about ready to go home when a grey figure dropped from the sky, sending Schmalch backward, tumbling onto his ass.

Dreg stood over him and laughed, a rusty sound that made Schmalch's backside pucker. The chivori's hand thrust down at him and Schmalch squeezed his eyes tight expecting a blow.

"What's wrong with you?" the scratchy voice asked. "Do you want a hand up or not?"

Schmalch opened one eye to find Dreg waiting to give him a lift. Pulled to his feet, Schmalch dusted off, wishing he'd worn less swish clothes to the Barnacle tonight.

"Can't see much." Rift materialized from the shadows, monocular in hand, her creepy chivori eyes glinting in the faint light like a stray cat's. "Two stories, lots of glass and lights, decorative façade. Patio along three walls, including seaside."

"Anyone home?" Dreg asked.

"Motion and shadows in three places. Could be more." Rift looked down at Schmalch. "So?"

"No soap," Schmalch said with a shake of his head. "Both stairwells end on twelve. There's a lift, but two big guys guard it. They gave me a hard time, told me it goes to the boss' place and nowhere else. They weren't too happy about me trying to use it, so

I left quick. I don't think they'll remember me. Oh, and there's two Abog with shock batons keeping the protesters out."

Rift crouched, slipping the monocular into her unslung pack and gazed up the side of the building. "We climb," she said after a moment. "Looks feasible."

"The façade is dreck, likes to crumble," Dreg said. "I made it up a few stories but decided I should wait for you."

Schmalch saw the gleam of white teeth from beneath the man's hood. He couldn't fathom why someone would enjoy climbing a building, especially one this tall. The idea made Schmalch nauseous. He hoped he didn't have to climb with them.

"Do they rent dinghies near here?" Head still tilted skyward, Rift motioned toward the Slaughteryards' wharf, a few blocks up the coast.

No one answered. Rift pointed to Schmalch.

"Oh!" Schmalch said. "Yeah, I know a place pretty close. Might still be open."

"Rent one, wait for us there." She looked away from the building and leaned over the seawall, indicating a spot where Rimadour Bay lapped the rocky shore below the Bung Building.

"What if they're closed for rentals?" Schmalch asked.

"Borrow it." Rift removed her cloak, stuffed it into her pack, and started climbing.

IDRA

Idra nearly backed out of the mingling room as soon as she stepped in. Daisy sat on a burgundy divan, back to the entry, eyes on a tall—for a puka—young man. Fortunately, she was still dressed, both hands in view.

Idra came up from behind, waiting until her lips nearly touched the puka's ear. "Daisy! I didn't expect you to be here."

Startled, Daisy recoiled with a sneer that went quickly flat.

Idra straightened and smiled.

"With that hold I just won, I thought I'd celebrate." The round puka pointed a ring-heavy finger at the tall young man, who looked bored as he watched a zoetically altered karju use her tail in curious ways. "I've been watching that one."

"Very…handsome." Idra tried to keep the inflection from her voice, but the word still sounded like a question. Pukas were small, green, and hairless, not attributes she sought in a companion. No matter the arrangement of their features, she found them unappealing. Not even when her libido was at its most urgent had she considered such an alternative.

"What brings you here?" Daisy pulled a nut-crusted kehtal stick from the floral embroidered bag on her lap and pointed it at Idra. "Sit."

"I'm meeting Imythedralin." She lit on the divan beside the puka.

"Oh really?" Daisy asked, hopeful note in her voice. "Will you be staying out here to share with us all or taking one of the private stalls?"

"Nothing like that." Idra scratched absently at a spot on her arm. "Just business."

"Too bad."

"He's all twitchy right now. Too much themot and not enough sleep. I doubt he'd be up to his usual standard."

Daisy chuckled. "Enough pleasantries. What do you want?" She bit off the end of the candy and chewed as she spoke. A flake of toffee clung to her chin before floating to the breast of her garish green gown. "We both know you don't like me much more than you like Flark."

Idra shifted her seat. She hated this sort of directness. She liked to approach topics like this obliquely, discreetly. "What I owe you..." Idra attempted similar candor. "Is there anything I can do for you, retrieve for you, broker for you to reduce my debt, Daisy?"

The puka left off chewing and studied Idra, one hand toying with the silk flower pasted to her scalp. Behind her, the mingling room doors swung open, ushering in a pair of chivori, who tumbled through the curtains of a private stall, though their enthusiasm was easily overheard.

"I did a little brokering for Flark and he made a reduction. I traded a particularly valuable artifact to Pitta for the same." Idra smiled and leaned closer, the way friends were supposed to. "I thought we might be able to make a similar arrangement."

Daisy returned to eating. "Did he try to back out after you'd already done your part?"

"Yes." Idra leaned away. Flark had tried to cut the percentage reduced by half. Only when Idra reminded him they'd had a witness—Imythedralin—did he acquiesce.

"Typical." Daisy took another bite of candy and sighed. "My eldest son Ghulf is an idiot. He washed out of Queen's College—as if such a thing could even be possible. He won't marry the girl he's gotten pregnant—says he wants to live the chivori way." Her face puckered as she glared at Idra. "All my gratitude to you and your kind for that. And he's fourteen and still living at home."

Idra blinked, waiting to hear the actual favor.

Daisy swallowed and took another bite. "Give him a job—a good one, not somebody's lackey—and I'll give you a reduction." She pointed the stub of the kehtal stick at Idra. "The better the position, the higher the reduction."

It never hurt to have a puka who stood to inherit so much as an ally. Idra could think of three mid-level roles ideal for such a person. Each had a good title, but the required work amounted to nothing more than talking with similarly neutered bureaucrats about what the functionaries were up to—and coming up with ways to gam things up. Even a complete douse could slip into one of those roles with no experience and collect a salary.

"I know the exact thing he'll be perfect for. I'll start my assistant on the documentation later today. Your son will work in City Hall and have his own assistant." Idra raised a glass and waggled it at Daisy. "What percentage would that earn me?"

"If it's as good as you say…" She fiddled with the daisy, mouth poked out like a fish's. "Twenty-five percent—with the guarantee you won't get rid of him for at least ten years."

"What if he quits?"

"Your reduction stands." Daisy picked up another kehtal stick and crunched. "That's probably what he'll do. Idiot child."

Idra extended an arm and they cemented their agreement.

A stooped karju man in spectacles and a fantastically expensive suit entered and held one of the mingling room's doors for a woman in bright red—pantsuit, shirt, gloves and all. Her white-blonde hair was swept up in a coil so intricate it could have belonged to a Mucha.

Idra cringed.

"What?" Daisy asked, looking around. "Oh, the Dobencourt matriarch. Gad, but that's a lot of red."

The pair settled on a cream sofa on the other side of the room. Pitta's well-painted face crinkled into a smile and she wiggled fingers at Idra and Daisy.

Because the red suit wasn't showy enough, Pitta had donned an antique headpiece. A fine silver chain skimmed her hairline, another traced the centerline of her scalp. At their forehead intersection hung a medallion stamped with voshari iconography. Below that, dangling so low it almost brushed Pitta's snoot, was a teardrop-shaped sand claret, a red stone the size of a thumbnail. Idra had seen the piece before—even tried it on—while picking through the crates stolen in the Yenderot's raid of the *Nimomyne*. As intermediary, the boodle had come to Idra first. Flark hadn't wanted to risk a raider clan knowing exactly who'd hired them.

Idra waved back.

"Ugh, she looks like a blood clot." Daisy said. "Which husband is that?"

"Lurtair. The second. A travelogue writer."

"How old is he? He looks old but I can never tell with karju."

"Not as young as Grehv. Not as old as Handsome. She likes…" Idra pointed to a pair of youngish karju across the room. "That age, whatever it is. After a few years, they get older, she gets bored, and she finds another one, puts the old ones to work taking care of her." Idra smiled at Pitta, who was still looking their way while speaking to Lurtair. Idra shifted on the couch, turning away from the yellow gaze.

Pitta was a member of one of Dockhaven's Founding Families and its current binnacle. The Dobencourts were the owners of most of the city's dry docks and retained one of the most influential chairs on the City Council, making Pitta a constant source of irritation to Idra. The Councilor was convinced her duty was to decry most anything the Mayor's office supported. Idra had made her only inroads after reaching an agreement with the woman's most recent spouse, Grehv. He'd served Idra as a source of information on Pitta as well as a connection to his former raider clan, the Yenderot. Without him, Idra would never have been able to make the connection for Flark. Grehv had been a beneficial ally—even if he did reeve like a horny bear.

"Pitta makes her spouses earn their luxury," Idra said. She knew the lifestyle. Her wife, the late Mayor Maryn Raan, had done the same.

"I couldn't tolerate one husband," Daisy said. "I don't know how she deals with three."

Pitta gave Lurtair a kiss on the cheek, rose, and started toward Idra and Daisy.

Bracing for whatever insults were coming with the Councilor, Idra crossed her legs and threaded her fingers together in her lap. The woman was worse than Imythedralin. No matter how she steeled herself, Pitta always managed to poke a sore spot.

Even before Idra had taken office, Pitta Dobencourt had rallied against her. The Councilor had tried to shame Maryn when she married Idra—though Pitta had conspicuously not appreciated similar criticism when she married Grehv. She was nearly apoplectic when Maryn died, leaving a will that indicated she wanted Idra, her last living wife, to complete the mayoral term, as was the city's tradition. Rimadour's heir, Til Nireer, had taken over when the city's founder died suddenly, and ensuing mayors had followed suit. Maryn had expected the same.

Pitta opposed. She spent nearly two months and mounds of silver on a campaign to add a law preventing spouses from inheriting the office, claiming the practice was irresponsible, the job required skill and training, but everyone knew her objection was aimed squarely at Idra. The situation could have stretched on for years had Idra's allies in the Merchants Guild and Shippers Association not proposed an amendment to Dockhaven's charter stating that the same logic be applied to the Founding Families, ancestors of those whose money built the city and whose reward had been a permanent seat on the Council. Much as with Idra's situation, tradition allowed each family elect their representatives internally, without vote from Dockhaven's citizens.

Pitta liked that option less than she liked Idra. The next day, she terminated her crusade. Two quarterns later, Idra was sworn in. Since then their relationship appeared cordial, though both took every opportunity to covertly taunt the other.

While Lurtair chatted with the be-tailed woman, Pitta lighted on a nearby fringed ottoman and patted Idra's knee in a matronly way. "You two look like conspirators. Discussing something interesting?"

"My onetime spouse and his twitching idiocy." Daisy left off ogling the young puka across the room and offered Pitta a passable facsimile of a smile.

Pitta drew in air dramatically. "The tenement implosion! Yes, I heard. We'll have to take a unified stance on this, Mayor."

"My assistant's already handling it," Idra said.

"Oh, you can't trust such a thing to Frung." The hand returned to Idra's knee, the subtlest of recriminations. "Think of how it will affect your campaign."

Idra shifted, dislodging Pitta's red-gloved hand. "Frung is capable. I've also spoken with the City Corps and put things in motion to prevent Flark from doing any further damage. The rest is just sorting through angry messages and planning." It was mostly true. "Flark has to be penalized, of course, but we can't call a Council meeting during the Sowers Festival, can we? And I wouldn't dream of making such an important move without the input of you and your colleagues, Councilor Dobencourt."

"Unexpectedly prudent, Mayor. We'll call a session early next quartern," Pitta said. "Let's hope you don't suffer too much in the odds thanks to this incident. Though *I'm* certain you had nothing to do with Flark's action…well, all our citizens might not feel the same. He *is* one of your most vocal supporters among the Rabble…elite." She said the last word as though she had bitten into a rotten fruit.

Though Pitta didn't have to worry about elections and campaigns that didn't stop her from meddling in them.

Idra had no such luxury. "Things will rebound as soon as *we* deal with Flark," she said with a smile.

At last check, Varyl, oddsmaker for the Caba Club, had deemed Idra a six-to-one favorite thanks to Flark's antics. Yesterday she'd been twenty-to-one. The Rabbles were her political base; she'd grown up as one of them. Flark was ruining that. After loudly backing Idra's campaign, he'd left her looking not only ineffectual but downright culpable, as though she'd paid for that support with permission to implode the structure, tenants and all. She wished the old toad's death would come soon.

"I suppose we'll see." Pitta turned slowly toward Daisy. "But what to do with Flark? We couldn't just toss such an important person in the Bag, could we? If his real estate holdings fell apart, that could devastate our city's less fortunate. Imt's eyes, he couldn't run it from prison."

Daisy choked briefly on the kehtal stick. "If Flark were thrown in the Bag—such a lovely idea—our eldest would serve as his proxy. Flark was keen in our divestment agreement to ensure I wouldn't be named." She snorted. "As if Tansy won't listen to her mother's advice."

Pitta closed her eyes and nodded sagely. Alternating lines of black and white were painted across her lids.

"And if he dies, Tansy inherits?" Idra asked.

Daisy flinched. Pitta looked at Idra, eyes wide.

"I mean, he's so old for a puka," Idra said. "Anti-agathics aside, of course."

Daisy smiled. "For now, yes. She's the only one of our children he didn't hate. Though the money gets spread around to all of them. *I* insisted on that."

Pitta's brows went up.

"Now, if you two are done picking the carcass of my

divestment," Daisy slid off the chair, "I'm going to offer that young man a ridiculous number of coins to do unspeakable things to me before this break is over."

ALIARA

The sun's last gasp glinted off lazy purple-grey waves of the Bay as Aliara scaled the Bung Building. The work was slow and precise, the kind of grating tedium no one considered when imagining the thrilling life of a Thung Toh operative.

Odors of cooking and snatches of conversation wafted from slender casements as she passed, residents within thoroughly unaware of her presence. The sporadic breeze whistled over Aliara and Dreg, shuffling her hair and snapping the loose tail of his coat as he followed her up. The building's cheap basalt-aggregate bricks gnawed at the tips of Aliara's fingers and the toes of her boots. Every few courses a chunk broke free in her grip. She wondered if the internal structure was based on something sturdier, or if Flark intended the building to last only through the balance of his paltry lifetime.

More than half-way up, the skitter of crumbling brick from below stopped Aliara. She shifted and looked down to find Dreg dangling by one hand, nothing but air below his boots. She took a step down and shimmied over, one hand stretched toward him. Dreg rejected her offer with a sneer. His free hand scrabbled against the blocks, little flakes tumbling away with each grasp of his fingertips. His face showed a mixture of fear and chagrin.

Dreg's fingers closed over a protruding brick and he adjusted, boots scraping for purchase. His hold whispered its intent an instant before breaking off, leaving a gash in his forehead as the hunk tumbled to the cobbles below. Dreg again dangled in space, silent string of curses passing his lips.

Aliara retrieved a spring-cam from her pack and waggled it at him; she could have a rope anchored in short order. He shook his head. The useless pride of youth. His fingertips probed the surface more slowly, digging into a deep seam between bricks. He latched on, clamped his feet into place, and gave a single nod.

Aliara stowed the cam and resumed her ascent.

She'd learned the delicate art of climbing as a child. Curled in the concave swirls of the candy-colored tower at Orono's mansion, she'd been able to see the Haven from Lower Rabble to Nest on clear days. It was the only place she could find privacy. She could cry, read, sing, do whatever she wanted on her perch without interruption. A few broken bones and uncountable bruises, but she had mastered the windless thing.

When Orono had disappeared, and Syl was announced as inheritor, well-to-do bootlickers invited the heir and his "young lady companion" into their homes. Aliara had practiced on their mansions as well—climbing their exteriors, cracking their safes, disarming their security. It had been an excellent education. She only wished she'd stolen more.

When young Syl refused Orono's bequest, leaving it in trust with then-Mayor Raan, the two of them were dumped on the streets of a city they'd lived in for years, but had only experienced from behind the high walls of estates. She acquired an entirely different education then.

Just shy of Flark's terrace, Aliara paused, listening to the activity in and around the penthouse. Somewhere inside, a melody engine was playing a maudlin ballad. Over it, a female puka's high, nasal voice shouted garbled words. The low rumble of a karju male replied.

On the patio above them, ringing thumps were followed by an irregular clicking that moved to-and-fro in short, spastic bursts.

Aliara recognized the sound of a clawed animal crossing stone, but the thump vexed her. She signed as much to Dreg using the Toh's hand cant. He nodded.

Aliara eased up, eyes level with the patio. An attack bird was amusing itself with a ball, knocking it around the terrace. A gich. Tall enough for Flark to ride if he was so inclined, it had a bulbous belly, long legs, and ropey muscles. Nearly as long as Aliara's arm, its thick beak curved into a vicious hook, and its talons were as long and thick as a rhochrot's finger. Like a child playing bumperball alone, the animal bounced the toy off the furniture and potted plants.

A gich was predictable, but only if it knew you. Sedate with their masters, the birds were almost as blindly loyal as Schmalch, no matter how poorly they were treated. To strangers, they were lethal. She'd never encountered one, but Aliara had seen scars on other Toh, heard stories of how the birds liked to kick and rip.

A bell rang in the harbor, the echo rolling over the patio in waves. The gich twisted its squat neck and cocked an eye into the twilight for a moment before turning back to its prey, chasing the ball across the stone patio away from Aliara and Dreg. Some douse had tinted all its white tailfeathers a soft pink, presumably to go along with the pink and blue of the patio cushions.

She drew a stiletto, aimed, and pitched. Unaware of the projectile hurling toward it, the bird ducked for its ball, knocking the toy off a potted rubber tree. Aliara's blade thunked softly into a chair cushion and dropped to the seat. The bird's head popped up, muscled neck twisting fluidly as it searched the patio for the source of the noise. It made a low throaty sound that turned Aliara's guts cold. She reached for her other stiletto.

A soft *tht-tht-tht* hissed beside her ear. The bird staggered forward, issued a surprised gulp, and dropped, a handful of steel spikes embedded in its neck and chest.

Dreg smiled, raised his needler, and shook it playfully. The steel barrel, thick as Aliara's forearm, was sealed on one end, the other covered in holes, needles hiding inside each. It looked like a salt shaker tipped on its side.

"*Paralytic*," he signed in the hand cant and holstered the gun. It was an expensive tool that required expensive ammunition. Effective, but no wonder the boy was always skint.

The exterior walls of Flark's penthouse were mostly glass that rose from knee height, the stone footing providing good cover should a puka need to duck a sniper. The seaward side was dominated by a solarium that included an immense plunge bath and a booth she assumed was a steam room.

Dreg pulled himself up, swung over the cabled patio railing, and hoisted her up after him. Accompanied by atonal whistling, a long shadow moved across the interior behind him. Aliara signed a warning. Dreg wrapped his arms around her, dropped to the ground, and rolled beneath the windows. When the whistling faded, Aliara slipped out of Dreg's grip into a crouch, casting a cautious glance through the window. Beyond the solarium, a bright light shone from a hallway, illuminating the polished white marble floor of a garish living space furnished in a jumble of what Schmalch would call "rich stuff."

She signed all of this to Dreg, who shifted to hands and knees and crept toward the nearest sliding glass door. While Aliara retrieved her stiletto, he eased the door open.

From the opposite corner of the patio, the click of talons and guttural warble of a second gich preceded its appearance. Dreg turned and drew his needler, raising it half-way before glaring at the pistol and awkwardly drawing a black-bladed knife from his boot with his free hand. He hadn't reloaded. The bird loped toward him and let loose a shudder-inducing screech. Dreg charged it in return, dropping to a knee-slide just before the creature could drive its hooked bill into his chest. His knife slashed the gich's ankle as he glided past.

In the penthouse, a brawny silhouette bounded from the hall to the patio. Aliara crouched in the shadow of a nearby planter, waiting for this newcomer to emerge into the moonlight.

A karju with a bulky mag-pistol burst from the open door and angled toward the fray. Aliara shot up, vaulted off a nearby patio couch, and catapulted herself onto the guard's back, driving both stilettos into the soft meat behind the collarbone on either side of his neck. The guard gurgled and took a step back before his knees buckled. She rode the crumpling body to the ground, abstractly registering a pistol shot as the dying man convulsively pulled the trigger.

The bird was still on Dreg. "Imt's eyes!" he swore, dodging a near-evisceration.

The gich leapt again, kicking at him with its wounded leg, talons barely missing as Dreg hopped and wheeled. Tattered from previous near misses, the boy's coat flapped around him. He dropped and rolled, coming to his feet on the bird's other side. The gich tried to switch attack legs to compensate, collapsing when the injured one gave out under it. A well-placed stroke and Dreg was splattered in arterial spray as his knife opened the gich's neck. The bird flopped twice and lay still.

SYLANDAIR

Tinted lumia bulbs daubed Pedestrian's dining room with a dilute gold, setting off the brightness of ironwood chairs and white tablecloths. Huddled in conversation over food more aesthetic than filling, the dinner crowd was beginning to fill the confined space. A pair of women enjoying bright-red vapor-crowned drinks paused conspicuously when Syl entered, only to return to their slurred debate with renewed enthusiasm.

Marthoth was nowhere in sight. Though Idra, Orilausko, and his own exhaustion had delayed him, it seemed Syl still had the advantage.

"Duke Imythedralin." The attendant appeared, every hair in place, every stitch of clothing costly. "Mister Marthoth left instructions to escort you to his private dining room. Our chef has prepared an exclusive meal. Would you follow me?" She smiled, batting lashes as black as his own to hide a hint of anxiety.

Syl and Marthoth had agreed upon Pedestrian, this year's selection to occupy the coveted bow dining room of the *Ipesia*. The space was well-lighted and extremely conspicuous. This unexpected change to a secluded locale heightened Syl's unease. Rejecting his host, however, was unacceptable.

"Of course." He gestured her ahead with a flourish.

The attendant led Syl down the aisle of the perfumed dining room toward the galley entry. In the instant before the leather-upholstered doors parted, he envisioned Marthoth waiting at a table situated between oven and block, the chef personally serving them a preliminary savory. Instead, the attendant glided through the bustling galley toward the spiral service companionway.

Syl paused, considering the last such staircase he'd scaled blindly. "Where exactly are we going?"

Waist-high to the second deck, the attendant crouched and smiled at him. "Deck seven. Mister Marthoth's private quarters."

Syl slid his hand to the back of his belt where his dagger waited. Comforted, he followed the attendant. They passed through a series of service closets occupied by employees, tools, dinnerware, and carts, each in a different state of industrious disarray. The higher they climbed, the more rapid Syl's pulse.

At deck seven, the attendant rapped on an overhead hatch, her knock barely audible over the racket from below. The door swung up and they emerged into a spacious cabin, enormous, night-chilled, and glassed on the fore, port, and starboard. The shadowed blues and spectral greys of the rugs and aft bulkhead blended seamlessly into the panoramic sea view off the bow. Marthoth sat at the dark aelde-wood dining table in a coat and scarf. The buttons of his red wool coat strained across his swollen midsection. The man was robust with wealth, though the unsettling swell of muscle still showed through the arms of his tailored coat. Through the opened fore wall, he scrutinized the busy Sound, where those he brought to frolic reveled, connived, and shamed themselves aboard the flotilla of vessels surrounding the *Ipesia.*

"Mister Marthoth?" the attendant said, her voice soft and polite. "Your guest is here."

"Duke Imythedralin," Marthoth said, gesturing Syl into the facing chair, a position that put his back to the sea and gusts of mounting winds. "I'm pleased we could share this meal together."

Syl sat. "As I am for being allowed to monopolize the attention of my busy host for a time."

"To what end Duke?" His voice held a hint of the Upper Rabble, near the stockyards. Squalid and violent, Marthoth had come far in life.

"I am in need of a reliable—and discrete—shipper," Syl replied.

Marthoth pushed out his lips, his brow rolling toward a scowl. His big hand dipped into his watch pocket. Syl heard a muffled click and the high whine of a mag-pistol jumping to life. Marthoth drew a delicate Querlin holdout and set it on the table, barrel mouth to his guest.

"I could be interested in expanding our routes into the Dominion," he said, "but first we need to discuss your involvement in Flark's mischief."

"I fear you find me at a loss," Syl countered, his aspect confused and subtly wounded. He'd spent hours at the mirror, perfecting each expression and gesture, readying control for moments such as this.

With a balletic wave, Marthoth rang the call bell in front of him. Javit scuttled from deeper in the cabin and settled her intimidating bulk on a hassock to Syl's left. She simpered like a child caught telling tales, her teeth as grey as the sclera of her eyes.

"You know of our recent troubles on the Tehtaemah route," Marthoth said.

"Of course," Syl said, "your travails are bound to be a source of gossip during the Festival."

Marthoth gestured at the waiting attendant, who came forward in a nervous half bow, putting herself at eye level. "Yes, Mister Marthoth?"

"Inform the chef we are ready to begin."

She nodded and disappeared down the service stair.

Marthoth snapped hairy-knuckled fingers, and a puka in a ludicrous red and grey uniform accented with silver braiding swooped in, depositing a morsel plate of cheese and *sklintara e cono*. Orilausko's prediction had been correct. When the puka poured green liqueur into narrow flutes before the diners, Syl caught his wrist, the servant's flesh pleasantly warm to his cold fingers.

"I would prefer something different." Syl released the man. "Caba, if you would."

With a curt nod, the puka and the drink vanished.

"I mean no offense," Syl said. "Quincitaba does not sit well with me."

"It's not a concern." Marthoth tapped his tiny pistol's butt with his thick trigger finger, eyes darting briefly to Javit. "How did you know there were artifacts aboard the *Nimomyne*, Duke? And don't bother with that dosh about your boy at the packet office."

"An odd bit I heard at the Onpuur reception while on break from our game last night. Chella Stond was gossiping about it." Syl watched Marthoth for any tells. The shipper had few reasons to place a contract on him. Still he was a possibility. "I wasn't sure of its validity until now. Were there actually the remains of six voshari on board?"

Marthoth chuckled. "No."

His gun remained on the table and Javit was placid. Should that change, Syl was ready to dash to the side rail and dive into the Sound.

"Apologies," Syl said. "I was merely using the information as a prod to fluster my opponents."

Javit snorted.

"If I may, what does all that have to do with Flark?" Syl asked. He refused to acknowledge the freezing air that was turning the quicks of his fingers blue, throwing fluttering tendrils of hair into his eyes, and stinging the backs of his ears.

"Karna's sudden defection, followed swiftly by these raids?" Marthoth's fists balled on the tabletop. "I have suspicions, Duke. I'd rather not say more."

"Understood." Syl licked his lips and considered his next words. "I am no admirer of Mister Flark. He haunts my penthouse, ogling my mate, eating my food, and prattling on about his repugnant conquests, both commercial and carnal. And now..." Syl shook his head. "I am certain you have heard of our conflict over the Heap."

Marthoth nodded.

"It is but one of the insults he has piled upon me of late." Syl plucked a roe-topped shrimp from the morsel plate. "Perhaps my plans for Isay are not the only endeavor in which we can collaborate."

Marthoth raised a brow and considered Syl for a long moment. Again, he snapped. The puka scurried forward and slid the glass wall closed. The frigid breeze vanished. Syl's shoulders relaxed as he drew in a full breath.

"Anything you could do to help me rid myself of the old barnacle," Marthoth said, "should opportunity present itself, would be appreciated. After the Festival, invite me to your next salon. We can resume our discussion of Isay's needs then."

Syl extended his arm and they brushed chilly fingertips across one another's palms.

"Now," Marthoth said, the fearsome gloom around him brightening, "let's enjoy our dinner. The chef is unparalleled in Dockhaven. Negotiations and squabbles should never spoil the enjoyment of a well-made meal."

"You're 'sposta stay in your room," Grub said. "I'll be out here, making sure you don't change that."

Karna gave the karju bodyguard her best scowl. She'd been studying Flark's management methods and that seemed like one of his most effective for cowing a subordinate. Grub didn't notice.

"I need to meet my friends. I want at least one Festival night out," Karna said. She tried to remain calm, but she hadn't been outside since she'd moved in with Flark. This tacky apartment was starting to feel like a prison.

"The boss said you're 'sposta stay right here, so that's what you're doin'."

"You can come along and guard me while we're at the Caba Club. Come on, Grub. I can finally afford to take my friends there, and you won't let me out." Karna had already tried tears to no avail. "I won't go to Marthoth's party. I'm not stupid."

"Right here." Grub pointed at the floor and slammed the door.

Karna changed the tin on the melody engine and opened the baffle. Grub hated *Marastrava's Coronation Suite*. He could keep her here, but he couldn't tell her what to do. Flark had made her lady of the house. She would be giving the orders, even if she couldn't leave.

She climbed the short steps into bed, tucked the antique Eitan-lace gown beneath her, and opened her book. In this volume of *Phantoms of the White Moon*, Dreagle's mother had been kidnapped and was being held by her cousin, Baron Barillion. Dreagle and his plucky band of adventurers had to find the Harbinger Stone and deliver it to the Baron in two sunups. All this while he and Carapina, Princess of the Insect People, were falling in love. It was the best one yet.

Being with Flark hadn't been what these romantic adventures had promised Karna. She'd hoped that once she found a mate, she'd no longer need the books, but life here had been nothing like she'd expected. It wasn't even like what her sisters had described with their boring work-a-day husbands. But Karna was homely and shy. She felt fortunate that someone as rich and important as Flark had chosen her. If she hadn't been so good with numbers, she'd still be stuck down there with the rest of Pukatown.

Karna picked up a little pink margle tart, round except for the flat spot from the baking sheet. She popped it into her mouth and bit down. The still-warm gooey center was sweet, better even than the fresh fruit used to make the treat. At least Grub knew how to bake. Even her mother couldn't make margle tarts that held their shape as well as his did.

Dreagle and Carapina had just entered the tunnels hidden around the volcano when Karna heard one of Flark's ugly birds shriek. They were terrible pets. She'd wanted a long-haired cavii, but Flark said it wouldn't live a day around the giches. He was probably right.

What sounded like a small banger came next, maybe Hereht was messing with the nasty birds. She hoped that guard would be gutted.

Grub hollered, "Hereht, everything battened down there?"

Book in lap, Karna listened for anything else unusual. Maybe Flark had been right to keep her here. She'd assumed it was because he thought she'd embarrass him around all those rich toffs, but now she began to doubt. She considered getting up and sticking her nose outside, but Grub would just threaten to hurl a kisselball at her to keep her in place.

"I'm going downstairs. You stay put," Grub yelled through

Karna's door.

She returned to her book. Carapina was beginning to overheat and Dreagle had just run out of water. Karna *had* to know how they'd get out of this one. The party had almost reached the spot where the Aessorel had hidden the Stone when Grub and Hereht started making a real ruckus. Karna slid off the bed to lower the melody engine's volume.

Her door swung open. A pair of chivori stood there. The woman looked around the room with a blasé expression, eyes brushing over Karna like she was another piece of furniture. The man wore a ragged coat half-spattered with red blood. Black oozed from a wound in his forehead, its path circling his eye, mingling with the red on his cheek and throat. He smiled, and Karna's insides went cold. She backpedaled toward the safety of her book and bed.

"Are you the bookkeeper?" the man asked. His voice was raspy, like he needed a drink.

Karna gaped. She'd fallen asleep. Yes, that was it. She'd fallen asleep reading her book and now she was having a dream.

"Are you Karna?" the woman asked.

It didn't seem like a dream; this seemed quite real. "F-Flark's not here," Karna said. She yipped when her calf bumped against the bed's puka steps.

"That's not what she asked." The man stepped into the room. "Are you Karna? Are you Flark's trull bookkeeper?"

Before she could think, Karna began to nod and caught herself. She shook her head hard enough for it to come loose. If these people wanted Karna, she definitely was *not* Karna.

"Oh, now, I bet you are," the male said in a singsongy way. He stalked toward her, that bowel-chilling smile still in place.

"No…no, that's not me. I'm…" Every name she'd ever known flew away. She dropped to the floor and rolled under the bed. "I'm H-h-h—"

"Tell me…" His voice sounded like he needed to gargle. "Do

you have to drink yourself into unconsciousness before you let Flark climb on top of you?" He crouched beside the bed and peeked under, still smiling at her. A curl tumbled from his hood. It seemed to be every color at once.

"H-H-Hoozie!" Karna shouted as she pushed herself into the far corner, where bed met the wall. A bit of the comforter's dangling fringe tickled her back. "I'm Hoozie, Flark's cousin from Lint Grove."

The man made a mockingly surprised face. "Oh, I don't think you are." He flattened his body and slid under the bed, pulling himself forward. "You're right where Karna's supposed to be."

Karna's backside bumped into the wall. There was nowhere else to go. The smiling chivori reached for her, and she kicked, connecting with his fingers.

"Sax!" the man yelled. He pulled his hand back, shaking it like he'd been burned. "Little quim tried to break my fingers. Do you know what these digits are worth to a man in my line?" He stared at her hard enough to bore holes.

"Stop playing." The woman's voice was muted by the bed.

Karna kept kicking.

"Gam off, Rift, or crawl under here with me and fish this little gash out." He swiped at Karna, catching one foot.

Karna kicked with her free leg, twisting painfully in his awkward grasp. She connected with something and the man swore again. He wrenched her ankle. Karna shrieked and the world went hazy with tears.

She'd made a terrible mistake. Flark was awful. He treated her badly. He only wanted her as an incubator for new heirs. He didn't even like her. All this luxury had been too inviting. She'd been so stupid.

She screamed and kicked harder. Something in her hip popped.

"I'm done with this." The man released her, slid out from under the bed, and stood. Maybe he'd give up and leave.

Karna heard a series of clicks then the man bent down again, aiming a strange-looking pistol at her.

"No, no, no, just take whatever you want," she cried. "It's not mine, and Flark can afford to replace anything."

The pistol made an odd, airy noise and points of pain broke out across her chest. In a heartbeat, Karna went limp. She tried to kick, scratch, even scream, but she was frozen, locked inside herself.

The man dragged her out from under the bed. She wanted to grab the bedframe, but her arms didn't even twitch. He put his hands around her throat, tightening slowly. Karna felt the air cut off. Her lungs ached. Her heart thudded. She could feel her face swelling like a blemish ready to pop. She tried one last time to swat the chivori man's hands away, but her body refused. Karna's vision went hazy-brown as she stared into that cruelly smiling face.

IDRA

Idra sat on one of the mingling room's viewing sofas watching a pair of tanned and topless karju women tease a nude chivori man who dangled from overhead-mounted restraints. One of the women, zoet tail twitching playfully behind her, looked away from her work to smile at Idra. Bored by the whole thing, Idra twirled a loop of hair around a finger and scowled at the flirt. Had she not been waiting on Imythedralin, she would have abandoned this tedious exhibitionism and retired to the baths immediately after Pitta and Daisy left. She crossed her legs and shifted focus to the leather lounge across the room where two chivori men went at it as though pumping water in a drought.

Idra had been waiting long enough that Imythedralin could have enjoyed three meals with Marthoth. He was no doubt wasting time fawning over their host, but anyone who kept tabs on local events knew that the shipper required no flattery. He wanted a hook in the far reaches of the Dominion. A deal with a duke on the edge of the world would be just the thing. Add Marthoth's recent losses to the Yenderot—which he did not and should never know were due in part to Idra and Imythedralin—and the meeting should have ended ages ago.

She eyed the hanging clock and released an annoyed huff. The interminable lyntyyl game would resume soon, and she'd have to wait until next break to view his newest offering.

"Master Orono used to share an Orasian witticism from the War of Dawn and Twilight," said a low, creamy voice. "The Orasians claimed that whenever they threw a group of chivori past their saypas in a cell together, regardless of number or gender, by morning, those prisoners would invariably be physically entwined. I paraphrase, of course. The actual language was far more coarse."

Idra shifted her gaze to Imythedralin's sleek face and let her mind roll back to the last time they'd been physically entwined. He was not without talent. If only he could keep his mouth shut. One word and she wanted to smack him in his self-important maw.

"Bigoted and more than a little hyperbolic as it is, the sentiment is not unreasonably inaccurate." Imythedralin's gaze swept the room. "Things here have grown rather banal since I last visited."

The woman with the tail made a gratuitous gesture in their direction. Imythedralin chuckled.

"Too many karju," Idra said, "playing at being us."

"Indeed. A certain lack of finesse."

Idra adjusted her face to an annoyed pout. "What took you so long?"

"You are fortunate I have arrived at all, Mayor. My meeting with Marthoth nearly end—"

"I'm sure it was very important." She dismissed him with a wave. "What is it you have for me?"

Imythedralin's face darkened. "Something for your collection. Circumstances have changed, however, and we have a mutual threat to discuss first." He glanced at the clock hanging high on the bulkhead. "We have some time yet. Follow me." He leaned out of the room, looked to both sides, and exited.

Idra checked her appearance in the mingling room's mirrors before trailing him through the café and up the twisting staircase to the sixth deck. He and the drab goby he called a mate had been given one of the few luxury cabins this year while Idra—the *Mayor*—was shifted to second-rate accommodations. Though not as pitiful as what the majority of guests endured, the cabin still fell far below her standards. She'd tried to obtain one of the staterooms for herself, but all her fits and yelling and threats had failed to sway the *Ipesia*'s purser.

Imythedralin opened the door to his cabin, entered slowly, and peered around the corner before striding into the main room. Idra followed, groaning involuntarily. A bow cabin like this with a huge bed, massive washroom, and panoramic view had been hers during previous stays. Last year she'd spent nearly half the party climbing in and out of the oversized plunge bath on the balcony.

She crossed to the glass wall and took in the wild activity in the growing darkness. Interspersed among the many yachts, vendors' boats from all over the Haven had anchored around Marthoth's barge, their launches ready to ferry customers to smaller vessels where they could buy clothes, food, jewelry, or any other thing they might dream up. All the ships' lights glittered against the Sound's almost-black water, their dance broken by the occasional wake and the shades of nocturnal seabirds daring enough to bob for lethargic fish. In the distance, set against the cloud-veiled moonlight, young baluuts swirled in the sky and dipped into the waves.

Imythedralin crouched to fiddle with the cabin's safe. Sprouting from the slit at the back of his jacket was the oil-rubbed bronze of a knife handle, ornamental patterns raised in the metal. Though Idra had only seen renderings, she recognized the style. Her breath caught.

"Is that—is it a Voshar dagger?"

"It is. A gift from Aliara." Imythedralin rose, drew the weapon. The crescent-moon blade was honed on both edges, hilt and scabbard intricately decorated. Idra reached for it, but he shook his head. "This is not what I have for you."

She began to protest, but Imythedralin returned the weapon to its sheath and his attention to the safe.

Idra fell back onto the bed, sea-blue duvet poofing pleasantly scented air around her. The room should have been hers. Marthoth was probably punishing her for some imagined slight. She considered ordering the Corps to throw Imythedralin in the Bag so she could take over his stateroom.

He cleared his throat, interrupting Idra's musings.

She sat up. Neatly arranged on the breakfast table was a chased-copper coffee set. All annoyance vanished. Idra slid off the bed and reached for one of the cups.

Imythedralin gently deflected her. "Not just yet. We have something more pressing to address first. Marthoth has somehow deduced that Flark is behind his recent difficulties, and he suspects we are involved as well."

Idra hissed through her teeth. The last thing she needed was another vendetta from one of the Haven's elite. "What did you tell him?"

"That I was quite sure you would not conspire with Flark, there is too great an enmity there. Nevertheless, we should be on our guard. I fully expect Mintryl to continue his investigations. Are we allies in this?"

She gave him a curt nod and again reached for one of the cups. This time he didn't interfere. It was so light and delicate, she had difficulty believing the set had survived so long in the desert.

"Authenticated?" Idra whispered as though a louder sound might crack the delicate metal.

"Yes, by Wuukuster," Imythedralin replied.

"I've never seen a complete set before. Hardly any marring." The tip of her lacquered nail traced the pattern of dancing desert flowers. "What did you pay for the set?"

"Immaterial."

Her eyes went to slits. "Why?"

He took the teacup from her hand and returned it to the tray.

"How much, Imythedralin?" Idra asked. "You know I'm skint at the moment."

"Not a worry, I require information, not coin." Imythedralin straightened a twisted strap on her dress.

"What sort of information?"

"I require the records of all vessels arriving and departing Dockhaven by air, sea, or Egress in the months of Danurak through Alsolon of 2048. Both those doing so legally and any caught entering illegally. On paper, not chit."

Idra gaped. "That's insane. That's…that's nearly forty years ago. I don't even know if the city's records go that far back."

"Nevertheless, that is my price." He picked up the set's decanter. He seemed to consider crushing it. The idea made Idra's toes clinch. "The set is yours when I receive the records."

Idra's mind raced through resources that might have the information he wanted—abandoned records rooms, ancient employees, ways to forge such ridiculous documents.

"I will know if they're real," Imythedralin added with a sidelong glance that made her shiver. "I have a reference point."

"Which is?"

He shook his head and raised the pitcher higher, scrutinizing it in the room's dim light. "That would be telling."

"Fine. I-I don't know what I'll be able to find, though. What if I can't gather what you want?"

"I have confidence you will." He lowered the pitcher, cradling it in his palm. "Are we agreed?"

"I'll see what I can do. Yes." Idra would hand this project off to her assistant. If anyone could locate those records in the chaos that was Dockhaven's archives, it would be Frung. "Yes, we're agreed."

Imythedralin returned the decanter to its tray and the set to the safe.

"You'll excuse me for a moment." He nodded toward the lavatory. "Oh yes, I almost forgot." Imythedralin paused a few steps from the washroom door, slid a hand into his pocket, and withdrew her necklace. "I had considered giving the piece to Aliara, but my darling girl eschews the pretty baubles. I present them to her, they merely tarnish in a drawer." He tossed the firestar to Idra. "You keep the pendant. It may call Flark's attention."

While Idra fussed with the necklace clasp, Imythedralin stepped into the lav, pushing the door to so he could continue chatting.

"My friend said Prenja was once quite the trade hub of southern Chiva'vastezz thanks to the Egress." His voice droned over the patter of urine against the basin, the sound conjuring images of the army of dibucs Marthoth must have installed onboard to deal with his guests' copious waste. "But I'm certain you knew that already, given your tastes."

"I'm quite familiar." Idra ran a finger over the silky duvet, then a palm, then she sprawled across the bed and purred. "Too bad it doesn't work anymore."

"The terminus? Yes, quite a loss. All alone there in the middle of the Lohaataa Desert… I was impressed the raiders even bothered w—" His voice cut off with a *yerk*.

Shoes slapped against the lav's marble floor, a rhythm too random to be any dance.

Idra sat up. "Imythedralin?"

He grunted, a suppressed sound unlike his dismissive tone she knew well. Something or someone slammed into the shower's glass enclosure with a resounding *clong!* A voice yelped.

"Sylandair?" Idra stood and took a tentative step toward the lavatory, staring at the narrow band of light visible through the opening.

The spastic tap dance continued. She heard more grunts and one half-spoken curse.

"Are you…all right?" Idra glanced toward the exit. She could run now, get help.

Glass crashed. Through the crack, she saw bits of shattered mirror spray across the seascape marble.

Idra gasped and hopped away.

Metal tinged and the sheath from Imythedralin's dagger skittered into view. Another *clong*, a muffled cry, and the room went silent.

Idra's breath was coming fast. Her hands and feet felt leaden, numb. She couldn't move, could only stare at that sliver of light. Whoever had just killed Imythedralin was coming for her. She needed to hide, needed to run out the door right now. She didn't—couldn't—budge, just stood there, nauseous and shaking.

The door creaked. The spell broke. Idra scrambled onto the bed, angling for the exit. Her peripheral registered a dark shape exiting the washroom as she slid across the slick duvet, tumbling onto the floor, tangled in the bedding. She tried to stand, twisting her ankle in the too-tall heels, and collapsed, eyes squeezed shut.

Gentle footsteps ticked up to where she lay.

"Help me move our unwelcomed visitor to the bathtub," Imythedralin said, his voice strangely rough, like he'd been gargling seawater.

Idra opened her eyes. He was standing over her, shaking. His hair was mussed, his clothes disheveled, his eyes wild. A black bruise swelled across his throat.

He extended a hand and hefted Idra to her feet. "Lest he bleed everywhere when I retrieve my blade."

ALIARA

"One down." Dreg grunted as he hefted the bookkeeper's limp body onto the bed. The face was mottled and bloated, the killer's hands imprinted around the throat. Strangulation was sloppy and cruel, too slow. The woman probably deserved better. It had been a pathetic kill and pathetic death. "There's five-hundred ladies."

Aliara flicked off the melody engine and made a slow circuit of the room, moving paintings and opening drawers in search of a safe. Targets often secreted their most precious valuables in the bedroom.

Sitting on the bed, Dreg gave Karna's flaccid face an absent poke. "Why didn't he take her with him to Marthoth's zootie?"

"Flark?" Aliara asked.

"Uh huh."

"Puka's aren't his preference." Aliara opened an armoire inexplicably filled with old, ratty sheets and towels. "Every Festival, he goes after any chivori in the mingling room who'll take his silver."

"Did he give *you* some coin?" Dreg snorted a laugh as he shoved Karna's body aside and stretched out on the bed, hands behind his head, and muttered, "Comfortable."

Aliara looked behind the room's lone row of books and found only wall.

"You wanna give it some use before we leave?" Dreg patted the space beside him. "Why don't you come over here and we'll celebrate our success?"

Aliara looked at him, one brow raised.

"Little Karna here?" Dreg patted the corpse's belly. "She won't care."

Aliara crawled onto the bed and straddled him. She bent close, lips almost brushing his, and ran a hand slowly up the inside of Dreg's thigh. His smarmy smile broadened. His eyes slipped shut as she found her mark.

They flew open again when she squeezed, his smile vanishing with a yelp.

"The jig," she said, punctuating each word with a twist, "isn't done."

"Sax! Let go, Rift! I need that." He almost succeeded in hiding the whine.

"Find what we came for." Aliara jerked her chin toward the door and released him. "Take what you want."

She slid off the bed.

Dreg cradled his bruised pride. "You could have just said no, you whinging quim."

When Aliara resumed her search, Dreg hustled out of the bedroom, cursing under his breath.

Aliara crossed to the closet's double doors. Inside, a two-tier rack of tunics and suits greeted her, row of shoes beneath—all of it masculine, nothing like the frilly gown Flark's unfortunate lover was wearing. As she checked for hidden compartments, Aliara's fingers found a crankless spindle protruding from the bottom of the side wall. She groped around a bit more. Inside the pocket of a moth-eaten, brown-striped robe she found the missing handle, fit it over the spindle, and turned. A panel popped back and slid aside. Inside, a fat black safe slightly larger than Flark himself was anchored in the concrete wall.

While Dreg banged around angrily in the rooms beyond, Aliara sprung the combination lock and scaled the safe's meager contents: a bag of loose gems, a set of miniature hand-painted tiles, and a short stack of photographs, the top one showing two nude chivori women. Only one of their faces was visible. Prurient or otherwise, photographs were valuable if only for the silver they contained. Their subject matter merely increased the price.

Toward the safe's rear lay three green leather-bound books labeled "Marthoth Air & Sea." Two contained columns of numbers. The third was filled with handwritten notes. She fanned through the pages, noting the names of several of Syl's more privileged and influential acquaintances. Everything went into her pack.

One retrieval complete. Maybe Dreg had found the mask.

SCHMALCH

From the Bung Building, Schmalch made his way up Bay Run toward the Runoff, a floater neighborhood down the shore from the Slaughteryards. Made up of anchored razees and shacks strapped to barrels, bottles, and anything else that floated, the area gave those without enough coin to buy land a chance to own their own home. Like all floaters, the Runoff was part of the city, but separate, its layout changing almost daily. People showed up, rolled out a ramp or gangplank, and called it home.

Before the Duke and Rift had taken him in, Schmalch had been particularly fond of lifting rowboats from a little rental shop called Tendle's Marine moored not-too-deep into the Runoff. It had a good selection, and the owners used to put out table scraps for the gulls just about every night. Schmalch had enjoyed many a meal that way, though he'd also nearly lost an eye to the squawking vermin the night the Tendles left out a gnawed-on hog hock.

The place was close to Rift's jig—or it would have been if the neighborhood was where it was supposed to be.

When Schmalch arrived at the public pier that had once led to the Runoff, he instead found a row of fenced-in half-buildings. Wind-kicked waves skipped in the Bay where the Runoff had once floated. Nothing but a handful of construction barges were docked at the pier. Illuminated by a lamppost, a sign lashed to the fence announced, "Ready for lease this spring." Smaller print below identified the project as new rental slips, shopfronts, and warehouses, courtesy of Flark. Seemed like everywhere Schmalch went lately, the bung was building something new or tearing down something old.

Schmalch hadn't visited the Runoff since he'd started his life as the Duke's assistant, maybe longer, yet he still was surprised he hadn't heard that the neighborhood had moved. It might now be lashed onto just about any other public pier—and there were a few dozen on the Upper Rabble alone—or the residents could have split up to find other neighborhoods. Either way, locating Tendle's would take too long. Considering other places to find a dinghy, Schmalch leaned against the squeaky fence.

"Who's there?" hissed a voice from a spot past the streetlamp's glow.

Schmalch squinted into the gloom. "Huh?"

"You heard me." A puka about twice his age strode out, cracking his knuckles one at a time, his shirt sleeves rolled up. The man was ready to fight. "Who are you?"

"Apologies. I was just looking for the Runoff." Schmalch smiled—though he wanted to run. "I'm Schmalch."

The man's shoulders relaxed. He nodded. "My apologies, not yours. We've had a bit of a time today, so I'm keeping watch." He extended a hand. "I'm Kibbe."

They grasped one another's wrists.

"What happened?" Schmalch asked.

"We lived at the Yinago. Now all four of us—and everything we could carry—are out on our backsides. A buncha Grey Boots scaled most of our belongings this aftermid, even my aapa's favorite chair. I was away looking for a new cuddy when they showed up, but that was pointless. Everything's been snapped up already." He closed his eyes and sighed. "But you don't care about all that. The Runoff's moved a few docks north."

Schmalch was in Pukatown almost daily. He should have known. He was getting lazy, not noticing the details like he used to. He didn't like the feeling.

"If you don't mind moving out of Pukatown, the Belvedor Inn generally has rooms." Schmalch handed the man the last couple Callas in his pocket. "That'll buy you a quartern or two in one of their small rooms."

The man called gratitude as Schmalch jogged away. He passed some fake beggars, faces he remembered from his days living among them. Even back then, they had better cuddies than any of Schmalch's mates. They didn't need the coin like Kibbe's family did.

A few piers past them, he found the Runoff, its network of dilapidated ships and homemade pontoons rearranged but still whole. The windows of most dwellings were darkened, their walkways pulled back for the night. A few businesses were still open, but not Tendle's. The shack's windows were shuttered and dark, dinghies chained together in rows, gangway retracted. Schmalch frowned. They hadn't done that last time he'd stopped by.

He backed up as far as possible and ran, leaping at the last moment, barely catching the rough-cut lip of their deck. A group of gulls cleaning out the evening's scraps flapped off with squawked curses. Schmalch pulled himself up, avoiding their scattered lime. His feet and pant cuffs had taken a good soaking, but he'd managed to keep most of himself dry. Schmalch rose, dusted himself off, and hurried around the platform to where the rentals were chained.

Learning how to filch a dinghy had been part of Schmalch's Spriggan education. Over the years, he'd scaled plenty of the little vessels for night fishing or just for entertainment. During a cold snap three winters ago, he'd even used one as firewood. Mostly, though, he just borrowed, returning them so they'd be there if he needed them again later.

He located the rowboats and nimbly scampered over one after another to the last in the chain, held in place with a cheap padlock. Schmalch took out the new lockpick roll Rift had bought for him. When she'd finally been able to get out of bed, they'd visited the

Haven's best locksmith, and she'd had the kit made just for him.

"You'll still need these talents," Rift had told him.

Schmalch had been so overwhelmed, he hadn't been able to utter a word to express his gratitude, but he was pretty sure Rift preferred things that way.

He looked up at the Bung Building. The odd window was lit on the lower floors, but the penthouse blazed with yellow light. Schmalch wondered what they were up to up there. Whatever it was, the bung probably deserved it. In some ways Schmalch envied Rift and Dreg the bravery and daring it took to climb a building like that. He could barely look out of his bedroom window without getting dizzy.

He popped the dinghy's lock and slowly unwound the chain, easing it into the water as silently as possible. The last few links slipped through his hands too quickly and landed with a splash.

A light flicked on inside the shack.

Schmalch dropped to the seat and rowed, aiming to hide behind a nearby pontoon-house.

Someone opened the Tendles' door and called out. "Who's there?"

Schmalch positioned the boat behind the building, hoping his wake wouldn't give him away. After a moment, he heard the door creak closed and peeped out from his hiding spot. The shack was dark again. Schmalch maneuvered the little craft quietly through the neighborhood, ducking walkways and overhangs as he rowed. Once out on open water he angled toward shore, intending to hug it until he reached the spot Rift had indicated.

The green moon was in aught tonight, completely hidden, but Dormah was nearly full, bathing the Bay in its white glow. The water almost looked like shiny fabric, decorated with ships and seafoam instead of buttons and embroidery. The wind grabbed little kips of the sea, kicking up tight, angry waves. The city surrounded him in a slow, rising arc, buildings smiling with broken-tooth lighting. It was kinda peaceful.

He pulled the oars into the boat and took off both shoes, emptying them of water and wringing out his socks. Stained and misshapen, they were ruined. He'd have to buy new.

Schmalch really liked living with the Duke and Rift, but they had so many rules. Sometimes he missed not caring about how dirty his shoes were or how recently he'd bathed. But he had a meal in his belly whenever he wanted one and a warm bed every night. And nobody belittled him or conned him out of his coin like Garl had when Schmalch had worked for him at the Barnacle.

Plus, Schmalch was working for a Thung Toh operative, which was real swish. Schmalch had heard stories about the group since he was a kid. A chivori at the orphanage had spun the best Thung Toh yarns. "If you see one making a kill," she used to say, the little ones gathered around her, "keep your mouth shut or you'll be dead too."

These days, Schmalch knew three of them. He had no doubt that Rift, Haus, or Dreg would have no problem ending him if he blabbed.

Something bumped the dinghy. The little boat tipped and righted itself, rocking back and forth like a baby's crib. Schmalch grabbed the gunnels and waited for it to steady. The bump came again, this time lighter, jostling the dinghy instead of almost overturning it. Schmalch leaned out cautiously and looked into the dark water. He saw only his own shadowy reflection, twisted by waves.

A smooth snout broke the water, sleek head and bright eyes rushing toward him. Schmalch pulled back, nearly toppling himself. The harbor whale chattered happily, dove under Schmalch's boat, and circled him. The animal was twice as long as the dinghy, but half as wide, its skin as grey as a chivori's, but shiny and thick. It popped up again beside him and opened its mouth, revealing a row of nubby teeth. People fed harbor whales or dumped scraps in the sea while anchored, so the animals begged for more anytime they saw a person. Garl had called them "the beggars of the Bay."

"I don't have any food," Schmalch told the harbor whale.

It didn't believe him, bobbing and chattering, performing for its meal.

"Shoo," Schmalch said. He grabbed an oar and waved it in the animal's general direction. "I don't have time to play."

The harbor whale dove in a high arc, displaying its broad flat tail and showering Schmalch in cold seawater.

DREG

While he rifled through the marble-topped child's desk for swag small enough to carry, Dreg contemplated revenge. After the twist Rift gave his critter, he was about as lathered as a man could be. Maybe he'd kick the quim off the wall as they climbed down, let her bounce off the rocks and sink, by Fext. Or he could give her a taste of the needler. He slid a malachite cameo of Piru off a pile of papers and into his pocket as he imagined drowning Rift, her tight body flailing and sputtering away in the plunge tub downstairs. His wounded critter stirred, the ache redoubling his anger.

"Find anything older than me?" Rift's low voice startled him.

Dreg abandoned his assault on the desk and straightened, searching his mind for a nasty retort. Before he could speak, she tossed a canvas bag the size of his fist onto the desk, palmful of semi-precious gems of good size and cut inside. These were older than Rift. He hadn't thought of that when he'd made the deal. Either she was mocking him for his blunder, or she hadn't thought of it either. He wasn't sure what do to next.

"From the bedroom safe," she said. "The rest was antique or useless."

Dreg cleared his throat and reconsidered his vindictive plans. "Grat," he said quietly.

He fished in an inner coat pocket, withdrew a collection of miniature pukas carved from different woods, and tossed them on the desk before her. If they were as old as he assumed, the set had been sculpted around the time puka sentience was accepted. Worn and oil-stained from handling, the little statues clattered pleasantly as he dumped them on the desk.

"Take 'em." Dreg didn't bother to mention the cache of sketches he'd found, every one featuring one or more chivori performing sex acts. He was keeping those—to sell or for his own pleasure, he hadn't decided. "The toad likes little stuff."

"Game pieces," she murmured, stirring the scattered figures with one finger. "Rare."

"Really?" Dreg leaned on the desk and studied the ugly little trinkets, half-wishing he hadn't handed them over. "What game?"

Rift made a "*tch…tch-tch…tch*" in the back of her throat then a bleating that seemed to come from her sinus. "Translates to 'wanton scandal'—a raunchy puka's game."

"You speak Pukar?"

"Pukas are overlooked and *everywhere*." Rift picked up one of the game pieces, this one leaning forward to deliver a good view of her cleavage. "And they love to share."

"They share what I want." Dreg gave her his best lip-curl. "No need for all those clicks and grunts."

Rift shook her head, half-smile on her lips.

"What?" he asked.

She tossed the busty statuette in her pack and scooped the other oddments in after. "Did you find a triangular board?"

Dreg watched her for a long moment. She clearly had an opinion about what he'd said. He wanted to ask, but there was no way he'd give her the satisfaction. She could stuff her opinion up her quim. He didn't care.

With an indifferent shrug, Dreg returned to the shelf where he'd found the miniatures. A soapstone triangle covered in colorful dots and squiggly lines sat there. He passed it to Rift. "Wait. A raunchy puka game? Isn't that contradictory?"

Rift actually laughed. "They'd like you to think so. The wealthy don't bother to pretend." She turned the board over.

On this side was a different layout of geometric shapes. Inside each was a pair of joggling pukas, their positions varied and creative. For such a dodder, Flark was certainly single-minded.

"Sylandair had a scandal set. This may be it." She slid the board into her pack's front pocket. Three green-bound books peeped out at him.

"You found the ledgers?" Dreg asked.

Rift nodded. "The mask?"

"Not yet, I haven't finished up here. And there's still rooms downstairs to check."

She turned to leave but stopped, staring at an old watercolor hanging beside the door. In it, a small group of pukas danced in a meadow. Some were eating fruit, some picking flowers, some playing around a beribboned pole weirdly placed in the empty field. Their sun-washed faces oozed glee, though when Dreg looked closely, their eyes *did* seem to stare out of the painting directly at him.

Rift drew both her blades and cut fissures into the hardboard canvas with the tips until the image was a disfigured mess. For a long moment she stood there, looking at her feet. Then she shuddered, holstered her blades, and strolled out of the room with a cat's calm.

The painting was ugly, even a little unsettling, but hardly that bad.

"I'll follow you when I'm done," he called after her.

Dreg stuffed the gem pouch into his pocket and peered out the window behind him at the patio below, where the first gich lay, limp and peaceful, the second one out of sight below the spot where he stood. Pansy had mixed a good batch this time; the bird hadn't managed a step before the paralytic kicked in. He'd have to grab a feather or two before they left, keep one for a trophy, take the other to Pansy as a gift. If the old apothecary didn't give him a cost break, he'd never be able to afford such a swish weapon.

Dreg checked his reflection in the glass wall, adjusted where necessary, and followed Rift. He found her downstairs in a room where the white moonlight poured through a lone round window set high on the wall. Dormah's brilliance painted highlights and shadows over and between the odd assortment of art and curios. The place was packed with enough archaic boodle to make Dreg thoroughly regret the deal he'd struck with Rift.

At the center of the room, the windows of an excessive dollhouse glowed warmly. It was mounted on a squat, brushed-steel plinth that dominated the space. He crouched and peered into its ballroom, where the light of a lumia chandelier exposed a stage littered with miniature instruments awaiting a doll ensemble. After the smut Dreg had found in Flark's office, this was creepy and incongruous. What kind of grown man found this sort of feck amusing?

Surrounding the ornate plaything were walls and shelves of relics, each piece worth more than the last. One shelf held nothing but tiny hand-blown glass lamps, a collection of child-sized gemstone rings and brooches on another, the next displayed paintings no larger than Dreg's thumbnail.

Rift skimmed the room, filching the odd bob but leaving most where it sat. She slipped a lapis statuette of Aessatal and a silver snuffbox into her bag, eyed a jeweled censer, but passed it by.

"What in the depths, Rift?" Dreg asked.

She looked at him.

"Why not scale it all?" He picked up the burner. Dreg knew a sliphand who'd give him at least thirty Callas for the stones alone. "Like this—it's worth quite a few ladies… Isn't it?"

"Take it."

He shoved the piece into his pack. "So, you pass…?"

"It's yours." She picked up a delicate bronze bowl that fit perfectly into her palm. Strange symbols were etched all over it in lines so fine they seemed cut by the Duin. "Voshar singing bowl."

Dreg swallowed, now genuinely regretting his deal. Something like that would set him up for two or three years. More, probably.

"I scaled one of these," Rift said, absorbed in the copper-inlaid linework crisscrossing the thin metal. "Tehtaemah." Her black eyes rolled up to him, great and empty. "Every one's unique." She blinked, her gaze refocused, and she slipped the bowl into her bag. "This isn't it."

Dreg watched her for a moment before picking over everything she'd left behind. He couldn't haul it all down during the climb, but he'd bindle it up and throw it into the harbor if he had to. He could dive for it later, no one the wiser.

His pockets and pack rattled merrily by the time Rift whistled at him from the shadows beneath the window. On the copper-tiled wall in front of her hung the Voshar death mask cased in a stone-inlaid shadowbox of black aelde wood, a voshari's face frozen forever in warm, silvery platinum. Surrounded by rough eddies of metal, the expressionless visage seemed to burst from the wall. The eyelids were closed, soft swell of the dead orbs beneath. The lipless mouth was subtly parted. The flat, wide nose popped from the middle face like a blister. Set at the center point between both eyes and the nose, was an oval of resin, this voshari's mesphor gland embedded within.

As he drew closer, it seemed to Dreg he could see each lash and coarse brow hair, every burgeoning spine along the lines of cheekbones and jaw. Drawings portrayed the voshari species with long quills on their chins and scalps. This one's were fine; it must have been young. Dreg wondered if the subject's age made this mask more valuable.

When Rift touched his arm, Dreg realized he'd been walking slowly forward, drawn inexplicably to the mask.

"Stop." She pointed to the floor.

The marble gave way to a fan of copper tiles, the death mask unreachable without touching them. Rift squatted and rifled through the tools in her pack, returning with what looked like a straight, metallic fid. She twisted a knob at its base and waved it over the tiles. Down its length, a line of tiny lights lit in succession, pulsing vaguely.

"Current's on," Rift said. "Enough to kill."

Two more steps and Dreg would have been dancing like a twitch, choking on his own tongue while his insides roasted.

When the jig was done, he'd ask her where she got the swank probe, a good addition to his kit. Or he'd just take hers if things ended the way he'd like.

Rift wandered away waving the probe around with deliberation, its lights flickering as she made her way toward the dollhouse. The closer she got, the more steadily the metal fid's light array remained lit.

"Power bank's over here," she said.

"In the dollhouse?" Dreg asked.

"The base." Rift kicked the platform gently.

They circled the structure—large enough to fill half of Dreg's cuddy—in opposite directions in search of an access panel or switch. They found none. The base seemed to be one continuous band of dull metal.

"You sure that fid is working?" he asked.

Rift didn't answer, just returned to waving her probe like she was spreading incense at a temple.

Dreg started opening all the doors and windows on the dollhouse in hopes one was a switch.

He'd just finished with the ground floor when Rift said, "Over here."

She was across the room, standing in front of a bronze bust of Saxelyt, its plinth tucked against the wall. The wand in her hand showed steady illumination. Rift looked down into the Duin's face, fingers tracing the curves and lines like a blind woman. When she reached the eye patch, she twisted it upward, revealing the Mistress of Guile's empty socket

Dreg chuckled, "No fuge?"

Rift shook her head and slinked a finger into the void. A crackle of muffled snaps sounded from the dollhouse base and the top glided away, revealing the power bank's caps and generator. Flark must have paid some manky puka to crank the thing every quartern to keep it charged.

Dreg found the cutoff lever and threw it. "We're clear."

Rift returned to the mask display. This time the wand stayed dark. She jerked her head toward the piece. "Check it."

Dreg almost balked before realizing that put the hunk of platinum in his hands.

He tapped a toe to the copper. When nothing happened, Dreg tried his whole foot and found it safe. He tilted the shadowbox gently away from the wall, checking for triggers before hefting the mask. It was lighter than he'd expected. The face was a little larger than his own, yet not as enormous as a rhochrot's. It was long and narrow, almost ovular. The detail was unnerving, the metal clearly pure. He stared at it, imagining the price this thing might net.

The mask's thin lips twitched closed, their corners tightened and turned up, like someone stifling a laugh.

Dreg started, nearly dropping the shadowbox. He stepped backward, stumbling into Rift, who pushed him upright before he fell on his stern. He mumbled an excuse and shifted into the moonlight, scrutinizing the mask, certain the lips had mocked him. He squinted, turned it back and forth, even poked it gently, but the strange face smirked no more. The moonlight must have hexed him.

ALIARA

Dreg held the mask up to the window, studying the piece, oblivious to all else. Aliara hadn't expected him to be quite so interested. Old dosh—worth well beyond what a sliphand would pay—didn't jibe with what she knew of the boy. At least it was keeping him occupied and quiet.

She crouched and opened her pack, withdrawing a bundle of thin rope, her harness, a pair of leather gloves, and a wooden box the size of an apple. Branded on the lid was the Thung Toh symbol, Ismae's moons in eclipse.

Dreg winced and made a small sound like a cat dreaming.

"Take this." Aliara offered him the rope.

Dreg looked like a man who'd expected death but received only a kick in the jugglers. He shifted the shadowbox under one arm, grabbed the proffered line, and stared blankly at the rope.

Aliara clapped once and Dreg looked at her, angry discomfort rising in his expression.

"Rig us for a rundown and pull," she said. "You have your harness?"

"What?" Dreg scoffed. "Do you think this is my first jig up top?"

"Do it seaside. Make sure Schmalch is waiting." Aliara removed her cloak from the pack, spread it on the floor, and tapped the center. "The mask."

Dreg hesitated and then handed her the box, "Anything else, Madame Binnacle?"

"Bring the bodies inside."

"Me? You want me to drag two giches on my own?" Dreg asked, petulance below the gravel of his voice. His hands balled, his face darkened. He looked like he might drop into a tantrum.

"And a man," she said, one hand ready on the stiletto invisible to Dreg from where he stood. "Bring me fingers. Or toes."

"What?" His face scrunched up, rage evaporating. "Why?"

"No trace." Aliara tapped the little box.

For a moment, Dreg didn't understand. When realization dawned, he took an instinctive step away, shaking his head hard enough to loose a curl of hair. "Blanch bomb? No. I've heard stories."

"Luugrar, right?"

"Among others," Dreg pushed the hair back into place, "but yeah, mostly him."

Aliara chuckled.

"I didn't sleep for a week after he told the one about the jig in the bunker in…" His gaze drifted away as he struggled to remember.

"Albaness," Aliara said. She knew the story well.

Dreg shuddered.

His discomfort was good. Only the Thung Toh was audacious enough to use blanch germs outside of a laboratory. While blanching a scene removed any trace, deliberately setting loose a spark-targeted microbe edged close to foolishness. Treating it as anything less-than-lethal crossed that boundary. At least Dreg showed enough sense to be appropriately terrified.

"The way Luugrar described the scene…dust and chunks." Dreg lay the shadowbox on her cloak and stalked out, his rant fading into a mutter.

Aliara shrugged. The bomb was an acceptable risk. As soon as the Corps saw blanch dust coating Flark's furniture and walls, they'd know something had happened, but it would take them months to sort out exactly what had occurred. With all flesh and bone consumed, investigators would need days to simply figure out who'd been killed. They'd never learn who'd done the job.

Outside, Dreg was grunting with effort, grumbling some derogatory generalization about karju.

"Kill that gich you needled," Aliara called to Dreg. She'd assumed his paralytic lethal but seeing it in action with Karna had proven otherwise.

She adjusted the shadowbox to a good center on her cloak. The face was beautiful, its features peculiar and unique. Before this jig she'd seen only drawings of voshari in Syl's childhood lesson books. Even then she'd found them fascinating. Their eyes, long and dark, were especially intriguing.

Aliara blinked.

Gone was Flark's gaudy room filled with collected-but-unloved trinkets. She was sitting at a table, simple lines and wild burled grain. A smiling woman sat across from Aliara, drinking from a cup that seemed to grow from her hand. Gloves and bodice showed no boundaries with the woman's skin, only a brief gradation of black leather to grey flesh. Thin-skinned wings twitched behind her, as deep a grey as the rest. Floppy curls the color of smashed berries tumbled into the woman's eyes, one iris as purple as her hair, the other hidden by a triangle of bark anchored in place by three brad nails.

"You're dead now." The woman raised the hand-cup to Aliara and winked with her missing eye. "Do you want not to be?"

Aliara blinked.

She was back in Flark's showroom, Dreg fumbling around in the parlor. The voshari's platinum face stared back impassively, unconcerned by her confusion, unwilling to explain.

"Sax's tit!" Dreg snarled.

A clatter and squawk, then the slow grate of dragging resumed.

Without looking directly at the mask, Aliara hurriedly wrapped the shadowbox in her cloak and worked it into her pack.

"They're all inside." Dreg crouched beside her, array of fingers, toes, and talons clutched in his fist.

"Already?"

"What?" he asked, tone tetchy.

"Never mind." Aliara retrieved the catalyst vial from the blanch bomb's box, removed its steel cap, and began squeezing blood from each severed digit into it.

The strange woman floated to the surface of Aliara's thoughts, winking, smiling, raising the hand that was a cup. Aliara had just seen the bust in Flark's gallery, her mind must have drawn from that image. Maybe some remnant of Ranaran's work had caused a misfire. Or Orono's fiddling.

Aliara closed her eyes and banished the image. "Your hand," she said when she'd finished juicing the corpse digits.

Dreg shook his head and stood. "You first."

Aliara set the vial on the ground, drew a stiletto, and pricked her finger, her black blood fouling the mingled reds. She looked at Dreg, who hesitated before drawing his boot knife. A quick nick to his palm and he completed the mix.

Aliara slung her pack, put on her gloves. "Ready?"

Dreg wheeled and ran.

Aliara uncapped the glass pyramid and poured the comingled blood onto the puce dust within. The blanch germs hissed and shifted as she poured, more drinking the fluid than absorbing it. Vial empty, she was up and running the instant the cap's seal squeaked into place.

SCHMALCH

Getting the dinghy had been no issue. Schmalch had taken more than one drunken ride in a filched boat. Keeping himself dry and clean in the process, however, had been a challenge thanks to the playful harbor whale. The beautiful jacket Sviroosa made for him was not only soiled by the lift operator's greasy finger and torn by those goons, but now it was also dripping wet and smeared with seafoam. Schmalch pulled a bit of sargassum from one pocket and sighed. Sviroosa would be furious. Or disappointed. He wasn't sure which would be worse.

A sudden splash spattered cold water on Schmalch and his mess of a coat. A rope dangled in the sea, its loose ends moving eel-like just below the surface. He looked up to see the all-grey man looking down from the top of the building. Schmalch waved. Dreg dropped the other end of the rope, this one swaying just above the scree line, and disappeared without waving back.

Schmalch waited for him and Rift to return and slide down the rope, but nothing happened. The silence from above stretched out, Schmalch's neck grew stiff, and he returned to watching the sea lap moonlit rocks.

A few dark pebbles skittered down the seawall and spilled softly into the water. Schmalch looked up in time to see Dreg and Rift mount the railing. For a beat, they hovered against the night sky like a pair of haints then they tipped forward and started running down the building. Schmalch gasped. They looked like the jykiini, shadow dolls coming for his spirit. He blinked until he could see their ropes. They slowed and seemed to float to the foot of the seawall. When they landed, Rift breezed over the slick rubble and pounced softly into the boat. Dreg slid and stumbled a few times, soaking the tattered tail of his long coat. He settled onto the bench behind Schmalch with a curse and the tinkling clatter of boodle.

"Row," Rift said.

"Where to?" Schmalch asked.

"Pier Road docks."

When they were back on land, Schmalch jogged after the pair's long strides, keeping close enough to listen to Rift's instructions. His arms ached from the row, but for fifty Callas, he would have spent all night ferrying them back and forth. He was panting when he reached the penthouse.

While Rift gave Sviroosa direction in the foyer, Dreg began drinking in the parlor. Sviroosa gave Schmalch a smile that turned instantly down at the sight of his filthy coat.

He hurried into the parlor. "C'mon, uh, Dreg."

From beneath the shadow of his hood, the chivori's grey eyes glinted in the low light.

"Pretty gloss living here, eh?" Dreg asked.

"Yeah, my first home since the Spriggans." Schmalch choked on the last word. He hadn't intended to share. "We're 'sposed to hurry."

"You like Rift's duke?" Dreg set his half-empty glass on top of the cellarette.

"Sure, yeah." Schmalch started toward the door that separated the new and old sides of the penthouse. The Duke had spent the winter setting up the new parts—a really gloss room he called the salon, an office, and new bedrooms for Schmalch and Sviroosa. He'd even let Schmalch decorate his own room. "Duke Imythedralin's kind of picky, but I'm learning."

"I bet he's soft, living around all this expensive feck."

"I've seen him get dirty." The image of the Duke cutting his way through Orono's horde floated through Schmalch's mind. "He can do things."

Dreg grunted.

Schmalch led him upstairs to one of the guest rooms. "Shower's in the lav. I need your clothes. Sviroosa's gonna clean and fix them. We're 'sposed to hurry."

Dreg pushed back the hood and yanked a leather thong from his hair. A chin-length clump of loose waves in brilliant ever-changing colors spilled out. It was like watching schools of reef fish swim through one another. Schmalch wanted to touch it.

"What happened to your hair?" he asked.

Dreg scratched his scalp with both hands. "Zoet."

"It's…it's really gloss." Schmalch had noticed the effect on the fuzz below the man's lip earlier but assumed it a trick of the light or the result of too many brews with Frabo and Yemenie.

"Grat." Dreg smiled, though his mouth barely turned up. "Rift doesn't care for it."

"I've never seen that one. At the Barnacle, it's mostly tails and horns and different-colored eyes when people get zoets. My friend Yemenie has a sub-seg-segm— she has an extra-bendy spine. And Garl's old partner had his eyes done permanently red. But all the colors…" Schmalch caught himself. "The clothes. I'm supposed to take them to Sviroosa. She's gonna have a lot to do on that coat for you. We'd better hurry."

Dreg tossed handfuls of shiny stuff from the coat's many pockets onto the bed. Schmalch bit his lip. He wanted to pick through it all while Dreg showered, but he had to move quickly. If he didn't, Rift might not give him the fifty Callas. He bit his lip a little harder.

When the pockets were empty, Dreg tossed the coat to Schmalch, the rest of his clothes followed.

"Don't scale my boodle." The chivori pointed at Schmalch as he stepped into the washroom. "I know every piece."

Schmalch hurried downstairs, deposited the clothes in the kitchen for Sviroosa, and raced upstairs to the Duke's closet. He picked a few things he'd heard the Duke complain of being too tight and ran back, tripping on a pant leg and jabbing a hanger up his nose half-way down the hall.

When Schmalch returned to the guest room, Dreg was sitting naked on the foot of the bed, skin flushed almost as dark grey as Rift's from the shower. Fully dressed and made-up, she leaned over him, comb in one hand, smearing some sort of goop into Dreg's reef-colored hair with the other.

Both chivori seemed unbothered by Dreg's lack of clothes. The chivori kids at the Spriggan Temple were like that too. If two pukas were in the same situation, one would cover her eyes while the other hid himself behind the curtains.

"Why can't I just put it up like usual?" Dreg asked.

"Pricey trulls style their hair," Rift said.

Dreg looked at Schmalch and rolled his eyes. "Why am I the trull?"

Rift jerked his head back into place and went at the damp tangle with a comb.

"Why not some friend from Chiva'vastezz in for a visit?"

"I tried to entice Sylandair from the table earlier," she said with the tone of someone repeating herself. "Everyone knows me, so you're the trull. I'm inciting envy…or offering a gift." She stood back and looked at her work. "Out-of-town friend rings false, risks questions we can't answer."

"Fine, but do I have to be a whore? Can't you just have picked me up at the Caba Club or something? A simple trawler?" He scooted a little closer, hands on her hips. "You seduced me. No money exchanged. Why not that?"

Rift slipped out of his grip, selected a black cosmetic stick from the dresser, and went at Dreg's eyes with it. When she was done, he looked an awful lot like some of the people Schmalch had seen come through the penthouse now and then. She picked through the things Schmalch had brought and tossed a slick blue shirt and black pants at Dreg, who was studying himself in the mirror.

The Duke's clothes were just big enough to be awkward. They made Dreg look like even more of a kid. Another reminder of life at the Spriggan Temple, where you took what was available no matter how bad it fit. Clothes were one of the few things people thought to donate to such a remote and ill-thought-of organization, but the stuff they gave was mostly old and worn out—and usually made for adults. All the little kids, too young to steal something better, took what they could in the best size they could find, rolling up sleeves and pantlegs.

Rift pointed at Schmalch "Get my—"

"Wait," Dreg said. "No. I am not wearing *your* gear."

"—black shirt," she finished.

Schmalch's face scrunched up as he tried to guess which one she meant. Rift wore a lot of black shirts.

"The one I was wearing when Sylandair disappeared."

"Oh, right." A few months back, Schmalch had found her in that shirt and little else, lying on the floor at the old Orono mansion. She had been out cold, the Duke missing. Schmalch didn't like to think about what happened after that.

He scampered to Rift's closet—far less stuffed than the Duke's—grabbed the black net shirt, and started back. On the way, Sviroosa stopped him with the basket of Dreg's clean clothes and boots, her eyes on Schmalch's ruined coat. He took the clean things, tossed Rift's shirt on top, and returned to the guest room.

Dreg grabbed the basket and started dressing.

Rift waved Schmalch over to the bed, where several things had been added to Dreg's shiny pile of boodle, including something big that looked like a thick picture frame. Schmalch stood on his toes for a better view. It looked like a face in a box, but no face he'd ever seen. For a heartbeat, Schmalch felt like the eyes had rolled toward him, but that was impossible; the lids were closed like the person was sleeping.

He chuckled. He wasn't even tippled and still seeing things.

Rift appeared at his side holding a pretty metal bowl. She ran a finger over the complicated pictures etched on the surface, and set it on the nightstand, far away from Dreg's dosh. Schmalch eyed the bowl, trying to decide if the lines were just pretty patterns or if they were supposed to be people dancing. Either way, he was sure the item was expensive enough to keep him in brews and new suitcoats for a year.

Rift took his chin in hand, turning him to face her. "Listening?"

Schmalch nodded.

She released his chin and pointed to the fancy metal face. "This is important."

He looked at it, again feeling as though the unopened eyes were staring back at him. The face was shaped strange—too round and too flat—the nose more like a bubble, no bridge whatsoever. Metal ripples around it made it look like someone had fallen asleep in the water.

"What *is* that?" Schmalch asked. He rubbed his own swooping nose, pleased to find it still in place.

"Voshar death mask," Rift said.

"Like the Duke's been talking about." Schmalch couldn't look away from the face. He'd never seen that much platinum in one place before. "The one he needs to keep away from…"

"Nihal Savesti. Yes."

Last autumn, Nihal had pretended to help the Duke and Rift. Instead, she killed Hergis, her brother, in the Duke's parlor, then ran off with a bunch of papers the Duke had inherited from Orono. Those papers explained how the old zoeticist had done his explosive experiment, the one that turned him into a monstrous bug. Schmalch didn't know why anyone who knew about Orono and his horde of bogy kids would want anything to do with those papers.

When he'd said as much, The Duke had explained that Nihal saw "flaws in several of Master Orono's hypotheses." She thought she could fix it, do it right this time.

Rift had muttered "hubris" and wandered off.

"Whether she fails or succeeds," the Duke had continued, "odds are Madame Savesti will do the same sort of damage as Orono, perhaps on a greater scale. We intend to prevent her from testing those theories."

"How?" Schmalch had asked.

"By keeping from her the components needed to complete her work." The Duke's grim face had shifted to a bitter smile. "Mister Haus is doing his part. Ours is to retrieve the mask. Without it, she cannot complete her metamorphosis."

Rift snapped her fingers, drawing Schmalch from the memory.

"Hrm? What?" He looked up at her.

Rift's brow scrunched. "Wrap the mask and wait in the foyer. An Ironclad carriage will be by soon to take you to the Bank."

Schmalch frowned. He didn't like visiting the Bank of Dockhaven. It was so cold and clean, and everyone looked at him like he didn't belong there. The guards standing around with their guns just make it worse.

"Why me?" Schmalch asked. "Why can't you do it on your way?"

"Don't want to be noticed there."

Schmalch shrugged. At least he'd get to ride in one of the Ironclad carriages. He'd only ever seen them on the street, never been inside where the rich stuff hid.

"Ask for box 3443. Put the mask inside. Lock up." Rift pressed a metal lockbox key into his palm. "Bring this home. Understood?"

Schmalch nodded and put the key on the clip Sviroosa had sewn inside his sodden jacket.

"What box?" Rift asked.

"Box 3443."

Rift nodded.

"Better?" Dreg interrupted, Rift's shirt stretched tight over his chest, the tattoo beneath blurred by the mesh.

Schmalch stepped back and studied Dreg's transformation. The effect was a little tough, a little feminine. If he'd seen the chivori in a club, Schmalch would have believed him an expensive trull, probably one who provided services he'd only heard about.

"You need a hat," Schmalch suggested.

DREG

The *Ipesia* floated in Lover's Sound, every window alive with lights and motion inviting Dreg to enjoy everything offered within. Bangers as varicolored as his hair ignited the midnight sky, their light revealing the barge's uncanny magnitude. From one of the balconies, a group lounging in a heated tub waved and hooted at the approaching launch while the crowd on the topmost deck danced in what looked like a garden grove, its trees salted with lights. When the breeze shifted, Dreg caught broken phrases from the ensemble driving the dancers. Decks below, a man stood at the main rail, pissing into the sea.

The launch's prow hopped as it cut through the growing waves of the Sound. Dreg pulled his coat tighter against the chill wind, thankful the weather had held off until after they finished their bit at Flark's penthouse.

Squeezed between Rift and a sweaty, mustachioed man on a narrow bench, Dreg tried to appear nonchalant. The closest he'd come to the extravagance that awaited was that lone, long-ago visit to Ruutad's *Spriggish Bym*. In his first year as a Toh, he'd splurged on a night in one of the Caba Club's translucent bubble-rooms after closing a particularly lucrative contract. Both experiences had been gloss, but nothing like this floating treat.

Dreg rubbed the lightly oozing scab on his forehead. With all the paint and paste Rift had thrown at him, she hadn't so much as attempted to cover the mark. He swore at himself for being so clumsy during their climb. Though she hadn't mentioned the incident, Dreg suspected the hair glop and eye paint were Rift's way of punishing him for his earlier blunders. As if the injury itself wasn't shaming enough, she'd made him try on the Duke's clothes, which made him look like a child in a handed-down temple suit. The shirt they'd settled on was tolerable, despite coming from her closet. Dreg enjoyed the way the old Salt Street Tribe tattoo on his chest showed through its weave, though not as much as he enjoyed the way Rift's high little bubs showed through hers. She'd changed into a filmy little blue-violet getup, and he hadn't exactly hated watching her strut around the penthouse while she dressed him like a dolly.

He glanced at her as she reached an arm over the launch's edge and ran fingers through the icy water, her eyes on the exploding sky. Sadly, her slim body was hidden by her long coat. Thoughts of having her—and ending her—drifted pleasantly through his mind. He could just push her overboard tonight. That would be simple. It was too cold for her to swim very far. Dreg chuckled to himself.

"Ready yourselves for docking," the boat's skipper squawked.

A banger burst above in a hiss of bright yellow and blue sparks, and the skipper jumped, jerking the wheel. The prow caromed off the barge's dock pads with a thump and everyone lurched in their seats. The man on the front bench flopped back onto Dreg's feet with a yelp. His friend recovered him amidst tippled giggles. Dreg received no apology.

"Nothing to fret about," the skipper called. "All safe now."

Rift watched the rest of the arriving guests disembark before she rose. The skipper muttered a welcome to the "duchess" and lent a steadying hand as she stepped off his craft. Dreg couldn't help but roll his eyes.

Rift stopped just outside the entry, her black eyes serious beneath the round brim of her grey hat. "Cabin first," she said. "Leave our coats, grab my shoes. Do your gawking on the way."

When they stepped inside, lights and sounds and smells assaulted Dreg. They stood on white-veined blue marble that gave the illusion of walking on water. Above, dangling crystals played at being stars as they circulated lumia light around the room filled with a chattering buzz louder than a swarm of chikka flies.

Dreg gulped it in.

A solitary woman in a short pink dress and cockeyed cloche that barely clung to her head spun drunkenly as the reception band played a tune popular the summer before. A troop of waiters with broad silver trays passed out bits of food and tall drinks. A proud-stomached man with spiky hair the color of starlight rolled dice and brayed something about the injustice of the game. On the stage, a big-armed karju danced and preened. His chosen zoet was fine green feathers that replaced his hair, ran down his spine, and sprouted from his forearms. Dreg wondered how he groomed.

Standing at one of the courtesy bars, ruby feather pin in place on the lapel of a slim black suit, was the Toh's liaison Traus, his pale grey hair as straight as the lines of his suit. Dreg didn't know why the man's presence surprised him; Marthoth's zootie was an ideal spot to cultivate clients. Behind him stood the burly blonde Muddler, another of the Toh's operatives. Dreg resisted the urge to wave.

Everywhere, Callas and jewelry glinted with invitation.

Rift gripped his forearm. "Try not to gawp like that."

Realizing his awestruck expression, Dreg rearranged his face into what he hoped was blasé. He snatched a tall glass from a passing waiter's tray and negotiated the crowd in Rift's wake. She led him up a grand staircase into a massive dining area, where a cream-skinned man with golden hair piled to almost twice his height played soothing music on a lavender clavichord. Toward aft, broad doors opened to reveal a scene straight from one of Dreg's more creative fantasies.

When he faltered there, Rift whistled at him. He chased her up more flights, down a short corridor, and into a corner suite at the fore. The all-glass outer walls looked over Lover's Sound. The rest were mirrors reflecting a bed large enough to hold five, exactly enough furniture for comfort, and a bar that could keep anyone tippled for a quartern.

While Rift visited the walk-in wardrobe, Dreg dumped his coat on the bed—ultramarine-and-white themed like most of Marthoth's barge—grabbed an open bottle from the bar, and stepped outside onto the balcony. The night air punched him, and he stood there alternately drinking and giggling. She joined him wordlessly, dark tips of her bubs sharp in the cold air. Looking at her, Dreg couldn't imagine how the Duke had chosen gambling over a good reeve.

His gaze drifted to her lips, tinted nearly as black as her eyes. He pulled from the bottle, grabbed Rift around the waist, and kissed her in the way that had buckled the knees of plenty of conquests.

Even while his lips were still on hers, Dreg regretted the move, worried how she might react. When he pulled away, her face was bland. She returned to staring at the glittering sky. He'd made no impression—a pain worse than any fid-wrenching rebuke she might've given him.

Dreg cleared his throat. "I thought we should get that out of the way," he said, shamed by the waver in his voice, "in case we have to put on a show later."

"You're clear?"

"Sure." He gave her a wry grin, but she didn't bother to look. "I'm thrilled to play your poovey for the evening."

"This kind of pretense…it's tricky not being yourself." She drew a deep breath, releasing it in a plume of mist. "Things change fast. Whatever happens, don't speak until you know the play."

Dreg hardened his face. "I can do the job—whatever it takes to close the contract."

"Good." Rift slipped into the cabin, threaded past the furniture, and ducked out the front door. Dreg chased after her, bottle in hand. She led him down through the twinkling blur to the gaming deck, where the Duke was ensconced at a lyntyyl table, chatting amiably with five grumpy players and a weary dealer. Rift slid onto the Duke's knee and went at his mouth like a hungry spa fish.

Across the table, a doddery lump of a puka shifted his attention from his cards to Rift. The target, Flark.

To one side of the Duke, a chubby puka woman scratched at her hairless scalp with stubby green fingers. The fake daisy pasted there threatened to fall off, but she righted it and returned to her cards. To the other side, a rhochrot with jolly, calculating brown eyes and a soft swoop of bright green hair smiled and winked at Dreg. Her skin was like dirty grey stone and so thick that had Dreg shot at her, his needles would have bounced off.

Flanking Flark were two chivori. One was an ordinary-looking man whose only notable features were a nose severe enough to slice bread and the sex appeal of a landed fish. He did nothing but stare at his cards like a bird hypnotized by a snake. The other was a woman who'd clearly put a lot of time and coin into her appearance. She was shorter than average and enjoyed exaggerated, karju-like curves. Though she looked better in person than she had in the news chits, Dreg recognized the Haven's Mayor Idra Carsuure. He'd thought her hair was gelid, but seeing her now, he judged it was a touch too grey to be a true white. Her bubs, big enough to fill a whole hand, almost jumped out of a dress that looked like fire made fabric. They had to be zoets. No chivori he knew looked like that naturally. She glanced up at Dreg with crystal-blue eyes circled in copper lashes and sneered.

"Vrasaj, Pet," the Duke said when Rift had finished. He nipped at her moonstone ring then turned, slate-blue eyes taking Dreg in from boots to spectral hair. "I see you brought me a kaleidoscope."

Dreg bit back a snide reply. They'd never met, though everyone in both Rabbles knew who the Duke was. The man was handsome to the point of beautiful, his movements precise, his expressions well-rehearsed. His clothes probably cost enough to pay a full month's rent for *everyone* in that flop Dreg called home—though the spiral-patterned purple scarf around his throat seemed a bit much.

They held one another's eyes until the Duke smiled.

"So glad you could entertain my darling girl," the Duke said, something biting in his tone despite the pleasant expression.

Dreg returned the grin. "My pleasure, Duke."

His gaze left Dreg, slid over Rift, and circled the table, pausing on each of the players before settling on the manky puka across from him. The smile never wavered.

"I believe you won that wager, Mister Flark." The Duke counted ten bars from his mound of boodle and slid them across the felt. "She did, indeed, return."

Flark scraped in the silver with a sly chuckle. "I know women. No matter the species, I know women."

"It seems you do," the Duke said, amusement in his tone.

"Can you take a break?" Rift murmured in the Duke's ear.

He looked from her to his cards and back again. "Difficult to say, Pet."

Rift stuck out her lower lip like a petulant child.

The dealer cleared his throat. "Duke Imythedralin?"

"Apologies." The Duke tossed bars into the center of the table. "I believe this will be my last round."

"The hold's not won yet, Duke." Flark's forehead wrinkled. "It's a big one."

"True, but my skills already suffer, and as you can see…" He ran a palm over Rift's thigh, eyes never leaving the old puka. "I have been provided an enticing alternative."

Flark made a noise like a boiling kettle as one hand massaged his domed gut.

"Besides, I would hate to take any more of your Callas," the Duke said. "You have such great plans for them."

Flark's annoyed bark became a coughing fit.

"Perhaps you should do the same, old friend," the Duke said. "Your green is going a bit grey."

Flark spat something unsettlingly large on the floor. He wiped his mouth with his sleeve and grinned at the Duke. "At least finish the round, Imythedralin. The dealer's going off shift. Perfect time for you to go do whatever it is you people do." His expression wasn't quite so disgusted as his tone implied.

The Duke sighed so loudly that everyone on this side of the room could hear. "Very well, Mister Flark. I will stay—but only until the end of this round."

Flark grunted, satisfied.

Dreg wondered how long this was going to drag out.

"Badger's stack," the dealer said.

Dreg knew enough of the game to understand the badger was the first position player, the goal was to lose all your cards, and play involved a lot of calculations. Beyond that, he'd never bothered to learn lyntyyl.

The puka lady stood on her chair and began stacking cards in ways Dreg didn't understand. When she was done, the Mayor did the same. As she piled her cards, she committed some unforgiveable gaffe involving botched calculations. The other players enjoyed a good laugh. The Mayor—out for the rest of the round and irked by the jabs—flopped back in her seat and crossed her arms, giving Dreg a fine view of her zoet bubs in their flimsy orange gown.

When the hilarity had calmed, Flark rubbed a dirty little bag trimmed with feathers and played his stacks. The pointy man and the rhochrot followed. The Duke counted out stacks until no cards remained in his hand. He'd won. The others cursed as they tossed unspent cards toward the bedraggled dealer, who produced a long, hooked stick and pushed the impressively large hold toward the Duke.

"You cheat!" Flark snatched a cane dangling from the table beside him and pinned the dealer's stick to the table. He pointed at Rift. "*She* brought you a card."

"Hardly, Mister Flark," the Duke said. "How would she have

known which one I needed? You have your good luck charms. I have mine." He again stroked Rift's thigh. "She is my bringer of fortune."

"You can't just make off with all that boodle, Duke." Flark released his lock on the dealer's stick. "Give me a chance to win it back."

"There are many days remaining in the Festival—"

"We play now!" Flark whacked his stick against the table, though the felt cover gave it less impact than he'd probably intended.

"I think not, Mister Flark. My most recent dose of themot has yet to wear off. I should take advantage." The Duke glanced up at Dreg. "We shall see if this one can entertain us until it does."

Dreg put a hand on Rift's shoulder. The Duke was about to blow their chance to be near Flark. Without even looking back, Rift brushed him off with one of the cruder gestures in the Toh's hand cant.

Flark grumbled something unseemly about the general dishonesty of all chivori before cracking a nearby waitress across her thighs with the cane. The woman shrieked and lurched forward, barely managing to balance her tray. Blackening welts rose just below the hem of her uniform's short skirt.

"Two more scorillion patties, a shot of khuit, and a brew—big this time," Flark demanded, "not like that dainty thing you brought me before."

"Sir, I haven't served you—" the server began, one hand protectively clenching her injury.

"Now!" Flark bellowed.

When the woman rushed off, the Duke tugged Dreg's sleeve. He crouched and the Duke pressed a full conch into his palm.

"Deliver this to that server," he whispered.

Dreg stared. This one coin would pay his rent for half the year.

"Ensure she receives that." The Duke released Dreg's sleeve, his brows low. "I *will* check later."

Dreg caught the server at the bar placing her next round of

orders. He slid into place beside her and offered the platinum coin.

She looked him over, mouth tight, eyes narrowed. "Just because I let some puka whack me with a stick doesn't mean I'm a trull. Not even for that much."

"It's from the Duke." Dreg jerked his chin back toward their table. "An apology for Flark."

"Someone *should* apologize for him." She grabbed the coin.

Dreg held tight until she smiled.

She tucked it into a pouch on her thigh then turned, showing off the rising black welts—and giving him a peek at the curve of her ass and just a hint of panty. "Every year he gets worse."

If this job went as quickly as he hoped, Dreg intended to come back and rub salve on those welts.

"And ickier," she continued. "It's awful serving him drinks, but I really pity anyone who has to deal with him in the mingling room. You should hear the stories."

Dreg mock-shuddered and they both laughed. He glanced back to the table.

Rift was watching him.

"Enjoy the plat." Dreg tapped the counter with a wink and jogged back.

"…can't set stakes appropriate to people of our stature," Flark was shouting when Dreg returned to the table. "It's not right for Marthoth to put limits on wagers. Everyone here can make their own decisions."

Based on some of the stumbling tipplers he'd seen wandering around, Dreg wasn't entirely certain that was true.

The Mayor groaned and dropped her head to the table.

"I believe he wishes to avoid appearing to have caused any becoming paupers." The Duke encouraged Rift off his lap and rose. "I am thoroughly comfortable with Mister Marthoth's rules. The *Ipesia* is, after all, his vessel."

"Wait, wait!" Flark groped for the cane, succeeding only in

knocking it to the ground. "I'm tired of lyntyyl, and Marthoth's low stakes rules… I invite you to my yacht to play some Billidoc Dice, Duke. Bring your woman and her toy. We'll set our own stakes—ones appropriate to people like us. Perhaps even wager with some land?" His hairless brows went up.

The Duke chuckled. "I have no interest in staking my land on the Big Island, Mister Flark. You know this."

"Oh, no, no, Duke. I meant the Heap. Play a few rounds on my yacht and maybe move on to bigger things than a box full of Callas."

The Duke made a show of considering.

"Imt's eyes." The Mayor groaned as she stood. "Let's take another recess while these two finish dancing."

The pointy man rose and gave his chair a cursory kick before stalking into the crowd. Everyone else remained, whether lazy or curious.

"It seems dull with only the two of us playing, Flark," the Duke said. "We have done that often enough at my penthouse."

"Fine, then I invite you *all* to my yacht—the *Wide-Eyed Lessee*—for gaming."

"I'll be there," the female puka said. "I want to see what awful things you've done to my lovely ship."

"A delightful idea, Madame Daisy," the Duke said.

Flark pointed a ring-laden finger at her. "It was never yours, and you're not invited."

Daisy grinned and plopped out of her chair. "Oh, I'll be there."

Flark's upper lip rose in a snarl as he watched Daisy trot across the gaming floor.

"Gratitude, but Mister Marthoth needs me here." Javit rose from the resting hassock and scuttled off.

"I'll join, but," the Mayor sighed, "I need a bath first."

"Each of the *Lessee's* six cabins has a full bath," Flark said, one brow raised. "You're welcome to use the owner's suite."

The Mayor's face squeezed in on itself. "Ugh, no. I'll be fine alone in *my* cabin. Unless you're planning to blow up Marthoth's barge with everyone still inside?"

"Implode, and they were warned." Flark dismissed her with a grunt and returned to the Duke. "I'll send Vesven with a launch to ferry you over to *my* yacht."

IDRA

Imythedralin had betrayed her. Idra was certain of it.

She'd been considering the possibility since he'd returned from dinner with their host. He'd claimed he told Marthoth nothing, but wouldn't it have been easier to deflect suspicion onto Idra and let the shipper deal with her? At first, she'd believed Imythedralin, but the more she considered, the more convinced Idra became. She'd even begun to suspect the assassination attempt in his cabin was all fiction—a play put on to secure her sympathy.

Idra cast glances this way and that as she moved through the revelers, certain that at any moment, Marthoth's goons would slip up beside her calmly and make her disappear, leaving Asah Onpuur to win the election unopposed.

Idra made sure her face showed none of these concerns as she worked her way through the gathered constituents toward the farspeech office, stopping at least two dozen times to hear their praises and complaints, resisting her urge to flinch every time a red-sashed crew member wandered near.

The first year he'd thrown the extravaganza, Marthoth had placed the farspeech office on the gaming deck, reasoning the location made it convenient. He'd failed to consider the noise. At the following year's Festival, he'd converted two cabins on the fourth deck. The location was far from silent, but the space was as quiet as one could hope for aboard the *Ipesia* at Festival time. It was also extremely inconvenient.

A cluster of young and rising business owners accosted Idra on the second deck. She'd heard their concerns before and had long-since memorized the associated palliatives. They naturally brought up the Flark situation, and she was able to truthfully tell them that she and Pitta had discussed the matter earlier that day. Incongruously, one man among them kept asking "How're the cards treating you?" as he gazed unblinkingly at her breasts. Idra was fairly certain he was so tippled, those were the only words he could recall.

Though she told him the cards were treating her well, Idra had been playing horribly, her mind on the election and her assistant's most recent message concerning the Yinago Tower. Flark had hurt her immeasurably with this implosion stunt. She couldn't fathom how he possibly believed what he'd done was acceptable to the city's leadership. The man was a menace. And he'd made her look like a confederate.

She truly hated owing the little scug anything. He was always showing up at her office asking for favors, implying he was going to change the terms of her loan, trying to turn the Mayor's office into his personal service. She had to lash that down.

Once she'd cleared the Flark obligation, Idra would do the same for Daisy, Callen, and Pitta. They may be just as important and powerful as Flark, but they were nowhere near as annoying—or unpredictable. The rest of her debts—smaller loans from smaller people—could wait.

Halfway up the next staircase, a tightly wound spiral, Idra paused to speak to a trio who wanted to know what she was doing about the terrible situation in the Lower Rabble. Upper Rabble, she corrected them, and assured each one that she *and the City Council* were addressing the Flark issue in due haste.

"By playing cards with him?" a pretty brunette woman asked.

"Not all punitive damage is visible." Idra's smile showed her pity for the woman's ignorance.

She'd learned the subtle art of politicking from her late wife and Dockhaven's previous mayor, Maryn Raan. The woman had been demanding, but she'd been excellent at her job. Idra had done her best to absorb all Maryn's skills, surprised by how often the techniques she'd learned as a dancer cultivating clients dovetailed with those of a politician courting voters.

Idra had been Mayor for a third of her life. After inheriting the title on Maryn's death, she had held it through two elections. In both, the Rabbles had been her base, Pukatown the key. She campaigned as a daughter of a trash mucker and a tram driver—one of their own made good. The voters not only bought it, they loved it, especially the pukas.

Flark was ruining that.

Idra didn't know what she'd do without this life. The Founding Families would never accept her into their society bereft of her title. Worse yet, without her mayoral bargaining power, Idra would be left to cover what she owed. She might be forced out of the Nest, have to sell her estate, maybe even liquidate Maryn's collection—*Idra's* collection.

Lost in thoughts of these potential horrors, Idra topped the steps to the fourth deck, turned the corner, and nearly ran smack into Lady Orilausko, owner of the Caba Club and one-time Seer of Dream and Waking. And one of Idra's few dear friends.

Ori had arrived in Dockhaven via the Egress more than two decades ago. Thanks to profound nausea and weakness experienced by the traveler, the system was used primarily to transport items of significant value, which were accompanied by an unlucky guard or two. So when Ori and the young, silver-haired chivori had plopped out of the Haven's terminus, dirty, wounded, and wealthy, it was unusual but hardly momentous. When the Corps spotted her Seers marks, though, the Commissioner notified Idra. Mystics were rare, those who'd joined the organization more so, and the few living in Dockhaven remained reclusive.

It had been imperative Idra cultivate the woman's goodwill. Most of Idra's constituents thought of Seers as prophets and fortune tellers, but they were *all* mystics possessed of a variety of occult talents. No matter the specifics of Ori's skills, Idra had reasoned, a mystic would be a valuable associate.

Idra had introduced herself, even set Ori up in an elegant apartment on the Big Island, but their friendship didn't bloom until Ori applied to renovate the Caba Club, having purchased it from the previous owner's heirs. Some of the Founding Families had balked at her plans to shift the dignified, exclusive establishment to a bawdier one, catering to appetites more often served on the Rabbles than the Big Island. With Callen Onpuur's Critter Pit operating only a few streets away from the Caba Club, Idra had seen no issue with approving the application. As usual, Pitta Dobencourt and her gaggle of cronies had blocked the vote.

By that time, Ori's silver-haired young man had left Dockhaven, leaving her without an ally. Minimal details of her exile from Chiva'vastezz had circulated, enough for Idra to know the Seer had been highly placed, but when Idra learned Ori had been the Empress' advisor, she knew she needed to be that ally. Even if Ori's subtle skills didn't lend themselves to Idra's needs, her first-hand knowledge of the Dominion's politics and personalities would be invaluable in negotiations—trade, treaty, or otherwise.

So Idra fought with an enthusiasm she didn't really feel for the project, leveraging the situation as an opportunity to deepen her association with Ori. She'd even hosted a last-moment negotiation between Ori and Pitta in her office a few days before the Council's hearing on the matter. That was when she'd learned that Ori's mystical talents were more impressive than a street mendast's chicanery and far more useful.

Though Idra learned her efforts were unnecessary—Ori could have easily dealt with the situation on her own—the Seer had appreciated her amity. They'd grown close, so much so that Ori had assisted with Idra's last reelection campaign. If only she'd stayed in Dockhaven. Idra could have used Ori's talents this cycle.

Marthoth's guests milling around them, Ori and Idra stepped apart, flustered and laughing at the unexpected encounter. Ori's hair, usually smooth and styled, was a wreck. The unblemished grey of her nose, cheeks, and ears was dark with chill.

"I was wondering if I'd see you here." Idra took Ori's shoulders and brushed ears.

"You know I wouldn't miss it, Iddy." Ori tucked something unseen into a pouch dangling from her elegant silver-chain belt. The leather was a dark amethyst to match her coat, the perfect contrast to her screaming-green gown.

Idra missed their trips to the tailor together. She'd dressed better when Ori lived here, before the woman's absurd move to Locnor.

Idra brushed a wisp of black hair from Ori's face. "You look like you're either having a terrible time aboard the *Ipesia* or a fantastic one."

Behind Ori, a karju man in striped trousers left the farspeech office.

Ori giggled. "The latter, but not what you think. I was on the upper deck. It's windy! One man even lost his hat." She fussed with the pile of hair that had once been a well-coiffed bun.

"Despite that mess, this…" Idra waved her hands over Ori's body. "…is amazing. Where do you get this sort of thing in that backwater?"

"You'd be stunned." Ori opened her coat and twisted, showing off the gown's shifting fabric and plunging neckline. "Prugor in Locnor Bay does most of my work these days. A rhochrot if you can believe. All that fine work with those cumbersome fingers!"

"She's quite talented." Idra would have been impressed with the work if it had come from the Haven's Cloth District, let alone a bucolic nor. "If I ever find time to visit your…your…what do you call it?"

"The Vale Collective."

"Yes, Vale Collective." Idra tried not to sneer at the name of Ori's quaint rural retreat for artists. It sounded abominable. "If I find the time to travel all the way to Locnor Bay, I'll have her do some work for me as well. That embroidery at the hem is stunning!"

"Yours is wonderful as well, Iddy. Gaamguud?"

"No, Itylmuud on Tailor's Row."

"Well, it's gorgeous. I haven't worn one of hers in ages." Ori tapped her lower lip and looked at the floor. "I'm staying in the city for a bit." She leaned closer and whispered. "Why don't we slum around for a day…have one of our trips to the Cloth District?"

Idra clasped her hands together. "Absolutely. I'll have Frung—"

"Tokimer must be with me," said a familiar booming voice. Their host, Mintryl Marthoth, strolled up.

Idra's gut clenched, but she held her smile. She hadn't expected the man himself to fetch her. Marthoth was huge, more than two-heads taller than Ori or Idra. Half of him probably weighed more than the both of them put together. He could murder her without so much as creasing his jacket.

Her gaze darted to Ori. If things became ugly, maybe she'd intervene.

Marthoth straightened his suitcoat and bent slightly to accommodate them. "I'm fortunate to find two such beautiful women in one place."

Idra and Ori murmured gratitude.

"I see you've been on the upper deck," Marthoth gestured to Ori with the glass in his hand. "I'm told several hats and scarves have been lost. Unfortunate for my guests, but good for the haberdashers floating around us. Where are you off to next, Your Ladyship?"

"Back to my room to find a brush." Ori made a half-hearted attempt to straighten her hair. Her cheeks darkened. Idra would have been equally mortified in her place.

"And you, Madame Mayor?" As brown and cold as the zhuuve

in his glass, Marthoth's eyes settled on her.

"It's time for my daily exchange with my assistant." Idra nodded toward the farspeech office. She tried not to look at his big hands or peek into his jacket for the butt of a gun or think about what he might do if Imythedralin had indeed given her up. "I tried having him visit each morning last year and keeping him with me the year before. This has worked the best." She chuckled casually and flicked an errant lock of hair over one shoulder. "Frung's talents lie in the office, not at my side."

"Good," Marthoth said reflexively, his tone practiced and disconnected. His gaze was already drifting over them, most likely toward other guests requiring his attention, though Idra imagined him watching an assassin slink through the crowd toward her, poison at the ready.

Marthoth's eyes returned to them. "I hope you're both enjoying yourselves."

"I need a nap…or ten," Ori said.

"Themot's the only thing propping me up," Idra added. Her face ached from the artificial grin.

Everyone chuckled as convention dictated.

"Ladies," Marthoth said, "as delightful as it is to see you, I must be going." He put a hand on Idra's shoulder and held her eyes for a long beat, squeezing uncomfortably hard before releasing her. "Perhaps we will speak later, Your Honor," he said and left with a curt bow.

The knot of anxiety in Idra's core did not relax. That squeeze had meant *something*, she just wasn't sure if it was related to the election, an awkward pass, or if Imythedralin really had spat out her name.

"Well, he is doing a fine job of masking his anger," Ori said.

Before Idra could reply, Daisy emerged from the farspeech office. She waved at Idra. "Don't let that squash-headed guard leave for the *Lessee* without me, Mayor," she called and trundled down the corridor.

Inspiration struck. Idra grabbed Ori's arm. "What are you doing after you fix your hair?"

"My dinner date for the bangers pointed me toward a performance of mid-century northern-Ossquere folk music in the main chamber. I'm supposed to meet her friend…who was it? I can remember the face…"

"Why don't you come with me instead?"

Ori looked at Idra, brows furrowed, bow mouth turned down.

"I'm going to Flark's yacht to gamble, and I could use some trustworthy support. You could…" Idra raised her brows and smiled.

Ori's affable expression screwed into a pucker of distaste. "I could help you win?"

"Well, yes, I suppose so, but that wasn't what I had in mind. I was hoping maybe you could…" Idra bit her lip and glanced at all the people milling around them. This wasn't a public discussion. "Things are complicated right now."

"Apologies, Iddy dear," Ori took Idra's hands in hers, "but I'm far too tippled to be of any use. Even if I could make a connection, the results would be unpredictable at best. Plus, you know Flark hates me. He'd throw me into the Sound before anyone dealt a card."

Idra shook her head, dismissing the request. "Of course. Go straighten that gull's-nest of a hairdo."

"Don't be so anxious." Ori released Idra's hands and cupped her face. "I'm sure you'll be fine. You always are." She turned and drifted away, disappearing amongst the well-dressed roisterers.

Idra drew a long breath and stepped into the farspeech office.

"Mayor Moocha!" the puka clerk called.

It had become Idra's moniker in Pukatown during the last election, though not one she relished. The idea of all these pukas calling her "mother" made her wildly uncomfortable. She couldn't afford to put a stop to it, though. The pukas loved to say it, so she was stuck.

"I was starting to think we wouldn't see you today." The little woman struggled for a moment to rise from her stool, but eventually gave it up. She was what Idra thought of as painfully pregnant.

"Oh, don't get up, Blura. A round just ran longer than expected." Idra offered the woman her most engaging smile. Remembering someone's name did more for Idra's odds than any new policies she might claim she'd make. Remembering a detail about them amplified that goodwill. "How are you feeling? Any more seasickness?"

"A little earlier. The wind's been whipping around the Sound." Blura patted her obscene belly. "The little one here doesn't like the roll of the waves."

A shorter, downright slim, puka came trotting out of the back area. "Oh! Mayor, I didn't know you were here."

"Blura and I were just talking," Idra said. "It's no problem, Frikka."

The thin puka stopped walking and narrowed her eyes. "Fritta. It's Fritta."

Idra gritted her teeth. She hated errors like this. People could excuse not having running water for two days, but they never forgot such simple slights. She'd been indulging too much. Blasted Imythedralin.

"My mistake," Idra said. "I met a Frikka a few days before the party. You both have the same beautiful eyes. My deepest apologies, Fritta."

The puka considered Idra for a moment before bursting into a smile. "Of course. My own moocha used to comment on my eyes. Grat for noticing."

The gallop inside Idra's chest slacked.

"So…the usual contact today, Mayor?" Fritta asked.

"Frung again, yes."

"Muurt's in room two. She just finished connecting these two who were having a fight, so she may be in a nasty mood. I could set you up with Lurnst in room one. He's just as discreet."

"I prefer to continue with the same conduit, grat." Idra strolled down the short corridor into room two, where a tremorous, elderly puka reclined in a white-cushioned chair.

Muurt was a generally unpleasant woman, so Fritta's warnings meant little. Idra had known Muurt nearly all her life. As a child, she'd been the Mayor's farspeaker during the last few years of Maryn's life. Her wife had trusted this farspeaker, so when the title of Mayor passed to Idra, she'd done so as well. The move had yet to be proven wrong.

"Princess," Muurt said. The nickname had once been an insult. After more than three decades, it simply was. "Let me guess, you want to talk to Frung about more tedious political drivel."

"What else is there?" Idra settled into the facing chair.

Muurt coughed into her wrinkled olive hand. "What about your precious antiques? At least those approach being interesting. Why don't we contact somebody about those?"

"No, it's Frung and politics. Apologies. And stop listening in."

"Right. Let's get it over with." Muurt closed her eyes and leaned back in the chair.

ALIARA

Syl led Aliara and Dreg hurriedly upstairs, not stopping for the usual conversations, only waving to those who greeted him. His smile was so forced it seemed almost sculpted.

Once they were safely locked inside their suite, he poured two glasses of caba and handed one to Dreg. Syl enjoyed a healthy drink before taking Dreg's chin in his free hand, tipping it back and forth, exaggeratedly studying his young face.

"Not terrible, Pet," Syl said. His diction had subtly softened and his appearance, while still well-kempt, was more disheveled than usual. He was even wearing one of Aliara's scarves as a cravat—a style he'd vocally disparaged in the past. "He has good bone structure, but the hair is a tad showy. I do not suppose you brought him here for us to play with though."

Dreg slapped Syl's hand away and downed his drink. Neither moved nor looked away.

"We're here for work," Aliara said, sliding into the room's only comfortable chair, legs curled beneath her.

"He *is* prettier than the last colleague you brought home." Syl grinned at Dreg and mouthed, "Haus."

He wasn't wrong. Victuur Haus was covered in so many scars and tattoos it was difficult to see the man beneath.

Dreg scoffed. "Everyone's prettier than Fist."

"What's this one's name?" Syl asked.

"Dreg," they replied in unison.

"Dreg?" Eyes still on the boy, Syl shook his head, chuckling. The Toh's bynames were a frequent source of amusement to him. "Flark is involved somehow, I assume, as you never before sought his company, Pet."

"Fat toad's the last target on this jig," Dreg blurted.

"You have a part for me to play?" Syl asked. "The little scug's been winning the hold too often. And as a business associate, he has demonstrated himself to possess an irksome lack of integrity. I would be delighted to play a part in ridding myself of him."

Aliara had expected as much, even if it turned out that Syl wasn't the source of the contract. Flark had long taken liberties—loitering at their penthouse, ogling her in the least pleasant of ways, and generally giving Sviroosa the dithers. His recent campaign to tear down their building was born from a deal gone off-beam. Aliara didn't know the details, nor did she care to.

"Just stay out of the way." Dreg's lip rose in a sneer. "Wouldn't want you to get shot, Duke."

"True." Syl edged a half-step closer to Dreg. "I have been bitten, sliced, stabbed, chained, poked, and most recently throttled, but not yet shot."

Aliara searched her memory but could find no instance in which Syl had been strangled. Her eyes went to the lavender cravat.

Dreg scoffed. "I'm sure it's rough being a toff."

"This one could be fun, Pet." Syl gulped the last of his caba and poured another. "Spirited. Shall we enjoy a little sport before we visit Flark's mighty boat?"

Aliara slipped out of the chair and studied her mate's face. His eyes were threaded with blue veins. His jaw clenched and relaxed in an erratic rhythm. He smiled far too much.

"How ossi are you?" she asked.

"Rather. Though not so inebriated as to be incapable." His speech was barely sibilant, but the ragged edges she recognized were there.

Syl withdrew a purple vial from his vest pocket and tossed it to her. It was half-full of themot. As Aliara snagged it with one hand, she drew back the other and swung, flat of her palm aimed at Syl's caba glass. He caught her wrist only a whit away from the drink—but he caught it.

"You see?" He lay his forehead against hers. "I am fine. What do you need from me?"

"You already got us on his yacht," Dreg said. "Isn't that enough? We don't need an amateur in the way."

Neither acknowledged him. Aliara watched Syl's face, his eyes. He was clearly exhausted, but he still was there, not yet locked up inside. That would come later—though she hoped that with Orono gone, this time it might not.

"We need the ship's layout, personnel locations." Aliara slipped back into the club chair.

"I will request a tour when we board. The little egomaniac loves to flaunt…and he has certainly spent enough time pawing over *our* home." Syl unbuttoned his vest, tossed it on the bed, and started on the shirt. "If he says, 'my yacht' again, I may thrash him myself."

"How many guards?" she asked.

"Two whom I've seen. Both karju, a woman and a man." Syl left the scarf in place as he removed his shirt. "They rotated every half day."

"Competent?"

"I suppose." Syl sat on the end of the bed and took off his shoes and socks. The scarf dangled at his throat like a lavender noose. "Flark has had little call for their services beyond running errands and the occasional poke with that blasted cane."

"We can try to take weapons on board," Dreg said. "Beg forgiveness if we're caught."

"I suggest carrying nothing more than what would be found on the common prostitute." Syl smirked, clearly enjoying the taunt.

"Anything else and they may guess you to be something other than what we present."

"He's right," Aliara said. "Keep your boot knife at most, everything else goes in the safe."

"Once we're there…?" Dreg asked.

"Finish the jig, then the guards." Aliara paused. "If need be."

"Yeah, maybe they'll want the Duke to hire them once their grubstaker's dead." Dreg huffed a laugh through his nose. "Any method in mind? Or is that your whole plan?"

"Get him alone," she said.

"Get him alone how?"

Aliara shrugged. She'd analyze the situation as it evolved. Dreg needed to learn to adapt to uncertainty.

"How would you feel about…" Syl frowned, sighed. "The old toad has often mentioned how lovely you are, Pet. He appears to enjoy a certain fondness for our species, gawking so at Idra that even she has grown weary of the attention. He mentioned you after you had gone." He affected a low, nasal voice. "'Your women are so nice to watch.' Or something of that ilk. Though he followed that accolade with a harangue on the splendor of the stalwart puka woman."

"You want to wager me?" Aliara asked.

"Or both of you. My impression is he prefers to be the audience. Distasteful though it may be, it would be the most expedient path. I am certain Flark would see it as a fine opportunity to gall me."

"We could work with that," Dreg said. "I found…" His eyes darted to Aliara, and he cleared his throat. "I found a stack of drawings at his penthouse. They back that up."

Aliara nodded. "Use us."

"Then I shall feel free to add you both to the hold if the opportunity presents itself." Syl turned to Dreg. "Though I am certain you brokered some sort of deal with my darling girl, now that I am involved, the terms have changed. I will see to the disbursement of any documents found—deeds, contracts, wills, and such.”

Aliara braced for Dreg’s complaints, but he only looked at her, colorful brows raised.

“Same deal otherwise?” Dreg asked.

“Anything younger than me,” she said.

“That you don’t take?” Dreg asked.

Aliara nodded toward her mate. “That *either* of us doesn’t take.”

Dreg crossed to Syl and both ran fingers across palms, their side of the agreement settled.

“Now,” Syl said, “I need you to fetch one of the *Ipesia*’s concierges.”

When Dreg started to object, Syl pressed coins into his palm.

“One for you,” Syl guided the boy to the door. “One for the concierge.”

“Where do I find a concierge in a zootie this big?” Dreg asked.

The door creaked open.

“I am certain you are resourceful enough to figure it out for yourself,” Syl said.

FRUNG

The farspeaker sat in front of Frung, eyes closed, body taut. The one the Mayor usually used liked to relax, but then she was ancient. It was an awkward moment, waiting for them to reach the proper person. Frung always felt like he should be talking or doing something to help or entertain, but farspeakers always complained when he did. Instead, he sat there obediently, quietly, and waited.

"Frung?" the farspeaker said.

"Yes, it's me, Mayor." Frung hated this mode of communication. Sure, they all took the Farspeaker Combine oath, and supposedly they only remembered snippets of conversations they connected, but the process never seemed secure enough to Frung, given some of the things he and the Mayor discussed.

"Any updates?" the farspeaker asked. It was the puka's voice, but Frung heard the Mayor's cadence and inflections.

He tapped his marking stick to the first item on his checklist. "There was a small scuffle—hardly worth mentioning—at the protest outside the Bung Building. The Corps carried off three young pukas, two males and a female. The rest of the protestors have remained peaceful."

"But they're still there," the Mayor said matter-of-factly. Only the farspeaker's lips moved as she spoke. The rest of her face remained inert. "You said the detained pukas were young?"

"Yes." Frung checked off item one.

"Wonderful. More years for them to remember me at the polls."
The Mayor paused. He could well imagine her expression as she
considered how best to mitigate the issue. "Was anyone killed?"

"What? No! I would have led with that."

"Good. Release the prisoners and send them home with some
food. What's next?"

"Demolition crews should be done removing…" Frung hated
saying this part. "…bodies by dusk tomorrow. The death total for
Flark's, er, implosion has risen since I messaged you."

The farspeaker's groan was so much like the Mayor's that Frung
almost laughed.

"How many?" she asked.

"It looks like two families were still inside. The last report said
eleven dead."

The Mayor groaned again. "Keep me apprised. What else?"

"As directed," Frung continued, glad to be past the
unpleasantness, "I have hired a puka artist to erect a small monument
to the loss—one that will not preclude reusing the property."

"The artist who showed last month at Duke Imythedralin's
salon?"

"Yes."

"Good. He'll owe me. Next."

Frung checked off number two. "Your odds have dropped
again. You're only a two-to-one favorite, according to Varyl."

"Sen—" Her voice caught. "Send notice to all the councilors.
We'll hold a special session to deal with the Yinago Tower situation
after the Festival."

Frung scribbled madly on his notepad.

"Schedule something. Be sure it's the twelfth or later. If they're
tired and haintstrung we'll never accomplish anything. Next."

"I'll also be scheduling around Pitta Dobencourt's party." Frung
picked up the invitation chit and stared into its eye. The images and
sounds from the elegant missive twirled through his mind.

"Of course she'd announce a party *during* the Sowers Festival," the Mayor said.

"It is a debut of her new acquisitions. She claims to have procured some Voshar pieces." He imagined the Mayor grinding her teeth.

"Fine. I'll be there. Next."

Frung ran through several other points, more of them related to the campaign than not. "That is all," he said as he checked off the final item.

"Not quite," the Mayor said. "Clear a day in my calendar for next quartern—the fifteenth or later."

"I think I can wangle that." Simple enough. Frung was accustomed to unexpected schedule changes. "Anything else?"

"Yes. I need you to locate all records of vessels of any kind going in and out of Dockhaven by air or sea during Danurak through Alsolon of 2048. Legal commerce as well as illicit. I need it all—on paper—as soon as possible. It's urgent."

The farspeaker blinked a few times as she closed the connection.

Frung shook his head, unable to comprehend the enormity of what the Mayor had asked.

DREG

Dreg slipped the catch at the nape of the tippled woman's neck, let the gem-laden necklace drop into his palm, and pocketed it. She'd glommed onto him outside Rift's cabin. He figured he deserved a little pay for the irritation.

"You smell like butter." The woman slouched against him, releasing a startled "yarp!" when Dreg pushed her into a round-faced karju woman strolling past.

He ducked into a passing group of identically dressed men before the tippler could right herself and grabbed the arm of the first uniformed person he spied, a sweating man who looked like he hadn't slept since Marastrava took the Norian throne.

"Are you a concierge?" Dreg asked the uniformed man.

"Porter," the man said, demeanor unruffled by Dreg's rough treatment.

"Where can I find a concierge?"

"They're all over." The porter waved his free arm, indicating a world laden with concierges. His jacket buttons strained against his soft paunch as he moved.

Dreg gave him a sour glare.

The porter sighed like he'd just been asked for directions to the sea. "They wear red jackets with silver epaulets, grey trousers, and grey hats. If you can't find one, try the main bar on the gaming deck. You can't miss it. They can help. If they're not too busy. Which is unlikely." He made a sound intended as a laugh. "Is that all? Because I'm already supposed to be on deck four and I haven't even completed my pickup yet."

"Sure."

Freed of Dreg's grip, the porter darted down the corridor, nimbly avoiding bustling employees and stumbling tipplers alike.

Dreg scanned the area in search of anyone wearing red. He passed over one sequined gown, two shirts—both worn under black jackets—and one overwhelmingly red suit before spying a woman dressed to match the porter's description.

Dreg slipped through the flow of people, following his target down the spiral stair yet not quite catching up. The companionway was congested with people talking, gesturing, even dancing. One man just sat on a step crying. Dreg tried calling to the concierge twice, but his voice was lost among the music and chatter.

First Rift sent him to buy brew for her puka, now her Duke sent him to find a concierge. This treatment was getting him lathered. Dreg was no one's errand boy.

At the second-floor exit, he caught a last glimpse of his target's bobbing tail of red hair as the concierge left the stairs. She wound past a wall of gamblers glued to their coin bandits and entered a swish restaurant encased in frosted piss-yellow glass, "Pedestrian" written across the door in antique block face.

Dreg followed her past the chance machines, barely avoiding an angry player's thrown coins, and went in after her. Décor was white wood, lighting and fabrics shades of yellow and gold, the furniture's simple designs more stylish than comfortable.

The attendant examined Dreg with pursed lips. "Welcome to Pedestrian," she said, barely sounding as though she meant it. "One to dine?"

"I'm…" Dreg paused, selecting his truth. "I'm expected."

"I see. You're meeting someone?"

Dreg nodded.

The attendant frowned. "Who?"

Dreg stretched to peer around her, scanning the room for any familiar faces. In the far corner, Muddler stood by a closed-door booth, the lights around it dimmed. Dreg could guess what was going on inside.

"Him." He pointed to Mud. "He's expecting me."

The attendant looked over her shoulder and stiffened. When she turned back to Dreg, her grey eyes were wide, though her expression remained composed. "You're certain *that* man is expecting you?"

"Yes."

Pedestrian's doors opened, and a cheerfully prattling group moved in behind Dreg.

"He didn't mention he was expecting anyone," the attendant said, gazing over Dreg's shoulder to assess the newcomers.

Dreg considered abandoning his efforts and heading to deck one in hopes a concierge was available, but it seemed unlikely. Even the porter had been dubious.

He glanced again at Muddler. Thung Toh operatives weren't supposed to acknowledge one another during a jig unless the meet was previously arranged or if contact was absolutely unavoidable. This, Dreg decided, fell into the latter category.

"He is. See?" Dreg waved to Mud, who hesitated before raising a hand.

Still skeptical, but unwilling to delay her more important guests, the attendant nodded and retrieved a menu from her podium. "Very well. Follow me."

Dreg stopped her. "No need. I'm not here to eat."

"Then stop holding us up," interrupted one of the newcomers. "I'm starving."

"And I'm almost sober," said another.

The group burst into laughter.

"I can find my way," Dreg said. "You take care of this lot."

The attendant gave him a sour-faced nod.

Dreg slipped past her into the dining space, where dapper toffs ate tiny food at tidy tables. Instead of visiting Mud, who was still watching, his handsome face quirked in curious amusement, Dreg found the concierge at the restaurant's mostly empty bar, talking to a petite chivori bym perched on a stool. Like Rift and the Duke, the woman was an ebhead, her hair black as an aught-moon sky. Her skin was so fair and perfect, it almost looked like silver, her face prettier even than the Duke's. The body beneath her chartreuse gown would keep him busy for days, especially tracing the ivy tattoos that climbed her arms and disappeared down the back of her dress. He wondered how far they went.

He edged past the pair and parked himself on the corner stool, offering a nearly complete view of the restaurant, and waited. No way he was letting this concierge get away again.

"He said no." As she spoke, the stiff bym toyed with the army of purple stones dripping from her left lobe.

"Correct. Mister Onpuur refused to see you," said the concierge. "My apologies."

"You had nothing to do with the decision." The ebhead woman put a hand on the concierge's arm. "You did well."

The concierge blinked slowly before nodding. "Anything else, Your Ladyship?"

Dreg's brows went up. She was a lady. That meant the Dominion. He was intrigued.

"One moment, Cirohl," the ebhead told the concierge. She looked over at Dreg. "Who might you be?"

Dreg glanced around, unsure at first if she was speaking to him.

"Yes, you." The ebhead smiled with a mixture of warmth and mischief.

"Your pardon," Dreg said, wishing he wasn't costumed as a trull. "I can think of several ways you could assist me, but I'm waiting for her. Duke Imythedralin sent me." He pointed to the concierge, who scowled back.

"Apologies, Lady Orilausko," the concierge said.

Dreg notched the name in his memory.

Behind the concierge, Pedestrian's attendant led the Mayor through the restaurant, heading straight for Muddler and the closed booth.

"No apology necessary, Cirohl." Smile now entirely genuine, Orilausko raised a hand, and the concierge quieted. "Come back when you've finished assisting the Duke. He is a friend, and I am in no rush."

The concierge, not bothering to hide her annoyance, turned to Dreg. "What can I do for Duke Imythedralin?"

Dreg slid off his stool and joined them, flashing the conch. "He didn't say, just told me to bring a concierge to his cabin."

"Is he there?" the concierge asked.

"He was when I left."

She hesitated, glancing toward the exit.

"I'll follow you in a few beats." Dreg tossed the platinum coin to the concierge and grinned down into Orilausko's lovely face. "Buy you a drink?"

"You should go with her." Orilausko's voice was smooth and firm. Her violet eyes held Dreg's, soft and deep.

He felt a little like he was falling.

"Don't you agree?" Orilausko asked.

She was right; he really should go with the concierge, but he couldn't peel away from those eyes.

"I'm already late to dinner with an old friend." Orilausko didn't seem to move, only the world around her. "You wouldn't want to delay me, would you?"

He shook his head. He really did need to get back to the jig. "I need to go with her," Dreg said.

"Then go." Orilausko touched his arm, and an almost imperceptible tingle raced through Dreg's body.

He shook his head and headed for the exit.

SYLANDAIR

"I am certain you are resourceful enough to figure it out for yourself," Syl told Dreg, gently encouraging him out of the cabin.

The boy stepped into the corridor, immediately accosted by an impressively tippled woman.

"I know you, don't I?" she asked, a little extra spittle behind each word. She draped herself over Dreg's shoulder and sniffed. "You smell nice."

Syl shut the door and returned to Aliara. He sat on the bed facing her, sighed, and removed the scarf, revealing the black welt circling his throat.

She shot to attention.

"Someone has taken out a contract on my life," Syl said. "I have been less than cautious in recent months. This situation may have been precipitated by my new projects in Isay or perhaps some of the deals I've been brokering here and in the Dominion—"

"Or Flark."

"Yes, he is certainly a possibility." Syl rubbed his throat, glad to be rid of the cravat. The sensation of it around his neck was too much like the thrall collar Orono had put on him last autumn. "I have silvered Isnarin's palm to uncover the source."

Aliara raised a brow.

"He informed me of the contract. Chella Stond approached him. He has agreed to dredge her for information."

Aliara scowled. She considered Chella's operatives sub-par.

Syl rose and offered her his hand. "Join me in the washroom?"

Aliara followed, staring at the young chivori's lifeless face so long that Syl thought she might check him prow to stern for the Toh's signature mark—the one hidden behind her ear—though he hoped she would not. Entrails already bulged from the wound Syl had delivered; jostling the body would undoubtedly shake them loose.

"I don't know him," she said at last.

"He assailed me from behind with the sash from his uniform," Syl said. "At least he had the decency to allow me to finish pissing."

Aliara's face cracked in a tiny smile, the one that said she was annoyed with him, with herself, and with the world, yet she still found him delightful.

Syl pulled her close and kissed her, warm and comforting in a way he had found from no one and nothing else. "I will keep you with me until this is resolved. I require no other protection."

"Good." Aliara pulled from his grasp and left the washroom, pausing at the doorway to cast a sly wink Syl's way before disappearing into the main room. Her filmy periwinkle blouse flitted to the floor behind her.

Syl needed no further invitation. He followed, closing the door on the corpse, hoping Dreg would struggle for a whale's age to find a concierge.

Aliara lay half-undressed and stretched across the oversized bed, a dark sea snake drifting on the waves of the duvet. She beckoned him with curled fingers

He gladly joined.

She brushed his wounded neck with soft, black lips, and the dull ache in his flesh seemed to dwindle. Her hands explored his back and chest before moving between them, toying with the buttons of his trousers. With a quick scissor of her legs, Aliara rolled Syl onto his back and smiled down at him, that quirky lift of only half her mouth reserved for him alone.

Her smile relaxed into a gasp as his hands found her.

He had spent far too much time at the lyntyyl table.

Aliara had collapsed atop Syl, face tucked against his throat, when someone knocked at the cabin door. Three raps, a pause, and one more.

"Dreg," she murmured into his ear.

Syl turned and ran his lips along the curve of her earlobe, lower lug to helix. "The boy is too efficient."

Aliara huffed a laugh and swung off him, redressing as Syl rose reluctantly and adjusted his appearance for less personal pursuits. He welcomed Dreg and the concierge inside, the young Toh's surly frown balancing the woman's pandering smile.

"My name is Cirohl," the concierge said. "I understand you required my assistance."

"Join me in the washroom, would you, Cirohl?" Syl asked, gesturing her in before him.

"Of course, Duke Imythedralin." The concierge's red ponytail bobbed with each step as she passed the mussed bed and stepped into the lav. The smile wavered as she took in the bloody mess in the tub, its gruesomeness reflected innumerable times in the shattered mirror fragments littering the floor.

"I was led to believe I would be safe from such mischiefs about Mister Marthoth's vessel." Syl tapped the blackened skin of his throat, though the concierge hardly seemed to notice. "It seems I am the exception to such prohibitions."

Dreg ducked into the washroom behind them, laughing at what he found.

"This is most unacceptable," Cirohl stammered after a moment. "No one is supposed to die on the *Ipesia*."

"Indeed. Yet this flagitious gentleman was lurking in my

washroom. He burst from the towel locker and attacked as I washed my hands." Syl guided the stunned woman back into the main cabin, settling her in one of the breakfast table's chairs. "I would hate to blot the name of Mister Marthoth's fine vessel by publicly exposing this incident. Naturally I would be delighted to keep this unfortunate occurrence to myself, but there is the…evidence to sort out." Syl put a hand over the concierge's. "Tell me, Cirohl, can you relieve me of this burden so I may shower without those milky eyes watching me?"

SCHMALCH

Schmalch felt as important as the Duke when the Ironclad carriage rolled up in front of the Heap. He walked carefully down the steps, parcel tucked safely under his arm, eyes squinted against the wind. Below, the driver watched him from a fore compartment high on the vehicle, little plumes of breath her only visible movement. Next to her, the busser scanned the area, weapon in his lap.

In Schmalch's past, he kept his distance from Ironclads. He'd seen what a blunderbuss did to the face of a stupid thief. Tonight though, *he* was the client. He'd be riding in armored luxury.

When Schmalch reached the last flight of steps, the driver slipped down out of her jockey box and opened the carriage door. She had crags around her eyes, brown hair poking from beneath her knit cap, and a scarf over her nose and mouth.

"Don't you get cold up there?" Schmalch asked. It may have been spring but just barely. Winter was trying to stick around.

"Sometimes, but numb fingers are better than an obstructed view." The scarf shuddered in rhythm with her words.

The driver bent to lower the folding steps. "Apologies, you might get a little cold too. Our last fare was attacked. No one hurt, but we had some glass broken." She pointed up to one of the barred windows. It looked like a caged mouth with broken teeth.

Schmalch climbed into the cabin. The barreled walls were upholstered like cush sofas. Schmalch guessed that was for when things got rough. The passenger would be all padded even if the coach rolled. He settled into the seat. It was warm.

"Toasty," he said.

The driver chuckled. "Sure, it's heated, but when we get moving, that wind will start coming in that window. You won't freeze to death, but I wouldn't take off my coat if I was you," she said, closing the door.

Schmalch nodded and tugged his hat over his ears. He sank back, set the wrapped mask in his lap, and listened to the driver climb into position. She and the busser exchanged muffled words, and something inside the vehicle clicked twice before settling into a low hum. The carriage rolled forward, wind gushing into the cabin through the broken window. Schmalch wished he'd thought to bring a muffler for his nose or even a scarf like the wise driver wore.

He was huffing warm breath into his hands by the time they crested the hill that separated the Big Island and the Pipe. The desalinization plant came into view out one window, its hulking shape outlined in Dormah's white light, every detail exposed, every shadow made weird. Thanks to the Duke, the crumbling parts of it were coming down, but the work was half-done now, leaving only broken walls and floors and the odd remnant of furniture visible. It was like looking into a corpse.

Through the other window he saw the Orono Estate. Across High Street from the plant, the property was nothing but empty walls now. It wasn't even named for Orono anymore, Schmalch reminded himself. It was the Imythedralin Estate. The Duke had torn down that nightmare building where Schmalch had been chased, where he'd almost been eaten, where several of his friends had died. He'd seen monsters there so terrible that they still woke him up every night, hoping Sviroosa didn't hear his screams. That plot of land might just be a bunch of flowers and trees inside a wall to most people, but Schmalch still saw the towering mansion, all glass and tiles and candy-tipped tower.

He squeezed his eyes shut as the Ironclad passed between the two properties.

"They're all dead now," Schmalch murmured. "No more bogy kids. No more monsters."

The package on his lap jumped.

Schmalch opened his eyes and stared at the parcel, which sat there like a parcel should.

"We just went over a bump." He'd been too busy worrying about past haints to realize it.

The package jumped again. Schmalch didn't just feel it this time, he *saw* it. The wrapped shadowbox started to shiver like it too was cold in the drafty carriage.

Schmalch looked around. They'd already passed the estate and the plant. A few people were out visiting still-open businesses. They all looked like they should. Everything else was normal. He wasn't hallucinating, and he was too cold to be dreaming.

Schmalch untied the string and peeled part of the waxed cotton away from the vibrating package. The instant moonlight touched the shadowbox, it went still. Schmalch gulped.

The mask opened its eyes. The blank platinum orbs within rolled toward him.

Schmalch flinched and the shadowbox wobbled on his lap, threatening to fall off. He clasped it so hard that his gloved fingers ached. If he broke the thing, Rift would take him apart bit by bit.

By the time Schmalch had secured the box, the mask's eyes were closed again, lids hiding the soft swell of the dead voshari's eyeballs. Schmalch stared at the face, daring it to move again. The eyes popped open. They were blank, no color or pupils, but the eyelids twitched as though it was looking around. Then they stopped. The mask was looking at him. He was *sure* of it.

The lips moved, slowly and stiffly.

Schmalch couldn't breathe, terrified and fascinated all at once.

"Bank of Dockhaven." The driver opened the door and folded

out the steps for him. "We'll wait here. How long you think you'll be?"

Schmalch hurriedly re-wrapped the mask, doing his best to tie the string with gloved fingers, and leapt out of the carriage.

The bank loomed ahead, thick walls, burly guards, and loads of cap-lights. All he had to do was make it down the long walk and into the building without losing or looking at the mask, and he'd've earned his Callas.

He swallowed hard. "Not long." Schmalch ran into the bank.

IDRA

Pedestrian's attendant had been a dancer. Idra recognized it in the way she walked, gliding with silent grace despite heels so thick they should have clomped with every step. It was the same carriage Idra had developed to keep herself from tumbling off stage during her years working for Callen Onpuur.

The attendant spoke quietly with a tall, handsome karju man, who stood by the last portside booth, watching Idra with a half-smile. She wasn't normally attracted to karju, male or female, but for this one, Idra might make an exception as she had for Maryn.

Returning to Idra, the attendant whispered, "He says their next guest has been delayed. If your business is brief, they can accommodate you."

Idra looked past the woman, returning the man's coy smile. "I only need a few moments of your friend's time."

The blonde man nodded and opened the booth, its ironwood doors polished to near-white. Idra dropped a coin into the attendant's palm and settled onto the gold felt cushion opposite Traus. The Thung Toh's liaison was lean, elegant, and attractive. His skin was lighter than his charcoal hair, his eyes fairer than either. He sat bolt upright, marinating in the same smugness as Imythedralin, though Idra found this one completely devoid of whimsey.

During the last break from the lyntyyl table, she'd invited Traus to dine in her cabin where they could have spoken more frankly. She didn't trust the privacy of booths like this one. Any member of her species could lay an ear against the exterior wall and listen in. Traus had insisted. Marthoth permitted him on board, the liaison had explained, only if he agreed to certain stipulations, one of which was that he do business only in his booth at Pedestrian. Idra suspected a lie but found it unwise to provoke anyone with Traus' influence.

She didn't like this Traus as well as the one who'd been in place when Maryn was still alive. That Traus had understood client relations, visiting when paged.

Unfortunately, during Idra's first term, that Traus had been shot five times in the chest while drinking brew in the middle of the Bitter Barnacle.

Soon after, an odd little man calling himself Luugrar had visited Idra with a single, simple request. He'd made no threats, didn't speak a harsh word, but settled into the red leather chair that faced Idra's desk and, looking like someone's rumpled grandfather, Luugrar had scared her blood cold.

When he'd left, Idra had followed his directions precisely. The City Corps ruled the previous Traus' death accidental. All evidence was misfiled and lost, some poor puka in the records room blamed—though she'd given him a generous severance.

A month later the new Traus had visited, lapel festooned with the same ruby feather pin his predecessor had worn. This new Traus had announced his expectations for working in Dockhaven, admired then questioned the authenticity of the Verduun watercolor in Idra's office, and left without chance for reply. Now he wouldn't even deign to visit her cabin, only a few decks up. The audacity annoyed her beyond words.

For this meeting, though, she would follow his rules.

"Traus, gratitude for seeing me on such short notice." Idra extended both hands across the table.

"I am quite accustomed." He clasped her hands briefly in greeting. "Impromptu meetings such as this one are expected at

Festival time, Mayor." He straightened his shirt cuffs. "What would you like to discuss today?"

Idra lowered her voice. "I need another contract."

"You need not whisper, Mayor," Traus said. "Not even the most gifted chivori could hear what we discuss within this booth." He tapped the wall beside him. "Baffled, courtesy of our host."

She cleared her throat and nodded. "I've been invited to Flark's yacht and…" She sighed and looked at the overhead. "I'm not sure he isn't planning to kill me…possibly Imythedralin, too, but the Duke can do his own hiring."

"You require personal protection."

Idra nodded. "Marthoth also may want me dead."

Traus didn't bother to look surprised. "When do you depart for Flark's vessel?"

"Soon. His big Dobencourt bodyguard will be here with the launch within an hour."

Traus frowned. "I would require at least twice that to notify an operative and allow them time to both prepare and travel here."

"I've known you for almost two decades, Traus." Idra leaned across the table. "I'm sure you already have someone onboard."

"I might." His pale grey eyes flicked to the booth's doors and back. He shook his head. "No."

"The big karju out there?" Idra guessed. He was perfect—muscular and intimidating but pleasant to watch. She closed her eyes and calculated the remains of her stake and what she could still afford to lose. "I can pay three bars." It was exorbitant for a few hours' guard duty.

Traus cocked his head and considered her. "My friend out there is *my* protection for this event."

"I only need him for the night."

"Yet he is unavailable. Perhaps you should consider taking one of your City Corps along with you. Isn't protecting you one of their duties?"

Idra snorted. She didn't need any corpsmen knowing her business.

"The Abog have a vessel somewhere in the surrounding flotilla," Traus said. "They might be of service."

Idra considered. An Abog at her side would be adequately intimidating, but she'd had poor experience with them in the past. One she'd hired had nearly provoked a fight instead of deflecting it, another had switched sides when offered more coin. She'd be better off on her own. Maybe she could cuddle up to Imythedralin's trull. He might be persuaded to protect her. If not, she could use him as cover if Flark did attack.

Idra opened the booth door and rose.

Traus caught her hand before she could leave. "Don't despair, Mayor. Allies sometimes appear when least expected."

SYLANDAIR

Concierge and corpse gone from his cabin, Syl allowed the shower to calm him, stilling the blurry high from exhaustion and intoxicants. His body was less battered than expected, though bruises mottled his neck, torso and arms, deep enough they would be with him through the rest of the Festival.

Despite accepting the bet with Flark against her return, Syl had been certain Aliara would be back on the *Ipesia* by night's-end. The boy—he could hardly be more than that—was a curious surprise, and Syl was eager to learn more of what had precipitated his involvement. If he had not known of the prohibition against killing fellow Toh and their family members, Syl might have worried Dreg had been sent to eliminate him as well.

Clean, coiffed, and ready to spar aboard Flark's vessel, Syl shook his head at his reflection in the standing mirror Cirohl had been kind enough to supply. The would-be assassin had almost had him.

Syl returned to the main cabin, selecting grey trousers and a high-necked shirt from the closet, topped with a black waistcoat festooned with bright blue dots and a short wool trench buckled up the side, scarf at his neck. He hated the fashion, but Syl would not give Flark the joy of knowing he'd been garroted.

Aliara and her young Toh had moved to the balcony. As he dressed, Syl watched them, figures set against the flotilla of glittering ships in the dark Sound. The frosty puffs of their conversation intermingled with the language of gestures known only to the Toh. Even hampered by bulky coats, they understood simple twitches of the arm or swoops of a finger.

Syl found himself disquieted by his mate's ease with the boy. She had been equally comfortable with Haus and all other Toh he had met—and the Duin knew they'd both indulged in extraneous lovers through the years—but something about the scene niggled at him. Perhaps it was nearly losing her, perhaps it was having her to himself for months, or perhaps it was the drugs and lack of sleep. Whatever the reason, Syl wanted to push the young douse over the railing and take Aliara in the night air.

He loathed the realization of his own jealousy.

Bottle of caba in hand, Syl stepped outside to join them and slid an arm around Aliara's waist. "Would you care for fresh clothes, Pet? A change does wonders for the outlook, and though fetching, these togs smell of…the Rabble."

She twisted to kiss him before slipping inside, her scant clothing dropping in her wake. Syl watched Dreg watching her.

"Lovely, hm?" Syl leaned on the railing.

Dreg realized he was staring and looked away, his cheeks blackening. "I suppose. For her age."

"You should practice your calumny." Syl refilled the boy's glass.

"My what?"

"Your lies."

Dreg offered a gesture of indifference. The ever-present glower and dark gash on his forehead detracted from what might have been an attractive face, provided one appreciated the ways in which flaws exaggerated beauty. He was the kind of bauble Syl would normally have enjoyed, but tonight Dreg was Aliara's colleague, nothing more. Syl wondered if the injury was her work.

"This is your first visit to Mintryl's party?" Syl asked.

"Yeah."

"Is that why you linked yourself with this job?"

The boy threw back his shoulders. "It was *mine* first."

"I see." Syl drank from the bottle. "Fortuitous you encountered Aliara. How would you have reached Flark otherwise?"

"I'd've found some way. This razee's not impenetrable."

"I suppose not. Though I doubt you would care for Mister Marthoth's treatment of the uninvited."

Dreg turned his back on the darkening sea and reclined against the railing, downed the caba, and waggled his glass for a refill. "If I'd been alone, I'd've netted the whole commission."

"Oh? How much did Aliara take?" She cared little for coin, but like Syl, she understood well its connection to power.

"A quarter of it." He gestured at Syl with his glass. "Enough to pay for everything you're wearing."

"I suspect otherwise."

Dreg snorted. "Exactly. Not like Rift needs it. *I do.*"

Syl chuckled.

"What?"

"It amuses me to hear her called that."

"Rift? That's the only thing I know to call her. Or did until tonight. Aliara." Dreg almost smiled, but stopped himself, brows furrowed. "Why 'Pet?' She's a lotta things. Somebody's pet isn't one."

Syl paused, glass half-way to his lips. The moniker was a private joke, one that began in childhood, bestowed by their warden Nushgha. He was not about to share such an intimacy with this fatuous boy.

"On that point we can agree. Now, about this…" Syl flicked the puff of hair below Dreg's lip. "You have altered it all?"

Dreg took another drink and nodded.

"Forever?"

"I'd have to go to the zoet parlor and have it changed again. Once was enough."

"Painful?"

"A little the first night, but mostly annoying. It all fell out, grew back like this. Itched like an ass on an ant hill for a quartern or so." He rubbed unconsciously at a patch of skin above his left elbow where fine hairs nearly imperceptibly shifted from orange to black to maroon. "I scratched myself bloody in a couple spots."

"Why would you do such a thing?"

Dreg shrugged. "Why does anyone get a zoet? It's gloss."

"Well, it is quite the phantasmagoria. Makes you unforgettable." Syl clicked the bottle against Dreg's glass. "Remember that, young Toh. Such recognition could be an impediment in your line of work."

Aliara emerged from the cabin, her hair slicked back, smudged circles around her wide-set eyes, her lips bare. The black dress clung to her like fog, its skirt covering only the merest necessities. On her feet were the familiar soft-soled black boots. No matter how many pairs of shoes he purchased, she preferred those. Though he sometimes played at complaining, in truth, Syl found her intractability charming.

"You look lovely," Syl said.

She yawned and stretched, revealing a hint of the matching panties beneath. A familiar, but no less pleasant thrill ran through him.

Aliara thrust a thumb toward the door. "Ready?"

"One moment. Grab your coat while we finish our drinks."

She raised a brow and went inside.

Syl's expression hardened as he stepped into Dreg. "If she does not pass safely through this jig, you will find I am not as pleasant as I appear." He straightened the boy's coat collar and patted both shoulders. "Now, shall we go win what we can from that insufferable puka before you end him?"

SCHMALCH

Sviroosa had left scraps out for the stray cats and a few of Schmalch's favorites were arguing over the meal by the time he reached the penthouse patio. He spent a few moments stroking the fur of a particularly runty brown tabby. She liked to be held. Most of them just skittered away if he reached for them.

He hadn't been able to stop thinking about the mask the whole trip home. He didn't open the package again before leaving it in the deposit box. It was just too creepy watching those metal lips move, those empty eyes watch him.

He whispered about the mask in the cat's ear, but she had no opinion, only purrs. Schmalch snatched one of the bigger scraps from the bowl and set the little tabby on the far side of the patio with the food. She gobbled happily, purring as she ate. He gave her a final pat and opened the front door. At least his cat would have a head-start on her meal if one of the others noticed.

Sviroosa was eating at the kitchen table. Schmalch climbed up on a stool and joined her. It had become their habit, and one he really liked. She was nicer when she wasn't cooking or cleaning or running errands. Sometimes he actually felt like she really listened to him.

"Where were you off to?" she asked as she ladled soup.

"The bank. Rift needed me to drop something off." He ate a spoonful. Vegetable. Sviroosa made great vegetable soup. He swallowed and looked at her.

He wanted to tell Sviroosa about the blinking mask, but he wasn't sure she'd believe him.

"It was this weird mask," he said.

"Oh really? What kind?" She dipped some bread into her soup.

"Voshar death mask."

Her lids batted furiously. "Those are *rare*."

"And spooky." Pebbles broke out across Schmalch's skin just thinking about the thing looking at him.

"What? Why?"

He opened his mouth and snapped it shut. If he kept it closed, he'd be fifty Callas richer and no one would think he was crazy. "It's only that it was weird seeing a dead guy's face is all. I, er, I wonder how they made it without destroying the body."

"What?"

"They poured metal over his face. Wouldn't he've burned up?"

She giggled. "It's more complicated than that. The Duke hosted an artist who could probably explain it all if you're interested."

"Oh." Schmalch nodded and they ate in silence for a few moments.

When she'd finished, Sviroosa said, "Leave your poor, beautiful jacket in my room tonight. I'll see if I can do anything to repair the damage you've done."

Schmalch choked a little on his soup. "I was working for Rift. I didn't know I was going to be working for her when I got dressed. I would have worn something else. Promise."

"It's fine." She leaned over and kissed his cheek before sliding off the stool. "I'll do my best to mend it. If it's hopeless, I'll make you another."

"Really?" He'd expected trouble, not a kiss.

"Of course." Her face brightened and she dug through her apron pockets until she produced a chit. "After you'd gone to the bank, a farspeech runner left this." She passed him the tin. "Also, a deliveryman dropped off a package for Duke Imythedralin. Were you expecting something?"

Schmalch shook his head. The Duke hadn't mentioned anything. He really hoped it wasn't another death mask.

"Well, I had him put it in the office." Sviroosa climbed her puka-steps and began washing dishes.

Chit tin in his pocket, Schmalch left the soup unfinished and went to the Duke's office. A mysterious package was more interesting than another message listing all the things he needed to do while the Duke was away.

A crate almost as tall as Sviroosa sat by the desk, shiny brass clasps and hinges holding the lid in place. Schmalch circled it. The only mark branded on it was from Marthoth Air & Sea; nothing to indicate it had come in from another island. He unfastened the catch and lifted the lid. Inside sat a building.

Looking down on it like this, Schmalch might not have recognized the Orono mansion had it not been for the bulbous, candy-striped tower. He dropped the lid, which snapped shut with a terrible clap, and stumbled backward, falling on his ass. Schmalch scooted across the floor until his back hit the wall.

He'd thought about it today—he'd even gone past its corpse—and here was the horror as though he'd conjured it.

When the Duke had demolished the place, Schmalch had been so happy. The things they'd all seen there were better wiped from the isles. He'd never wanted to see it again.

Schmalch couldn't imagine why the Duke would want this thing in his house.

He sat there too long, staring at the crate, replaying images of those horrible creatures, before he remembered the chit tin in his pocket. Maybe that would explain this nasty thing.

He withdrew the squirmy zoet and held it to his eye, stroking its rutted spine. The Duke's smooth voice blew through his head, the tone soured the way it was anytime he didn't like what he was about to say.

"Vrasaj, Schmalch. First, you should expect a package to be delivered by Mister Marthoth's runners this evening—if it has not already arrived. Leave it in my office. Unopened. I will see to it when I rise after the Sowers Festival."

Schmalch mentally chided himself. He should have used the chit first.

"On the dawn of the thirteenth," the Duke continued, "an Ironclad carriage will arrive to transport you to the Bank of Dockhaven. Retrieve whatever is in box 3443. The carriage will wait for you. Do not let this parcel leave your possession. It is integral to our attempts to locate Madame Savesti. Take a weapon if you think it wise."

Schmalch groaned. He wanted to stop Nihal Savesti too, but he really didn't want to have to be around that mask again. Just thinking about it gave him the dithers.

Until then, he would enjoy himself. He was going back to the Barnacle.

PART TWO
WIDE-EYED LESSEE

SYLANDAIR

Before ferrying them to Flark's yacht, Vesven had subjected everyone to a search, the only losses being the boy's boot knife and a holdout pistol concealed in Daisy's cleavage. Though Aliara, Idra, and he had been wise enough not to bother with an attempt, the bodyguard had been annoyed by Syl's insistence on bringing a valise. After a thorough berating by Flark and a gentle search of Syl's case, Vesven had allowed them aboard.

Before they'd so much as removed their coats, Flark ordered the *Wide-Eyed Lessee* taken further out from the flotilla around the *Ipesia*. It would be far easier for their host to make them disappear away from the many eyes of the Festival goers. Daisy's apprehension of the maneuver was clear on her face. While Idra tried to hide hers, Syl drew on his confidence in Aliara's skill to prevent any sign of the same in his countenance.

After a near-interminable tour of his vessel, Flark herded them to the upper deck of the yacht. The enormous multi-tiered carbuncle was alive with yellow light that could only have come from capacitance power. Choosing cap-light over lumia was a boast of wealth—a showy statement that Flark could afford the waste. Syl wondered exactly how many hours members of the crew spent sweating over the generator cranks each day their employer was expected to be aboard. He also wondered how a man obsessed with all things miniature had wound up with such a hulk of a vessel.

Instead of sharing intriguing facts such as these, the bung had inundated his guests with the dubious provenance of every appalling artifact and artwork onboard. He also felt it necessary to share exhaustive anecdotes of the many unsavory sexual exploits he witnessed and enjoyed throughout the vessel's garishly decorated chambers. Daisy had laughed at most, deemed several untrue, and generally enjoyed ruining their host's tour. Whether she did it to put him off his game or purely for pleasure was inconsequential; her effect on Flark's mounting agitation was welcome.

The yacht's topmost deck was a vaulted affair of paneled glass, though despite this greenhouse-like design, it featured no plants or flowers, only Flark's ubiquitous tinselry. Pink and blue lumia tubes wrapped the base of a modest bar, the same were concealed just under the lip of the expansive pool, coloring the steam that rose from its surface like captivated snakes. The water consumed all but a few strides worth of the deck at the aft end, a narrow walkway surrounding the rest.

Flark hustled Syl, Idra, and Daisy to a circular, felt-topped gaming table. Dreg made directly for the bar, Aliara his shadow. Vesven and Mabiyn—the other bodyguard whose name Syl had discerned thanks to Flark's raving about her incompetence—did their best to look at ease while standing near enough but not too near their charge.

Aliara lolled at the bar like a woman with no particular task in mind, comfortable and just a little bored. Syl knew she was actually assessing every word and movement of the group, letting alternate scenarios of assassination and escape play out in her mind. Throughout the tour, Flark had massaged her posterior in ways that would have earned him a shattered wrist under normal circumstances. She'd allowed Flark to misbehave for the evening, to be at ease with her presence. Though Syl was pleased to see Aliara slip back into her profession so easily after months away, he would have gladly broken Flark's hand himself had he not been attuned to her ruse.

When they had settled in, Flark barked for the steward, D'Nell, a nervous woman met during the tedious tour. She arrived with a plate of uuha. Before Syl could remove his gloves to select a morsel, Flark slid the plate of cream-and-crab-stuffed seabird eggs in front of himself and crammed a pair into his mouth. He then coughed on the rest.

"D'Nell!" Flark barked when the steward turned to leave. "Bring another plate of this and some of that pie from this morning. My guests are hungry."

Despite being famished, Syl had no intention of eating leftover pie Flark had already had the opportunity to sneeze on.

The steward murmured assent and hurried down the companionway steps.

"Panoply," Syl called to Dreg, "make yourself useful and bring us a bottle of caba and some glasses."

The boy bit off a snipe and rummaged behind the bar.

Flark stopped eating long enough to shout, "Vesven! Open the radiators."

The ginger man did as commanded, and warm air steamed in from vents set at intervals across the floor.

Flark rubbed his hands together. "Ah, much nicer, eh? You'll be out of your coats in no time. I have a boiler, one deck down, heated by a dozen exotherms for the sake of the pool deck alone." He waited for impressed reactions that did not come. "You really should get yourself a yacht Duke. You never know when you're going to need to leave the Haven in a hurry. May as well do it in comfort."

Syl raised his eyebrows and affected an amused chuckle.

Dreg arrived and did his best impression of a server, though it was clear the boy had never once waited a table, and possibly had never seen a table waited upon. When Flark grabbed another handful of eggs. Idra rolled her eyes, turning her head away from the repulsive gobbling to watch the *Ipesia*'s twinkling lights.

"So, what did you two bring that's worth the deed to the Heap?" Flark washed down the uuha with a gulp of caba and released a sharp belch. "Remember, the place is a Skeln Emat design, you don't see cantilevering like his anymore. Expensive for the Rabble. Could be worth an undeveloped plot on a better islet." He glanced sideways at Syl.

"This *expensive* building," Idra said, "is the same one you've been in my office ranting about tearing down for the past season? The one you called 'the worst sort of death-trap?'"

Flark harrumphed. Daisy tittered.

"I will not be wagering property, however…" Syl retrieved a paper-wrapped piece about the size of a dinnerplate from the valise he had brought on board. "I did bring along a few items. Together, these pieces are of equal—if not greater—value than your portion of the building in which I reside."

Flark's face brightened. He wiped his hands and mouth with the cloth provided by D'Nell.

Syl unwrapped a tray. Like its still-hidden mates, it was resin, shaped by the finest savant beetle wranglers of First-Epoch Chiva'vastezz. The surface was smooth, almost pure black, and subtly translucent. The edges were crimped in soft waves that imitated the sea, the details so intricate they seemed frozen in the moment before break. It was like looking into a water-filled quarry.

Flark ran his tongue over drooping green lips.

Idra leaned closer, her drink ignored in favor of the antiques. Old objects, especially beautiful ones, were the Mayor's favorite subject outside of herself.

"Miniatures." Syl removed another piece from the valise. This vanity set, so tantalizingly small and old, would have been a worthy trade for the lower levels of the Heap had Flark been willing to sell. The set would do as a wager instead. Brush unwrapped, Syl placed it face-up on the tray. Its bristles were still intact, the house sigil still in place. "A three-fifth-sized vanity set. A child's most likely, but the perfect size for a puka lady."

"From?" Flark asked.

"Are you familiar with Prenja?"

"Your people's lost city with the dead terminus. Of course."

Idra scoffed. Prenja was a passion of hers. Flark's blunt and inaccurate terminology for such a beautiful and faceted civilization had clearly offended her. The Cataclysm had left the once-verdant city without rainfall for centuries, its soil turned to sand. The city had not been lost; it had been abandoned to the desert.

"A crass but mostly accurate assessment." Syl unwrapped the comb and added it to the tray. Only two teeth were missing. "Through some creative channels, I have obtained this set, First Epoch. That is my wager, easily equal to the Heap." He added to the tray an unblemished perfume bottle in the shape of a geyser then removed his overcoat. Refreshing at first, the steam heat was becoming overbearing.

"Doubtful, Duke. That's seaside property." Flark pried his eyes off the vanity set and turned to Idra. "What do you have?"

Syl knew Idra had nothing with her of significant value. "The firestar our Mayor is wearing is a Pre-Occupation setting by Kolesa," he said before she could speak. "A pity the Orasians executed her for offending the God-Emperor by being born minikin. She made such beautiful pieces, and too few." He smiled at Idra, holding her eyes, hoping she was alert enough to follow his lead.

Idra retrieved the pendant from her cleavage, holding it out for Flark's inspection. She was not without guile after all; there was a reason she had remained mayor for two more terms after merely inheriting the role.

Flark narrowed first one eye, then the other as though he could appraise the piece from across the table. "If you say so Duke. Fine, Mayor, that's your stake. Maybe Pitta'll buy it off me."

"I'll put up that piece of land off Salt Street," Daisy said, "the one you've been pestering me about for months."

Flark frowned.

"It's valued at twice what the Heap's cost you—penthouse excluded, of course." She rapped the tabletop with a knuckle and gave Flark the eye. "That's Big Island property."

"I approve," Syl said.

Idra nodded.

Flark's nostril's flared and he smacked his tongue against the roof of his mouth. "That may be fine for these two, my sweet Pricklefoot, but if I win, I want something different from you."

Daisy sneered, "What?"

"You give up your shore tenements south of the Heap. Those should have stayed in my holdings. You must've drugged me before our settlement meeting."

Daisy smirked. "Done."

"Satisfactory." Flark chuckled at his divested wife and yanked a clattering pouch of dice from his coat pocket, setting it alongside the ubiquitous charm bag. "Did you know I played Billidoc Dice with a group of Bankal raiders in the days before I bought my first building?" he asked.

"You?" Idra laughed. "Gaming with the Bankal?"

"I was born into a Billidoc clan. You didn't know?" Flark looked from Syl to Idra, not pausing long enough for a reply. "When I was old enough for my junket, they dumped me in the Haven with my clothes and a few coppers. Can you imagine what that was like?"

"You might be surprised," Syl said.

Flark chortled and gobbled more uuha. "You'll pardon me if I'm skeptical—" He cut short the intended barb as Aliara—sans boots, dress, and coat—dove into the pool. She made almost no splash.

ALIARA

When he returned from doing a shabby job of serving caba, Dreg slipped onto the stool beside Aliara. "How long do you think we'll have to wait?" he whispered.

She shook her head and signed. *"Hush. Listen."*

He grunted and reclined against the marble bar top.

Dreg had begun chafing almost as soon as they boarded, suggesting direct attacks at any hint of an opportunity. They'd had a number of heated exchanges in the cant. When he'd advocated killing everyone on board, Aliara had reminded him that only she still possessed a weapon, and if he didn't stop trying to be binnacle, she'd use her bane on him.

"…imagine what that was like?" Flark had moved on to some tedious story of his childhood.

"You might be surprised," Syl said.

Like many, Flark had consistently underestimated her mate's acumen and determination. During the years he and Aliara had lived on Dockhaven's streets, Syl had been able to contribute to their survival thanks to Reye, Orono's ancient groundskeeper. Instead of lecturing Syl on botany as their master had directed, the haggard old man often spent their afternoons teaching Syl sleight of hand, the reading of faces, the rules of every game worth betting on, and the skills needed to win them. Without that knowledge, Syl and Aliara would have been even worse off during those years.

"You could go sit on the toad's lap," Dreg whispered, "and see if he'll go someplace alone?"

The longer she stayed with Dreg, the more he'd chatter. Aliara rose, stripped, and dove into the pool.

The water was warmer than the air; Flark's bevy of exotherms were doing a fine job. She swam the pool's length in long slow strokes, the sensation smooth and easy. She'd been a douse longer than most children, hadn't learned to swim until an early jig on one of Orono's vacations. Even then she'd only picked it up because the alternative had been drowning. Her instinct had been to give in to the water after the estate's guard hounds had chased her into a lake. She might not have fought so hard to live if not for what Orono would have done to Syl had she never returned.

Aliara rolled onto her back. Dormah was high, its white face only beginning to wane. B'hintal Dadeyah was aught, invisible but for the stars it blocked. The roof was glass, metal ribs arcing down from a segmented ridge beam making it seem she swam inside the carcass of some vast sea creature. Steam became heavy droplets running rivulets down the panes, making the stars and moons beyond waver and shift. A thick cable was strung through the ridge segments, like a cord through a spine. Aliara's gaze followed it to aft, where it led down to a hand-cranked windlass. If necessary later, they could roll back the roof for a quick, albeit cold, escape.

Wind gusted outside, and the yacht responded with the slightest of lurches, stirring the pool. Water splashed its melody in Aliara's ears, the pleasant vibration running through her lower lug, her jaw, her entire skull. Of all the things Syl had done to the penthouse while she was bedridden, why not a rooftop pool? She'd suggest it when they returned home next quartern.

Aliara closed her eyes and went limp, her body following the pool's sway, the boat's sway, the sea's. Water muted the gamblers' bickering voices. She almost felt peaceful. The last time she'd felt this weightless, a man in a green jumpsuit had been carrying her across a battlefield. She'd had a hole in her chest. She couldn't breathe.

With a sharp gasp and a splash, Aliara stood up in the pool. Only Dreg looked her way. She waved him off, rolled onto her belly and swam to fore, lolling there, studying the tableau, refusing to think about the domed operating room and the surgeon with silver-spring hair.

Distantly, she could hear Flark boasting of not only besting Bankal raiders, but also escaping them. She found it difficult to imagine Flark walking at a brisk pace, let alone outrunning a roomful of angry raiders.

Across deck, Dreg had turned his attention to the old puka, staring at him like an osprey ready to tear its prey from the water. She couldn't remember ever being as impetuous as this boy, but then her patience had been learned in childhood. When she'd wanted a doll, Aliara had spent a full year stealing napkins and ribbons at just the right rate to not be noticed. The wait almost always had its reward.

This was why she was binnacle. With him in the lead, they both would have been shot and tossed in the Sound by now. Luugrar was right—Dreg lacked experience, needed seasoning. This jig would have killed the boy had he attempted it alone.

Things needed to play out naturally between the gamblers. Syl would keep their attention until he found an opening. A little privacy, and all Aliara needed was to get close enough to lay a hand on Flark. She rubbed the black nut of foreign flesh in her palm, the retracted needle a textured whisper beneath her skin. The toxin would take Flark quickly, his death would appear as no more than an old man's heart betraying him at last. Daisy and Idra would make fine witnesses to his growing agitation, and Aliara had no doubt the crew had long observed much of the same.

The guards were doing a poor job of appearing nonchalant. Mabiyn leaned against the railing, just out of reach of Flark's cane, eyes to the sky. Vesven lurked a few steps away from the bar, hands behind his back, pretending to scan the Sound. Aliara would need

Dreg if the pair became a problem. Both had pistols strapped to their hips. A crease in Vesven's trouser leg above the boot-line revealed the knife tucked there. Mabiyn's skinsuit left no room for such subtleties. Unless she pulled a garrote from her cuff, the pistol and two roast-sized fists were her only weapons.

The players continued bickering. Flark still wore his ridiculous fleece-lined coat, but the rising temperatures had all the chivori out of theirs. Syl seemed tired, his edges sharper and quicker to cut, but he was playing his part. He'd had far more experience at it than she. Aliara had once seen him play for four days straight, more liquor and drug than blood in his veins. He defeated a roomful of more-respected players and killed the first one who'd drawn a weapon in protest. Syl's knife had been lodged in the man's skull before the pistol left its holster.

She rolled onto her back and swam toward the bow.

"I had a curious experience my first evening in Dockhaven," Flark blurted, loud enough for people on the mainland to hear. "I stayed at a dump called The Bucket of Blood. You know it?"

Idra groaned. She'd hoped his story was over, but Flark had only paused to watch Imythedralin's lackluster mate disrobe.

Even after knowing the duo for years, Idra still couldn't fathom why Imythedralin insisted on showing up to events with that woman on his arm—she had no sense of status. To Idra's mind, being a Vazztain duchess would make tolerating Imythedralin worthwhile, but this creature always made a production of not taking the title. Idra would gladly be known as Duchess Carsuure of Isay. With such a title, even Pitta Dobencourt would have to treat her as an equal— or at least with far less condescension.

"I believe I do," Imythedralin said. "A few blocks from The Triangle, correct?"

"That's the one," Flark made a face adjacent to a smile. "I own it now."

"You must be quite proud," Idra said. "I've seen actual chum buckets more appealing than that tavern."

Flark's voice dropped a step. "Maybe next you can tell us of your rise from the Rabble, Mayor. Do you still like to dance? I hear Callen has an opening down at his Critter Pit. You're a little old, though." He leaned back in his seat and studied Idra. "Maybe you'd still be good for warming up the crowd."

Idra crossed her arms and withheld her urge to separate Flark's stunted ears from his weirdly round head.

"I was put up that first night with a group of Bankal ashore between raids," Flark continued. "I had no choice in the matter; it was that or sleep outside with the cats. They were tippled enough to find me amusing, so they included me in their game of Billidoc Dice."

Idra's gaze wandered to the young chivori drooping off the bar, his eyes on the gaming table. A glass of khuit dangled from one hand, a shot that likely cost more than he'd earn on an all-day shift in the *Ipesia*'s mingling room. Idra wondered how much Imythedralin's mate had paid. The physique was there, but there was something odd about the face, like it had been put together from other faces. She hadn't decided about the hair quite yet.

If she won, maybe Idra would steal the trull away from Imythedralin and have a night to remember. The unattractive ones always worked the hardest.

She didn't really want the Heap; property in the Rabble was more trouble than she had time for, but Imythedralin would pay well for the building. Maybe she'd keep Daisy's Big Island properties if they didn't seem too difficult to maintain. And the vanity set would fetch a high price—provided Idra didn't decide to keep it. Either way, she'd be able to pay off Flark and still have a bit leftover for her other creditors.

She flinched when Flark sneezed loudly enough to stir Ruru from her depths.

He blew his nose on a monogrammed hanky. "You catch all that, Mayor?"

Idra had no idea of what he'd said, but she'd be trussed and put to sea if she'd admit it. "Yes. I know the game, Flark."

"Me too," Daisy said. "Now, can we play or are you going to make us sit through another half-fib first?"

Flark's face darkened for a moment. "I warn you, Duke, Mayor, I have a talent for Billidoc Dice." He chuckled. "I won a great deal of money from those Bankal. They nearly killed me for it, but I escaped. It was an auspicious beginning. Bought my first property with the winnings, the narrowest building in the Haven. You chivori wouldn't be able to lay on the floor crossways. It's still down there on the Prick. I lease it to a family of eight pukas."

"Indeed," Imythedralin said in a dubious tone. He stopped picking compulsively at a thread on his shirt cuff and leaned elbows on the table. "Have I ever shared with you the motto engraved in the hearth stones of the inglenook in Isay's ducal manor house?"

Momentarily baffled, Flark shook his head. Hooded eyes and flaccid lips, he looked like a drunk baby.

"'Hold yourself above all others and your world will fit in a tear.'" Imythedralin's eyes rolled up from the cuff. "It loses a bit in the translation from Old Vazztain, naturally."

Flark brayed laughter. "Leave it to you to be duke of a duchy with a motto about crying."

Daisy groaned. "You short-masted buffoon."

"Shall we discover the true depth of your skill?" Imythedralin tented his fingers beneath his chin. "Let us say whoever has the best of five rounds wins the buildings, the vanity set, and the pendant?"

Flark's eyes went wide. He wiped amused tears from his cheeks.

"Best of ten rounds then?" the Duke countered.

"I bring you onboard my ship, feed you, give you drinks, and you want to just reeve me and leave?" Flark said.

"You invited us for this purpose," Imythedralin said. "You were very specific."

"You're backing out of this deal too?" Idra asked.

"We'll get to that wager eventually…eventually," Flark said.

Idra jerked her hand away as he tried to pat it.

"Let's start with some friendly rounds of dice before we move to something bigger." Flark's brow lowered. He smiled.

Daisy sighed. "If we're not wagering what we agreed, then what?"

"I need another drink." Idra and her empty glass headed for the bar. She'd had enough of their endless haggling.

Imythedralin's boy was still there, eyes pinned to the players at the table. He didn't have the disconnected gaze of a trull. There was something predatory in the way he watched them. A tattoo showed through the mesh of his shirt, stylized script she recognized as the Salt Street Tribe's mark. Perhaps Imythedralin had brought this one along for another reason.

By the time Idra slid onto a stool opposite the ersatz trull, he was playing his part again, caba bottle ready to serve. He looked better up close, though she really couldn't decide if she enjoyed or loathed the zoet hair. It was tacky and showy, the sort of thing a washout zoeticist sold to drunk dockworkers for a month's pay, but there was a hypnotic quality about it. Idra wondered how it would feel against her thighs.

"So, you're being paid to watch other people play games?" She leaned forward on the bar, offering him an influential view.

The trull paused to appreciate her as he filled a glass. "I suppose so," he said, tone abrasive.

"What part of the city are you from?" she asked.

"Lower Rabble." He handed her the drink. "Why?"

"What are they saying about the election?"

He chuckled at the disintegrating linchpin of her life as if it was an amusing flicker watched on a rainy afternoon. "They're not too happy about the Yinago Tower coming down. I saw them blockading Flark's building earlier today. Not sure they care as much about the dead families as that it might be them next time."

"Flark does it," she waved the caba glass at him, "so now any landlord can?"

"Exactly." He brushed a wavy strand of red-green-orange-blue hair from his face and returned the bottle to its place. "Their lives are pocky enough. Now they have to worry about being crushed in their sleep."

Idra took a long drink, tilting her head back to improve the trull's view. When she set the glass down, she smiled invitingly. "You'll be voting for me, right?"

"I like the Onpuur woman."

"Asah Onpuur? You want your city run by a gang boss' heir?" Blood pounded in Idra's skull. With Asah at the helm, the city would collapse in on itself in a year. She reached across the bar and tapped the tattoo on the trull's chest. "You think your Tribe would appreciate that?"

"Former Tribe." He pushed her hand away. "Mayor for a daughter or no, the other bosses would send Callen Onpuur to Ruru before they'd let him have their territories."

"Trulls like you would be giving her father half, getting kicked to death by his Sweeper scugs, or in the Bag. Is that what you want?"

"No, but…" He put both palms on the bar and sneered smugly. "You *are* letting bungs kill their tenants…"

Idra slapped him.

"Themot?" Imythedralin called from the gaming table, lavender vial in hand. Behind him, Flark was snorting yellow dust off his thumb knuckle.

Leaving the trull to rub his jaw and snicker, Idra returned to the game.

SYLANDAIR

The themot was making his teeth ache.

Syl retrieved the dicebag from his inside pocket. His set was resin, transparent enough to display its lack of weights, the sort welcomed at all tables. On his many visits to the Syl's penthouse, Flark had often tried to play with opaque dice, despite Syl's steadfast rejection. The puka was untrustworthy in every way and enjoyed flaunting it.

Syl dropped the tens in the cup, shook, and tossed them into the glass-walled tray Flark had provided. Two landed lightly, three hit the walls, and one bounced out, bumping into Flark's dice cup. Syl retrieved it, scowling at his sloppiness. He would be unable to play the errant die this round. He selected two of its valid mates, their numbers consecutive—what the game referred to as "cargo"—and moved them into position in his die rack. Flark selected two cargo and one dead die from his roll. Daisy had a set of two matching numbers, or "passengers." Idra's had nothing.

"The Mayor has no cargo!" Flark laughed and wagged a plump finger mockingly at Idra. "Not even a passenger! There's no way I'll give you what you need. Don't even bother with negotiation." He clicked his tongue and shook his head, looking to Syl for support. "This is what happens when you let a woman shoot for herself, right?"

Daisy made a sound of displeasure.

"My opinion on sex and randomness remains as it was with lyntyyl." Syl gestured around the deck, from one chivori to another. "Remember, ours is a species undifferentiated for the first years of life."

Flark's nose wrinkled. He'd expressed his distaste for the chivori sexual maturation process on more than one occasion.

"You rolled first position, Mister Flark," Syl said. "What would you trade to complete your cargo? Negotiate with me."

Flark rubbed his charm bag between thumb and fingers as he considered first his dice then Syl's. "Gimmie your two or six and I'll do the same for you next time around."

Turn of play during the negotiation phase switched directions with each round. He had made such deals with more honorable players in the past, but Syl was no dunderpate. He leaned on the table. "Why would I believe you would hold up your end of our bargain when that round arrived?"

Flark indulged in the pretense of offense. Syl slid two useless dice to him.

Syl's negotiation with Daisy went well. He contributed three bars to the hold in exchange for gifting her one useful die. Daisy reached a similar agreement with Idra, but Flark did not let the Mayor speak, just shoved two inconsequential dice at her.

"My turn." Flark played his last two with the others in his rack, ending with a run of three cargo and two dead, useless dice.

Syl added his final pair to the trio, giving him four cargo.

Flark snarled.

"I may not have had cargo, you hateful little toad, but I have passengers." Idra said, placing her dice.

Their numbers matched one she had played earlier, giving her three passengers. It was not enough to win, but the tie aggravated Flark. The old puka went for his cane, succeeding only in knocking it to the floor. He swore and commanded Vesven to fetch, all the while blaming Syl's poor negotiation for his loss. When Syl reminded him that outwitting your opponent was the central strategy of any game, Flark remained unassuaged.

"Cozeners!" He waved a finger at Daisy. "You gave him that die. You two are cheating. Is she gonna split the hold with you, Duke?"

"Yes, Flark," Daisy said, amused annoyance in her voice, "this pittance is *so* important to me that I struck a deal with everyone but you before coming aboard."

"Perhaps my companions and I should leave." Syl rose from the uncomfortable chair and glanced at Dreg. The boy was at attention, obviously bothered by the possibility of departure while Flark still drew breath. "This event has not been as pleasantly diverting as anticipated."

"Sit down," Flark said, "unless you want your penthouse to take an eight-story drop."

Everyone was silent for a moment.

"You realize what you're doing with all this implosion dross, don't you, Flark?" Idra blurted, palms on the table, halfway out of her seat. "You're ruining what little goodwill this city has for you. I'm not going to support any more of your projects." Her voice rose as she spoke, blood darkening her cheeks. "I've been helping you all these years—nearly half your life, you goby! You built your empire under me as mayor—before that too, when I was Maryn's wife and spoke on your behalf. You'd be nothing but a fleetless, beached Billidoc without me." She flopped back into her seat and spread her hands. "Now you do this to *me*?"

"And you took every bait. You think you're so clever, Carsuure, but my Uncle Furdoc's goat could outwit you." Flark narrowed his eyes, leaning as far forward as his ridiculous coat allowed. "I told you to approve my Slaughteryards project."

"You were just going to build more of the same. I won't have my city littered with those monstrosities, looking like some pile of hideous Tehtaemanian pottery." Idra stood and aimed a long, lacquered fingernail at the puka. "I helped you on your way up, old man. I can send you back down."

Daisy watched the exchange with a grin. Syl settled back into his seat.

"You'll be out of this election before the Festival's over." Flark smirked. "Especially if I continue to throw my support behind you *and* raze the other two buildings you convinced the Council to approve. Maybe I won't even bother to warn those tenants."

"You may ruin her, Mister Flark, but Idra is correct," Syl said. "She could damage you as well. Our Mayor enjoys several more months until the election. She could do many things in that time… especially if she had the backing of another individual with *some* influence in the Rabble."

Flark affected a wounded expression. "You'd do that to me, Duke?"

"Without question." Syl reached for the nigh-forgotten hold, collecting his meager winnings.

Flark slammed his cane on the hold, pinning the box in place. "That's not yours."

IDRA

Idra filed away Imythedralin's suggestion of publicly backing her campaign and enjoyed the surprised glare he gave Flark. Their host was playing the same tactic he always did, changing the agreement as the situation shifted. It was infuriating, and she had allowed this overblown slumlord to get away with it for far too long.

"Four cargo wins over three cargo or three passengers. There's no getting around it, the hold belongs to Imythedralin," Idra said more vehemently than intended.

"One of them bounced off my cup," Flark said matter-of-factly. "That entire roll doesn't count."

Daisy scoffed. "He didn't play that die. That's a poor ploy, even for you."

"I am unfamiliar with that precedent, Flark. Perhaps you should have shared all table rules before play began." Imythedralin turned her way. "What say you, ladies?"

"He's knows he's wrong," Daisy said. "The old bogsquatter's head sinks further into his shoulders whenever he lies."

Idra smiled at Flark. "I've never heard of that rule either."

"You two-copper trulls!" Flark's bellow sparked a coughing fit. Bits of spittle and phlegm peppered the table and everything on it, even the leftover pie. "Vesven, throw these dried-up quims into the Sound."

Dobencourt's nephew hesitated.

"Now!" Flark roared.

Eyes fixed on Idra, Vesven stepped forward, bent, and murmured in his boss' ear.

"I don't care if she is the mayor or if it would inconvenience that cunt aunt of yours!" Flark yelled into Vesven's ear. "No one accuses me on my own ship!" He gasped for breath before settling into an eerie calm, his huge, wide-set eyes narrowed to threatening slits. "I'm no cozener."

"A swindler? No, not you Mister Flark." Imythedralin growled, his smile so sour it curdled Idra's stomach. "I simply cannot imagine you would cheat at dice or perhaps void a pledge, leaving your facilitator without due commission."

Daisy covered her mouth and snickered.

"All you did was get two people in a room together, Duke." Flark flopped a hand toward Idra. "Imt's eyes, I already knew the woman!"

"But not to whom she could, in turn, connect you," Imythedralin said.

"I would have found another way without you."

Imythedralin's hands curled into fists. He leaned toward Flark. "Neither of *you* knew what Marthoth was transporting beyond construction materials."

Idra bit back a rebuke. Imythedralin was slipping, forgetting his audience. Daisy's raised brows and slack jaw told Idra she was assembling the pieces, formulating a way to snatch a share for herself. Idra had seen him exhausted before, just as tippled and ossi as he was now, and still he'd come out on top. Maybe it was tonight's attempted throttling or his confrontation with Marthoth, Idra wasn't certain, but Imythedralin was frazzled.

"So, you knew a little information? I put up the capital." Flark snarled, displaying the uuha remnants stuck in his teeth. "You didn't earn such a high fee."

"One item, Flark?" Imythedralin lunged forward, leaning on the table as though ready to wring the bung's neck.

Idra was disappointed when he caught himself and relaxed back into his seat, smoothing his long black tail of hair. Watching Imythedralin strangle Flark would have made fine entertainment.

"A single artifact out of the dozens Mister Marthoth's vessels carried," Imythedralin said. "It seemed a suitable commission."

"Seems reasonable to me," Daisy said, as though she'd always been a member of their venture.

"What piece?" Idra asked.

"You think I'm a gudgeon, Duke?" Flark said. "That mask's a rare piece."

"The mask?" Idra gaped at Imythedralin. "You were getting the mask?"

She'd inspected the haul before delivering it to Flark. The mask had been stunning, so perfect it seemed to move under her covetous scrutiny as though the funerary artists had captured more than the creature's countenance. But then she'd been drinking a lot that night. Flark was right, the mask was beyond rare, it was unique. In all examples she knew of—whether private collection or museum piece—the amber tear set between the two eyes had always been cracked or missing. This one was whole, the voshari's mesphor gland intact. It was the only viable sample of the species' spark known to exist. Its value was inestimable, though she'd never admit any such knowledge to Flark.

If the pilfered crates had not been sequentially marked, Idra would have kept the mask—stowed inconveniently in crate nineteen—for herself instead of the paltry finds in the final one. At least in Imythedralin's collection it would have been appreciated; she could have seen it from time to time. In Flark's hands, she'd never so much as glimpse the piece.

"You've already appropriated two boatloads of Voshar antiquities," Idra said. "Isn't that enough?"

Imythedralin raised a brow at her.

"Three when my contract's done." Flark said.

"My price was but one item—" Imythedralin began.

"That mask was the finest piece, and you both know it." Flark slammed his palm against the table. The antique perfume bottle tipped, wavered, and fell with a soft *klonk*. It rolled across the tray, bumping tenderly against the brush's ancient bristles.

"I would appreciate it," Imythedralin said, voice dry as the Prenjan desert, "if you would refrain from affecting my vanity set. If you should happen to win it this evening, then you may flail about all you like."

"*She* took enough to pay you both," Flark said. His perpetual frown turned to a sinister grin as his brown eyes rolled toward Idra.

"What? My payment was the debt reduction," Idra said. "We agreed on the amount beforehand, Flark. Or are you backing out on that as well?"

Flark smirked at her, stroking what passed for a chin. "Are you so stupid, Mayor, as to think I didn't know you stole from me? Imythedralin's information said forty-two crates. Do you think I can't count?"

Idra's skin pebbled. She pulled her coat over her shoulders and crossed her arms. She'd balked when Imythedralin had first brought Flark to her. He knew she could connect the puka to Grehv, who in turn could connect him to the Yenderot. She wished she'd stuck to her instinct and not allowed herself to be persuaded. The lure of a debt reduction had simply been too great.

"It must have been the Yenderot or Grehv," she suggested. "They handled everything before me. I received forty-one crates, and you were delivered the same."

"Poor bluff, Mayor," Flark said. "Should I have Vesven go fetch my uncle's goat to see if *he* believes you?"

"I wish those Bankal had caught you and slit your throat on your first night in Dockhaven," Idra said. "I'm sure you cheated them too."

Flark's smile dropped. His enormous nostril's flared. "Vesven!" he bellowed. "Bring me my pistol! The Bildvald!"

SYLANDAIR

"Boss, I don't—"

Flark caned his bodyguard in the shins, hard enough to make Vesven wince and steady himself on the table.

"Aye, I'll get your gun." Vesven limped toward the stairs, attempting to hide his anger.

Daisy reached for the holdout in her cleavage before recalling its confiscation. Idra nearly left her seat, settling back into place when Mabiyn blocked the stairs, hand on her pistol butt. Dreg's lounging posture had straightened while Aliara swam lazily toward the near end of the pool.

"Mabiyn! Roll back the roof!" Flark belched gloriously and dropped out of his chair like a moist glob of unrendered fat.

With a last stern look at Idra, the bodyguard began cranking the windlass. A low ratcheting filled the tense quiet, and a chill wind burst in from the bow. The roof gradually retreated toward aft, each segment receding in on the others.

Syl resumed his coat before assisting Idra with hers. As with her former spouse, Daisy had never removed her wrap. Pukas did not care for cool weather.

"What is it we are doing here, Flark?" Syl asked, voice raised over the retracting roof's clatter.

Aliara's swimming quieted. She leaned against the deck near their table.

"You all think I'm such a cozener," Flark said, working his way toward the pool. "We'll play something none of us can cheat at."

Vesven emerged from the companionway, wooden box in hand. He opened it and displayed the contents to Flark. Inside lay a fine long-barreled competition pistol, its polished surface adorned with cityscapes of the Haven.

"Bildvald-built with engraving by Shostle." Flark picked it up, turning the gun against the moonlight in appreciation. "I assume you all know what that means. Can't get one like it anymore—the maker's lost most of his fingers and the artist died last year." Flark cackled. He gulped his drink and turned to Daisy. "I commissioned it just after our divestment." With a nasty smile, he thumbed the weapon's power stud.

"What *exactly* do you propose?" Syl asked.

"Send that trull your woman brought to the starboard side of the pool," Flark said.

"You will not murder my entertainment for the evening."

"*Pfft*. It's not like anyone would miss him." Flark rolled his big eyes and displayed the weapon, small dial nestled on the side of the power box. "It's a competition pistol, Imythedralin. Variable velocity. He won't be killed, just a nasty bruise. He'll still be able to suck whatever it is you might want him to suck later on."

"Still, hit an eye and I've lost him for the evening," Syl said.

"He'll be fine. We'll give him different things—fruit, pottery, tinned food, what-have-you. Over three rounds, each of us takes a shot. A point a hit. You lose two if you hit the trull. Most points, you win." He spread his hands magnanimously. "No way to cheat."

The splash of Aliara's swimming resumed with a *whoosh* as she pushed off the aft wall.

"And we are wagering what?" Syl asked. He turned his coat's collar against the wind and rolled his aching wrist. The weather wouldn't allow him to forget its break in that monstrosity of a house last year.

"The stakes we settled on earlier." Flark waddled slowly toward the narrow port deck ledge, waving them along behind him. "This is a better show of skill—a more verifiable competition—than dice."

Syl raised a brow.

Flark groaned with exasperation. He thrust the pistol toward Syl. "Here, I'll let you shoot first."

Syl took the weapon. Aiming at the distant lights of the *Ipesia*, he inspected the sights, confirmed the velocity was set to low. He had never target shot with Flark; they had no actual knowledge of one another's skill. For Syl, shooting was a pleasant pastime, one he engaged in often. While Aliara was bedridden, his assistant and he had spent many late-autumn and early-winter evenings on the roof, Schmalch hurling dross into the air for Syl to snipe.

Syl displayed the piece to both women. "Ladies?"

Daisy nodded approval. Idra merely shrugged.

"We accept," Syl said, "pending one condition."

Completely retracted, the roof clanged into place. Mabiyn returned to her post at the rail, sweating despite the temperature drop.

"We shoot, one of us wins," Flark said. Set against the vastness of the Sound, his voice sounded hollow, as though soaked up before the words reached their ears. "What possible condition could you have?"

"Before a shot is fired," Syl said, "you produce the Heap's deed, ready to sign."

DREG

Dreg watched the moons' lazy race across the sky and considered what was about to happen. He stood on the narrow bit of deck that ran its way around the pool, hastily repaired coattails flapping in the wind, Rift's carefully crafted hairdo a memory. At least if he survived, no one at the contract house would doubt his mettle. Still, he didn't look forward to being hit with one of the shots. Even dampened, he could lose an eye, a tooth, or fracture a bone if the strike was right.

Across the deck, his would-be assassins muttered to one another. Rift swam in the pool between them, nothing but black panties separating her from the warm water. The tube of lumia circling the pool's rim made her the most visible thing on deck. She cut through the water with the same languid ease of all her movements, the scars covering her body distorted by the water's sway. He wondered if she'd earned them all on jigs like this.

Flark's male guard was perched on a stool at the bar, holstered pistol displayed at his hip. His face plainly told his displeasure with the turn of events. The female stood beside the Duke, hugging her coat close. Flark had insisted the Duke shoot first, which put her charge one body away from her protection. She, too, showed her annoyance.

"Oi!" the male guard shouted. He tossed a piminee fruit when Dreg turned. "I'll pass you another if any of them manages to knock it out of your hand. And if you're still standing." He chuckled darkly, and Dreg had little doubt he'd seen this sort of activity before while in Flark's service. "I bet you thought you'd made a few easy Callas this evening. Well, Tokimer's favor to you."

Dreg looked at the fat fruit in his hand. It was large, maybe three times the size of his fist. In these circumstances, it seemed far too small.

"Ready?" the Duke called, voice dissipating in the wind.

Dreg held his arm straight out to the side, piminee balanced in his palm, fingers flat. "Yeah," he called back.

The Duke raised the pistol. Dreg stared at the black mouth of the barrel and his balls crawled back into his body. He closed his eyes. Beneath the sea's slow lap and the buffeting wind, he could hear the click as the Duke chambered a round. Dreg pictured a slug striking his chest, the impact knocking him over the rail and into the sea. They wouldn't look for him, probably just call the steward to take his place.

A crack echoed across the Sound. The fruit flew out of his palm, splashing into the sea moments later. Dreg breathed again.

"Oi!" Another fruit came his way.

He hadn't pissed himself. That was good. He held out the fruit obediently.

Flark stopped rubbing his threadbare charm bag all over the pistol and aimed.

"That coat's distracting," Flark called. "Take it off."

Dreg set the piminee down and did as ordered. Without benefit of the roof, the night air seemed to blow through him. His body shook and he willed himself still. Even for a tippled shooter, a motionless target was easier to hit than a trembling one.

He wished Rift would just bane the target and be done with it. If he'd been binnacle, this contract would have been closed hours ago.

Dreg hoisted the fruit and tried to divert himself by imagining the old puka playing with that enormous dollhouse, but he could only focus on the pistol.

The shot cracked and Dreg heard a soft zip to his right. The fruit remained in place.

Daisy burst into laughter.

"Exemplary," the Duke said. "It seems you may owe me a building soon, Flark."

"He was shaking!" the bung shouted. "Make that trull hold still and I'll go again."

"Oh no," Daisy said, wagging a finger. "We each get three, you said so, and you're sticking to it this time. You missed, you grumpy old bogsquatter. You're the one who made him take off his coat. Of course he's gonna shake."

Rift swam up to Dreg and leaned on the pool's edge beside him.

"You're flinching," she said.

"Yeah, I'm being shot at by a bunch of toffs who consider me disposable," Dreg said.

She pushed off the pools edge, water rippling over her, and signed, "*Don't watch them.*"

"Ready?" the Mayor called.

"Yes!" Dreg replied and raised the fruit.

He looked down at Rift swimming in lazy strokes toward the other side of the pool. Steam serpents rose from the warm water around her. He deserved more of the payout on this contract. No one was shooting at Rift. All she was doing was splashing around half-naked in warm water while he froze his jugglers off.

The Mayor fired. The piminee wobbled and fell, but bounced off the handrail into the pool. Flark insisted the hit didn't count because their wager had been to knock things *into the sea*. Though that stipulation hadn't actually been voiced, everyone capitulated when it became clear Flark wouldn't let things move forward until the Mayor had been denied her point.

Daisy sighted the piminee, one eye closed, tongue poking out of her mouth as though it helped her aim.

In the pool below him, Rift rolled and dove, giving Dreg a fine view of her ass.

The pistol cracked and pain burned hot and sharp in Dreg's shoulder. His arm hitched backward, fruit flying into the sea.

"Son of a dibuc!" Dreg screamed, grabbing the wound. Instead of ebbing, the pain was growing more intense, seeping into his chest, numbing his arm.

"Two points down already!" Flark choked out between guffaws. "See what happens, Duke, when you give an old woman a gun?"

Dreg inspected his chest. A thin line of blood oozed from a rapidly swelling welt. The area around it grew progressively blacker, the bruise already large enough to envelop part of his Tribe tattoo.

"You shot me!" he shouted.

"Quiet," Rift said as she paddled toward him.

He lowered his voice. "The old bag shot me."

She pushed herself out of the pool and studied the wound.

"Two points?" Daisy shouted from the other side of the pool. "I'm one down."

"What?" Flark's shrieked. "How in all the isles do you figure that?"

Dreg winced away when Rift's fingers brushed the rising weal.

"It's nothing." Rift shrugged. "Sore for a few days."

"I'm twitching bleeding," Dreg said. "I'm not doing that eight more times."

"Didn't you say, 'whatever it takes?'" She actually laughed. "*This* is what it takes."

Dreg's mouth snapped shut. He hated having his own words thrown back at him. He shoved Rift into the pool and would have gone in after her if the movement hadn't set off a cascade of pain across his chest and back.

Rift swam away, smiling. Dreg cradled his wound and imagined a host of punishments for her condescension.

"I knocked the piminee into the sea. One point," Daisy argued with tippled logic. "But I *did* hit him. So, minus one."

The Mayor tried to step back from between the bickering duo, but the walkway was so narrow all she could do was press herself against the rail.

"You had to actually *hit the fruit*," Flark shouted. Even from this distance, Dreg could see the old puka's face darkening with exertion. "You hit the trull. It doesn't count. You're two down. Unless we all drop dead in the next few moments, there's no way you can win."

"You had such a fit about knocking it into the sea," Daisy said. "I knocked it into the sea."

"What do you think, Duke?" Flark asked.

"I fear I have to say two points down," the Duke said. "Given your most recent revision of the rules, the implication was that we would shoot the piminee in order to knock it into the sea."

Daisy looked up at the Mayor, who offered a shrug, nod, and head shake. Everyone thought she agreed with them, so she solved nothing. It was the first time Dreg could understand how she'd stayed in office so long.

"We require impartial judgement," the Duke said. "Pet?"

"Oh no," Flark said. "She's not part of this, she doesn't get to decide anything."

"Very well." The Duke cupped his hands around his mouth, unnecessary at this distance, and shouted at Dreg. "What say you, Panoply? Is Madame Daisy two points down? Or merely one?"

Dreg took his hand from his wound, the bruise broader now than his palm, and offered them all a rude gesture.

"I fear our target has sided against you, Madame Daisy," the Duke said laughingly. "Shall we continue?"

The compulsory gloating and grumbling followed, but soon the pistol was passed back to the Duke.

"Vesven, another fruit," the Duke called. "We're ready."

Dreg gritted his teeth. He'd agreed to the contract, agreed to whatever it took. He just hadn't imagined voluntarily being shot would be part of the jig. What good did slick repute and a little coin do him if the next shot put out an eye? Those were expensive to regrow.

Dreg splashed a little water on his wound.

"Don't go dribbling your nasty blood into my pool," Flark chided.

Dreg spit in the pool.

Rift floated up at the gamblers' feet. She touched the toe of the Duke's shiny shoe and murmured something.

The Duke spread his arms. "Will you resume your duties for double your agreed-upon price for the night?"

Dreg pushed himself to his feet. He wasn't sure what that meant, but he'd be sure the Duke or Rift paid him something when this was over. "Fine, but I'm wearing my coat."

"Agreed." The Duke showed Flark his palm before the puka could argue.

"And I'll have to use the other arm," Dreg added.

"Most understandable."

"She does it again and I'm done."

The Duke nodded.

Dreg awkwardly slipped into his coat and raised the fruit with his unwounded arm.

"Aim carefully, Duke," Flark said. "The boy wiggles."

The Duke smoothly raised the pistol and fired without pause.

The fruit tumbled into the sea, little bits of its tangy pink meat spattering the side of Dreg's face. He was pretty sure he actually had pissed himself a little that time.

"He seems still enough to me," the Duke said.

Dreg added the Duke to his fantasies of punishing Rift.

Flark squeezed his charm bag like a goat's teat before firing and succeeding. He spent some time thereafter congratulating himself.

When the Mayor raised the pistol, Flark bawled, "If you win, Carsuure, I think I'll just keep my deed to the Heap. That might begin to cover the cost of the crate you stole."

The Mayor looked sidelong at Flark, pistol wavering slightly in her hand.

"We'll renegotiate who owes who what after the Festival. Go ahead and take your shot." Flark flicked his fingers casually at her.

The Mayor hesitated. She looked down at Flark and spoke softly. She was obviously pleading, though Dreg couldn't make out details. The Duke's face went hard. Even the divested wife kept her yap shut. Something had shifted in the already tense mood.

"I was visiting Pitta Dobencourt to do some relic trading." Flark attacked before the Mayor could resume her firing stance. "Odd thing, she already had a Voshar singing bowl. She said she got it from you. How could that be, Carsuure?"

The Mayor lowered her pistol slightly. If she shot now, she'd hit Dreg in the legs or gut. "Wh-what do you—?"

"Maybe I'll do some socializing at Dobencourt's party next quartern and ask her." Flark scratched his hairless chin, matching brow rising. He turned to the Duke. "Maybe I'll take you *both* down. A few words with Pitta, a few with Marthoth… See what hap—"[22]

The Mayor pivoted and fired.

ALIARA

Red-brown material exploded from the back of Flark's skull. His face puffed up and darkened. When his features went slack, the puka's corpse flopped face-first onto Syl's shoes.

The Mayor yelped and dropped the gun.

Aliara dove, slipping beneath the water to come up at pool's edge alongside Mabiyn, who held her weapon half out of its holster, her indecision apparent. She was looking to Vesven for advice, surprise in her eyes, when Aliara grabbed her booted-ankles and pushed off the pool wall. Already stunned, the guard dropped without cushion or catch. Mabiyn's head smacked the deck on the way down with a hollow *klonk!*

Aliara opened her bane gland, its needle unfurling from her palm.

Someone shouted "Oi!" but she didn't look as she wrapped her hand around Mabiyn's throat. The needle punctured skin, venom pumped, and with a single convulsion, Flark's bodyguard went limp.

Aliara let the body float and took stock. Dreg had neutralized Vesven; the guard's face was splattered with piminee meat, broken stem of a caba glass protruding from his throat. Syl and Daisy were easing the shocked Mayor toward the aft deck.

Aliara pushed out of the pool, her warmth steaming away into the chill night, and slipped back into her clothes, boots, coat, and hat. She joined the others at the gaming table.

Finished rifling the corpse's pockets, Dreg rose and strode toward them, his boot knife in one hand, Vesven's pistol in the other.

Daisy was doubled up with laughter. She wiped tears from the corners of her eyes and grinned at Syl. "When you took me to see Traus, I knew it'd feel good. I just had no idea how good. Best hundred bars I ever spent." She tried not to giggle but failed. "Unless I need to pay the Mayor now too?"

"I do not believe that will be necessary, Madame Daisy," Syl said. He pulled out a chair, angling it toward Idra.

"Imt's eyes," Daisy swore. "I'm so glad the old bogsquatter's dead I might pay you all."

"Yes." Syl smirked. "When arranging this little presentation, Mister Flark failed to consider that low velocity or otherwise, having a competition pistol placed against your skull will still kill you."

Daisy settled the Mayor into a chair. "Oh, Idra, you've earned my vote."

The stunned woman didn't seem to notice.

Syl busied himself polishing Flark's leavings from his shoes with a napkin.

Coat on and hair a wreck, Dreg slipped into place beside Aliara.

"So, what do we do now?" Daisy asked, looking at Syl as though he did this sort of thing daily.

"We make this go away," Syl said.

"Sink the ship," Aliara said. The Mayor's impulsiveness had rendered the previous cover story useless. She removed her coat and hat, passing them to Syl. "Take them. I'll meet you at the launch."

Syl nodded and Aliara started toward the companionway, waving Dreg after her.

"No, no, no, no." Daisy raised her hands, palms out. "Wait."

Everyone looked at her. The ship was hers now. It was hideous, but worth plenty of silver, little surprise she wouldn't want it sunk. Aliara's eyes rolled up to Syl. He would have to convince Daisy that as purchaser of a Thung Toh contract on Flark's life, it was in her best interest to sink the vessel.

"Madame Daisy, I realize this vessel may have sentimental attach—" Syl began.

"Oh, we'll sink this tub," Daisy said, "but first, let's clean out his cabin safe. Flark likes to keep his deeds close."

"Do you know the combination?"

"I used to, but I'm sure he changed it since we were divested." She raised hairless brows and shrugged. "I can still try."

"Pet, it seems your skills are needed elsewhere." Syl returned Aliara's outerwear, took off his coat, and passed it to her. "I shall assist our young friend in sinking the vessel."

Aliara glanced at the glassy-eyed Mayor. She didn't want to be stuck with that mess any more than she wanted to leave Syl alone with Dreg. Before she could protest though, Syl was halfway down the companionway. He winked at her and disappeared belowdecks. She was stuck.

She turned to her charges. Daisy seemed giddy, almost youthful without Flark weighing on her. The Mayor's pert face was slack with shock, cosmetic smeared, the wave in her hair deflated. Aliara saw only air behind her eyes.

Alaira drew a slow breath. Scale Flark's safe, lead them to the launch. She could manage the pair for that long.

"We go down two decks, hit the bow cabin, then head straight to the launch," Aliara told Daisy. Flark's exhaustive tour had amply revealed the ship's layout. "Move quickly. Understood?"

Daisy nodded.

"I lead." Aliara pointed to the empty-eyed Mayor. "And she's your problem."

IDRA

"Abandon ship!" Daisy shouted, slapping one of the cabin doors with an open palm as they passed.

The puka held Idra's hand, dragging her down a terribly decorated corridor. Idra gave no resistance. She was mesmerized by the hasty strut of Imythedralin's mate preceding them. The motion of her body, the sound of the puka's shrill, nasal voice seemed distant and subdued, the events playing out around her like snippets from the action flickers Idra had saved coppers to watch as a child.

She'd been certain her small appropriation from the *Nimomyne's* boodle had gone unnoticed. How many conversations had Flark sat through smirking at Idra, aware she'd pilfered the forty-second crate? How long had he been waiting for the right moment to taunt her with the knowledge?

Flark was going to expose her dealings to Pitta. When an inquiry laid the details bare, Idra would be lucky to go back to dancing at the Critter Pit—at least there she'd still be on the Big Island. And if Marthoth found out she'd brokered the deal that had robbed him of shiploads of goods—including so many irreplaceable artifacts— she'd be lucky to breathe long enough to dance anywhere.

She'd *had* to shoot Flark.

Idra hadn't fired a pistol in years, though she'd once been a good shot. Callen Onpuur had given her a little silver-plated holdout on her first night in the back booths at The Triangle, the most popular of his Rabble clubs.

"As tiny and mouthy as you are, Iddy," Callen had said, "somebody's gonna try to kill or plunder you. Don't hesitate to use the gun. Pretty soon, we'll get you augmented, tune you in to what our refined clientele wants. You'll be working at my Critter Pit in no time, earning real coin. Until then, keep the piece where you can reach it, preferably where they can see it. Catch?"

He'd shown her how to load and fire the palm-sized weapon, but it had been Idra's choice to learn to use it properly. After she nearly shot the ear off a particularly insistent tippler, Idra had taken lessons, monthly visits to the range thereafter. Until she'd married Maryn. After that she'd spent less and less time in the Rabbles until finally, Idra had stowed the pistol with her delicates and consigned the range to distant memory.

Target shooting was like sex, though; once you learned how, the skill never really left you.

Imythedralin's mate stopped in front of the door at corridor's end. She was taking Idra to the owner's cabin, that hideous bow space Flark had gloated about heavily during the tour. Idra stopped walking and shook her hand, trying to free herself from Daisy's grip. She needed to leave, to get away from what she'd done, not hide in Flark's abominable owner's suite.

Daisy wheeled on her. "What now?"

"I don't want…" Idra's words drifted off. She watched Imythedralin's slag fiddling with the door.

"Neither do I. It's an awful pink-and-blue nightmare in there, but we're gonna empty his safe, Idra. Don't you want to do that?"

Somewhere inside the vessel, a string of shots went off. Idra's mind evoked the hiss and snap of Flark's competition pistol, the recoil vibrating up her arm into her jaw. Idra squeezed her eyes shut and saw the bloody hole she'd blown in the back of the ancient puka's skull. She'd hired plenty of lives ended, but never before committed the act herself. The experience was repulsive.

Imythedralin's mate popped the cabin door open and slipped inside.

"That woman drowned Flark's guard," Idra whispered.

"One of them, yes," Daisy said. "The trull took that mountain of a Dobencourt out with a fruit and a caba glass. Pitiful." She chuckled at her pun.

"Vesven…" Idra gulped pooling saliva. "Vesven Dobencourt is dead?"

Daisy nodded.

Idra retched sour caba onto the swirling pastel carpet.

The puka made a sound of disgust. "Not much solid food today, huh?"

"She'll…she'll *destroy* me," Idra whispered. She wiped her mouth with the back of her hand and sunk to the floor alongside her vomit. Pitta wouldn't just send her back to the Lower Rabble stalls, she'd send Idra back to the sea.

Daisy sighed like a parent with a recalcitrant child. "We're gonna fix everything, Idra. Just like the Duke said, remember?"

Idra closed her eyes again, searching for the memory, but saw only Flark's gore dribbling onto Imythedralin's shoes. "No," she whispered.

Daisy put hands on her hips and took on a lecturing tone. "I won the yacht from Flark. He went berserk, going on about how he'd rather sink the *Lessee* than let me have it. He snatched Vesven's pistol and stormed away. His guards followed. Soon after, the ship started to sink, and we shooed everyone off." She spread her hands and raised hairless brows. "You'll be a hero. Pitta will never know you had anything to do with Vesven's death. So, pull yourself together."

Idra opened her eyes. It seemed too simple. "She'll know."

"Fine. Think about this then: When I get back to the *Ipesia* with the contents of Flark's safe, your debt to our family is paid. Does that help?"

Idra's lids fluttered. The idea seemed more like something she'd read than something actually happening to her, but it was still better than anything else that was happening at the moment. She nodded.

"Good. Someone should have shot Flark in the head years ago." Daisy winked at Idra. "Now stand up and help me retrieve my children's inheritance."

Idra got to her feet, poking a hole in the train of her gown with one of her needle heels. She'd adored this gown. Another casualty of the evening. Its loss made her want to cry.

"I know a tailor who can fix—" Daisy began, cut off by the screech of strained metal as the *Wide-Eyed Lessee* shuddered and dropped toward the bow.

ALIARA

"Abandon ship!" Daisy was yelling so loudly Aliara's jaw ached from the vibration. She clenched her teeth to still her lower lug, but it only subdued the din.

The Mayor, while still dazed, had been motivated to walk under her own power so long as Daisy led her along by one hand. The stunned woman's gait reminded Aliara of Orono's children, lifeless yet moving.

This jig hadn't gone as expected, though few ever did. Aliara almost regretted that she'd not been the one to end Flark. He'd been so bothersome for so long, watching his odious light wink out would have been satisfying. There was, however, something amusing about the Mayor eliminating him. Idra, for all her bravado, was a weak person propped up by the strong around her. She may have had poor impulse control, but Idra had a boundless talent for surrounding herself with effective people. Taking action on her own for once had unsurprisingly left her adrift.

When they reached Flark's cabin, Aliara slipped the lock and glanced back at her charges. The Mayor was more alert, her head bowed in murmured conversation with Daisy. She remained pale, a little wobbly in her unwieldy shoes. Still a liability to be monitored.

Aliara looked up when a chain of gunshots sang through the vessel. Syl and Dreg killing the propulsor, she guessed. An unfortunate, but understandable precaution.

She left Daisy and the Mayor to their conversation and ducked into Flark's cabin, a pale-hued study in ugly. Crouched on her knees in the middle of the pool of slick pink bedding, she swung open the mirrored headboard's center panel, revealing the safe behind. The bung had been audacious enough to show it off during their tour.

The combination used on Flark's penthouse safe worked on this one as well. Aliara dumped a pillow onto the floor and stowed the boodle in its case. She retrieved a handful of high-clarity gems, an unlabeled vial of blue liquid, three silver icons, a resin box of platinum conchs, and a portfolio filled with papers and photographs.

Inside a red-flocked box pushed to the rear she found a silver medallion and matching chain, Saxelyt's image raised from the burnished surface. It was solid, the diameter of Aliara's palm, and as thick as two stacked Callas, worth maybe two bars. The darkness of oxidation lurked in every crevice, giving the Duin's face an almost lifelike depth.

"You're dead now." The words echoed. "Do you want not to be?"

Aliara shook her head. This was her first jig back, her first pairing with Dreg. She'd experienced a hallucination, she told herself, one brought on by the stress of returning to work or adjusting to her new organs, maybe even a side effect of Ranaran's many palliatives. Aliara's mind had latched onto the bust of Saxelyt she'd seen in Flark's collection, inserting the Duin's image into her delusion.

She shook her head again. It hadn't felt like a hallucination. It had felt real. And strangely familiar.

Metal wailed. The vessel pitched to fore. Someone deeper in the ship screamed, and everything not nailed down skated across or crashed to the deck. Aliara slid off the bed with the silk blankets, landing on her hands and bouncing into a crouch.

Syl and Dreg had done their work. That left little time to collect her charges and meet Syl at the launch.

Aliara rose and worked her way up the sloping deck to the

corridor, where Daisy and the Mayor clung to the bulkhead handrails, eyes wide.

"Move!" Aliara shouted. Sagging pillowcase in one hand, she ran toward them as quickly as the ship's increasing tilt allowed.

The others struggled toward the stern alongside her. The Mayor, more lucid now, was forced to stop and remove her shoes at one point, though she refused to drop them. Daisy fell twice; age, stature, and circumference making her climb especially awkward. When the ship lurched to starboard, the puka toppled across the corridor. Barely missing the Mayor, Daisy landed in a rumpled green heap a half-step behind her one-time charge. With much swearing, she righted herself and crawled after them.

Aliara helped them both through the exit hatch and into the launch, where the steward and a couple others waited. Syl was absent. Dreg too. She stared at the hatch as though she could penetrate the hull. Their tasks should have dovetailed. They should have been here by now. But then ops never went as planned.

She'd give Syl two hundred heartbeats before seeking him.

DREG

Without explosives, Dreg had only one idea for the sinking of ships: open the propulsor inlets and flood the bilge. He was surprised when the Duke agreed. The task would be cold, unpleasant, and potentially dangerous, but it was by far their most expedient option. He just hadn't expected the well-dressed toff to bite.

Dreg looked down at the long, wormy zoet sleeping in the bilge water. It looked peaceful, harmless, but he knew that was an illusion. During his brief career as a Yenderot raider, Dreg had found himself more of a drudge than a bandit, spending his time in the mankiest parts of the ship while others did the plundering. One of his primary jobs had been tending to the ship's dual propulsors. As he and the Duke stared down at the dozing creature, Dreg could only think of a fellow tender named Gairba. While scrubbing the beasts one day, she slipped and fell into the bilge water with the pair of pale zoets. One woke and slurped Gairba up. Her muffled scream lasted only a breath before the creature jettisoned what was left of her out the other end, gore sprayed across the compartment's aft. The instant the ship returned to Dockhaven, Dreg had taken his shares and left. Life as a cog in another's machine was for the dibucs.

If he or the Duke were sucked into this one, their best-case scenario was to be vomited back out with a few broken bones. But that was unlikely. Dreg shuddered and squeezed the grip of Vesven's mag pistol. The idea of taking a ride through a propulsor was horrifying. He wasn't going down there while that twitching thing still sucked water.

"Is there a problem?" the Duke asked.

Dreg shook his head and raised the gun. He wasn't sure where to aim, but enough shots and he'd hit something vital. He fired down the worm's length, aft to fore, until the clip was empty. With each shot, the propulsor convulsed and twisted, its dorsal mouth flapping, tentacles waving spasmodically until the long body shrunk in on itself like a withered sponge. White fluid oozed from the wounds, clouding the bilge water and filling the hold with a fusty fish odor.

Dreg shoved the pistol in his belt, swung onto the ladder, and settled his bare feet on the tender's walk grating, shivering in the below-decks chill. They'd been wise to leave their heavy garments with Rift, but he couldn't help but wish for the warmth of his coat and boots.

If they survived this, he was going to enjoy the finest treats the *Ipesia*'s mingling room had to offer.

The Duke dropped down beside him. "How may I assist?"

"Now that the propulsor won't try to glom onto them, we open the regulators." Dreg pointed fore and aft where narrow ladders rose from the walk, leading to polished valve wheels. The equipment was toffed-up compared to the *Twilight's Blight*, but it was the same in principal. "Crank the wheel full open." Unsure if the Duke would catch his meaning, he added, "Left until it stops."

The Duke grabbed the ladder and swung around him toward the aft regulator.

"Wait for my signal." Dreg made his way to the bow ladder and scrambled up.

In place, he locked eyes with the Duke, who nodded.

"Now," Dreg called and jerked the wheel, his shoulder wound grousing with the strain.

The sea roared in below him, hungry to fill the void. By the time the valve was full open, the chill water covered the tender's walk. He dropped off the ladder and tried to follow the narrow path, now obscured by surging water. He'd almost reached the Duke, who was mounting the exit ladder, when the ship lurched downward at the bow, stealing Dreg's balance. He swayed, grabbed air and pitched into the icy deluge.

Dreg's body stalled. For an instant, he was paralyzed, able only to stare into the rising sea around him in astonishment. An age passed before he felt his heart beat again, and he pushed his way to the surface. The water sloshed into his mouth, bringing with it the foul flavor of bilge brine and propulsor blood. He gagged and spluttered. For an instant, panic took control then on instinct, he rolled onto his back, seeking the dwindling pocket of air between upper deck and flood. Buoyed up from its bilge grave, the bulk of the propulsor's limp body pressed against his back, threatening to clamp him against the overhead.

Then it moved.

A tentacle looped around Dreg's leg and with a quick jerk, drew him deeper into the chill. He groped for purchase with numb fingers and kicked the half-dead creature. It held tight. His detached brain commanded him to call for help. He obeyed, opened his mouth and tasted rank saltiness. His vision dimmed. Part of him understood he would die here. Rift—who had only had to open a twitching safe— would claim the whole commission.

Something brushed Dreg's numb knuckles then twined through his fingers. A hand. Dreg clamped on. A second hand circled his wrist and pulled. The propulsor countered. Dreg's limbs strained from their sockets. With a pop that echoed through his body, Dreg's shoulder came out of joint. He screamed into the sea and kicked at the clinging tentacle with his free foot. In response, the dying propulsor coiled its tentacle further up his leg and yanked. His hip popped free, the ankle felt loose and disconnected. They were going to pull him apart.

He kicked with his free leg again. The propulsor tugged, and

Dreg's boot slipped off. He shot to the surface, gasping for air, spitting foul seawater, and the Duke pulled him from the flooding bilge, tugging a little too enthusiastically on Dreg's dislocated arm. The man's lips were blue, his face paler than normal, and like Dreg, he shivered as though palsied. His fine clothes were ruined. Dreg couldn't quite reconcile this man who'd saved him with the one he'd met earlier.

The Duke hoisted himself onto his feet and offered Dreg a hand. "We need to move quickly."

Dreg vomited the repulsive amalgam. "My arm," he whispered. His hip had popped back into place, but the shoulder remained loose.

The Duke grabbed Dreg's wrist, braced himself, and tugged. Dreg howled, pain shocking him back to life. The Duke hefted him to his feet, still spitting and hacking, and urged him up the companionway to deck two and the docked launch. The ship shifted with a sharp groan of steel and canted hard to starboard. Dreg hit the bulkhead with a whoof and a whine. Above decks, people shouted and wailed.

"Up we go," the Duke urged him up the companionway.

Dreg tried to pull himself up, but his arm wasn't working. The hand of the other one kept slipping. The water was knee-high. Dreg slumped against the bulkhead. "I can't," he moaned.

"For the rest of the Festival, you can milk your injuries for all the attention and affection you please, and I will attest to your reliability no matter how egregious the lie," the Duke said. His tone was dark, more serious than Dreg had yet heard him. "Imt's eyes, I will even pay your way when we get back to the *Ipesia*, but you need to climb!"

Dreg tried again, but each time he made it a couple rungs, his arm gave out and he slumped back onto the deck.

The Duke grabbed his shoulder. "Let me."

Dreg stepped back and the Duke climbed up. For a heartbeat, Dreg was sure the man was going to leave him to drown. Then his well-manicured hand extended down through the hatch.

"Can you reach me?" the Duke asked.

Dreg hopped once, brushing the Duke's fingers, then again, catching the hand.

The Duke helped Dreg onto the deck and down the corridor toward the exit. Every step was agony, but the quickly rising water drove him through the pain. Out the aft exit, he could see Rift and the others waiting in the launch, shouting, urging them to rush.

He'd barely made it onboard safely when the steward released the davits and the launch dropped into the sea. The propulsor throbbed, and the small vessel struggled to escape the *Lessee*'s downward tug. The sea absorbed the deck they'd just stood on, its dark water burbling around the floundering vessel. The launch hesitated until they cut hard to port, breaking free of the ship's pull. Behind them, a chain of massive bubbles rushed to the surface, and in a huge gulp, Flark's yacht disappeared into the Middle Sea.

SCHMALCH

A few days before the Sowers Festival began, the Duke called Schmalch into his office after a card game with Flark had turned into shouting. The bung had left the penthouse promising to tear down the Heap or die trying. When Schmalch entered the office, the Duke was standing at the bar, downing shots of khuit.

"This is an important lesson to remember, Schmalch." The Duke raised a finger and turned around. His eyes were hooded, his mouth a hard, straight line. Schmalch hadn't seen him look like that since Rift got hurt. "Do not trust anyone or anything in which you have even the slightest doubt."

Schmalch nodded, mentally repeating the words if not fully understanding them. It was a concept he'd learned long ago at the Spriggan orphanage, but one he'd never been able to express.

"In my urgency to prevent Savesti from obtaining any voshari spark, I put my trust in someone I knew to be duplicitous. Now I must handle Mister Flark as well as retrieve my property. To do so I will need to nurture a relationship that would not naturally blossom." The Duke set his glass on the bar, returned to his desk to retrieve a ratty old book, and passed it to Schmalch. "Take this gift to Madame Daisy's abode. Invite her to dine with me prior to the festivities on Marthoth's vessel."

That lesson in mind, Schmalch knew he'd have to unwrap the

Voshar death mask when he retrieved it from box 3443 at the Bank of Dockhaven. It was unlikely anyone would have known the artifact was stored there, let alone broken into the building, then the vault, and finally the deposit box, but then there were thieves like Rift. He'd have to check the mask before bringing it back to the Duke, and that idea made Schmalch a little queasy. That moving mouth had haunted him the rest of last quartern, the blank-but-watching eyes bursting into his mind at the most inopportune times. A couple nights back, he'd even lost a bunch of coin to Yemenie and Frabo because he hadn't been able to focus.

The Ironclad had been waiting for him just before dawn as the Duke had promised, and though Schmalch had tried to dawdle in the lobby, the bank manager had spotted and remembered him quickly. After delivering a few welcoming words that didn't feel like they should be for him, she took Schmalch back into the vault, her shoes ticking against the brushed-metal tiles.

A clerk looked up from her customer as they passed. Her type usually scowled at him. This one smiled.

As the manager led Schmalch between a pair of well-armed guards and into the shiny metal room, a low metallic *whirr* built in the air around them like angry bugs with metal wings. The closer they came to box 3443, the louder it grew. The manager didn't seem to notice; she did her bit and left as though the tinny echo was normal. The instant he heard the door snick shut behind her, Schmalch climbed the puka steps and pulled the deposit box from its slot. It was vibrating so hard it tickled his hands. He drew a long breath, opened the box, and lay the wrapped package on the table.

This had to be the mask. What else would be making noise like that? It looked the same as when he'd put it there days ago. He didn't really need to unwrap it to confirm…but the Duke's caution echoed in his head. What if somebody had wrapped a windup toy and made off with the Duke's swish prize? Schmalch would look like a fool bringing that back. He'd never pay off the loss. His kids and their kids would still owe the Duke.

Schmalch untied the twine, peeled back the waxed-cotton flaps, and looked into that platinum face. The vibration stopped. It was just a shadowbox lying on a table, nothing mystical about it. The face was such a weird shape, the nose almost absent. The work was so detailed, he could see creases in the skin around the lipless mouth and oblong eyes, even hairs on the temples and chin that were so thick they looked like rhochrot quills.

Schmalch leaned in a little closer. The mask was neat when it wasn't trying to talk to him. No wonder the Duke wanted it. Schmalch had never seen anything like it before—history and anatomy weren't the kinds of lessons taught at the Spriggan Temple—but this time, it was just a mask. It didn't move, didn't try to talk to him. He'd just imagined all that nonsense.

"I was just tired," Schmalch said, the words reflecting off the vault's walls.

The lids fluttered and opened. The unseeing eyes rolled toward him, so alive Schmalch was sure he could see the subtle bump where color was supposed to be. The lips worked awkwardly like slugs moving through paste. And something in that translucent golden drop between the eyes wriggled and danced like the worms he'd seen in scat.

A chill stole through Schmalch. The last time he'd felt that way, someone had called him "food." He wrapped the mask and ran out of the bank into dawn's dim glow and almost leapt into the carriage.

The driver, a grizzled old man who liked to spit, leaned in after him. "Back to the Heap?" he asked. "Or you got s'more stops?"

"Back home," Schmalch said. "No stops."

The driver nodded, shut the door, and scrambled up the side of the carriage to the jockey box.

Schmalch arranged the wrapped mask on the seat facing him, as far away as the vehicle's layout allowed, and did his best to ignore its presence, even when it started vibrating again.

He jumped when the driver opened the carriage door. The package went still. Schmalch cursed at it under his breath as he climbed to the penthouse. Sviroosa was in the kitchen, elbow-deep in sweet-smelling dough. The Duke was finally awake, she said, and expecting a guest for the morning meal.

"He has work for you before you leave for breakfast with *that family*." She looked up from her baking and offered something approaching a smile. "He's in his office."

The Duke was dressed and groomed as swish as always, but his desk was a wreck, littered with dirty and broken objects strewn around a crate. So much packing straw was scattered through the room that Schmalch suspected Sviroosa would still be finding bits of it for months.

"Did you examine it first?" the Duke asked when Schmalch presented the hastily rewrapped shadowbox. When Schmalch nodded, the Duke took the package and set it on his chair. "What did you think?"

Schmalch searched his mind for something sane to say. "It's, er, a lot of platinum."

"Indeed." The Duke chuckled. "I have never before seen one in person."

Schmalch wanted to ask, "There are others?" but the Duke moved on too quickly.

"This parcel needs to go to Wuukuster." He tapped the crate on his desk before snatching something that looked like an old pair of scissors and wrapping it in the stringy packing. "I require his expertise in authenticating these artifacts."

Schmalch nodded. There'd barely been a quartern lately that he hadn't picked up or taken something to Wuuk's shop. The Duke loved his old stuff and Wuuk made sure everything really was as old as it was supposed to be.

"What is all that?" Schmalch crept closer, leaning his chin on the desk's edge.

The Duke tucked the wrapped scissors into the crate and selected a triangular board from his desk.

"That's a scandal board!" Schmalch said, thrilled to recognize one of the pieces.

"It is. It may even be the one I lost to Flark over the winter." He swathed the board in packing material and tucked it into the box. "We shall see."

"Where'd you get it?"

"All these items are gifts from Aliara."

Schmalch tried to appear suitably impressed, though he was pretty sure he'd seen a few of those "gifts" in Rift's boodle from the Bung Building.

"When you deliver this crate, tell Wuukuster the other package he and I discussed has arrived." The Duke nodded to the still-sealed mask and began wrapping the scandal pieces, a group of nearly naked puka women. Schmalch blushed involuntarily at their presence. "He will tell you what day I should expect him and if he has any special requirements."

"And I'll tell you."

"Yes."

The Duke picked up a pretty bronze bowl. Schmalch had definitely seen this one in Rift's boodle. The part he could see showed a copper-inlaid picture of two four-legged, four-armed people, narrow tails waving behind them as they chased a big lizard whose thick tail left trails in the sand. All had shiny black stones for eyes. Bits of green and red paint splotched the metal.

"What is that?" Schmalch asked. He wanted to touch the bowl.

"This is a Voshar singing bowl," the Duke said. He wet his finger in the drink on his desk and ran it around the lip of the bowl.

The whole room filled with a low, rich tone Schmalch felt in his guts. It was beautiful.

The Duke stopped playing and licked the caba from his finger. "Each is unique, and each produces an almost perfect tone."

"Can I try?"

"Gently, it is very delicate." The Duke placed the bowl on his desk.

Schmalch dipped his finger in the dark-red liquid and ran it around the bowl's thin rim. The sound seemed to run up his arm and into his face. It felt like a soft tickle. No wonder the chivori liked it.

"What's the picture of?" Schmalch asked.

"Those are two voshari—Pre-Cataclysm, of course. I suppose they are chasing some food source native to their lands, the remainder of which is now Tehtaemah." The Duke turned the bowl around, showing Schmalch the full hunting scene.

More voshari were busy trying to box in the lizard from their side. They all had those thick hairs on their cheeks and chin, but longer than what was on the mask. Finer hair was on their heads and shoulders, even a bit on the tails. Their faces were similar to the mask, but arty, like the paintings the Duke called "representational."

"The images on each bowl tell a story. This, however, I have no explanation for." The Duke tipped the bowl, showing Schmalch its bottom. A series of circles inside circles inside circles, bumping up against other circles inside circles covered the bowl's whole underside. "The scholars say no two of the patterns are identical."

The doorbell rang. Both looked at the office door.

"I'll answer it," Schmalch said. "Sviroosa's kneading dough."

"No, I will see to the door." The Duke rose and nodded at the mess on his desk. "Finish packing these items and take the crate to Wuukuster immediately. Ensure the foyer is unoccupied and the salon door closed before departing. My guest would not approve." He smiled and straightened his jacket. "I will not require your assistance again until aftermid."

Schmalch grinned and got busy wrapping. Maybe he'd take Fohmsquah to the Char and Claque for some tea and a show after breakfast. She deserved some time away from the refugee family members nattering at her all day.

DREG

The moons were almost gone, the sun's light a gentle warmth on the horizon when Dreg stepped out of the Belvedor Inn onto the bricks of Grammour's Bow. He looked up the street at the dim glow of red-tubed lumia from the unwashed window of Yartair's Food Counter, turned, and strode toward the always-open diner, the flavor of greasy eggs and half-burnt flimmel root already on his tongue.

Not once since he'd moved to the Belvedor had Dreg found Yartair absent from his post. He'd been asleep in a booth a few times and often napping at the counter, chin in his hand, but he'd always been there. If anyone came in at odd hours, though, the cook got lathered. "Now I have to heat the stove for just one meal. *One meal,* chivori," the gnarly old karju would say. "Do you know how much it costs me just to fire that thing up?" It seemed like a miserable life.

Dreg stopped by the Food Counter's door, peering through the grimy window. Yartair was sitting in a booth, head tipped back, mouth open, snoring. Though he was pretty hungry, Dreg walked on. The meal wasn't worth an upbraiding. He'd pick up some biscuits at Pinchknuckle Bakery. He might even feel generous and buy a bag to share with Luugrar and anyone else lurking at the contract house.

At the cross with Anchorage Way, he paused, studying the Heap, half its bulk hanging precariously over the sea. He *could* check if Rift was awake yet. She'd probably want to be there when he shared the details of the jig with Luugrar. But it was early. *He'd* slept for nearly two full days. At her age, Dreg couldn't imagine how much sleep Rift would need after a quartern-long zootie. He rubbed absently at his shoulder, still achy after the fiasco on the yacht—though the bruises had earned him loads of sympathy in the mingling room.

Dreg shook his head. No, he wouldn't bother Rift.

He headed down the shore toward the Prick. The boardwalk was quiet this early, only a few vessels lighted in the harbor. The news callers were starting to settle into their posts, and Dreg caught bits of stories about the rise of Flark's inheritors, the Mayor's odds in light of her heroics, and the various flotsam found in the Sound post-celebration.

The morning-shifters started stirring from their hovels, the sun subtly cresting by the time Dreg reached Pinchknuckle, where a comical loaf of bread greeted him, its shape and leering smile outlined in a glowing tube of lumia. Dreg stepped inside, headed straight for the counter, and ordered a full bag from the doddery bakery clerk. She commenced stacking biscuits in the bag at a sluggish pace, tallying aloud as she added each one.

Immersed in watching her, Dreg started when a nasal voice spoke from behind.

"I didn't think you'd keep it."

Dreg turned around, willing the old woman to move faster. Unanticipated conversation was not on his agenda this morning. A skinny puka with sallow green skin stood there grinning, pastry in one hand, its oozing jelly threatening to drip onto the floor. Like always, Boit's clothes hung on him awkwardly, as though the tailor didn't know the proportions of the person she was sewing for.

"Keep what?" Dreg asked.

"The hair." The puka's laugh sounded like a squeaky door. "None of us could believe you did it. Then it all fell out. You looked so funny."

"Yeah, well, it grew back. What're you doing here so early?"

The old woman announced the fifth biscuit.

"I know a rhochrot apprentice who'll ink me for free if I get there early so she can practice." Boit pushed up one of his too-short sleeves, revealing an obviously new tattoo, his skin swollen and piney around it. The angry colors wound down his arm like some rotten vein.

"What is it?" Dreg asked.

Boit squeaked with amusement. "I didn't think you'd been gone that long. It's Salt Street. See, here's where the desal plant sits." He pointed to the crook of his elbow and traced the line toward his wrist, pausing at odd little globs of color. "And that'd be the Tribe's squat, and there's the aerodrome, and didn't you used to live somewhere around here?"

The sixth biscuit dropped into the bag with a soft *foof* and a muttered announcement.

"And that would be North Point," Dreg slapped the puka's wrist. It was unsettling to see how little Boit had changed. He was still obsessed with the Salt Street Tribe, still had the same hollow eyes, still wore the same stretched-neck shirt. Dreg suddenly needed to get away from his one-time crony.

"Yeah, she's inking that one next quartern," Boit said. "Then she'll start with the detail."

Dreg turned to the bakery clerk. "Can you hurry that up?"

"Seven." The woman scowled at him.

"That's enough," Dreg said, reaching for the bag. "Just give it here."

She stepped away from the counter and out of his reach as her tongs groped for another biscuit. "Eight."

Dreg quietly cursed the nasty old quim.

"Did you see Seiroh and Vindyl the last time they were here?" Boit took a bite from his pastry, big brown eyes pinned on Dreg, watching for any hint of reaction. A smear of jelly lingered below his lip.

"When was that?" Dreg kept his face bland. He didn't particularly care if Seiroh drowned in Ruru's womb, but he wouldn't object to seeing Vindyl again.

"It was…" The puka shrugged. "Can't remember exactly. I know it was at least a quartern before the Festival. Everything's a blur around the Festival, eh?"

The clerk announced the ninth biscuit.

Dreg considered telling Boit about the swish blur that had been his Sowers Festival but decided it unwise. He wasn't sure how to explain winding up on the *Ipesia* without mentioning why he'd been there.

"Seiroh seemed to think they'd be back in mid-Inbar, but I haven't seen them yet," the puka said. "He said something about stopping in port to make deliveries."

"Deliveries of what?"

Boit's bony shoulders lurched as he swallowed. "He asked where you were. None of us knew what to say. Not even Jova. Where *have* you been?"

"Ten." The old woman dropped the bag on the counter. "That's twenty-two coppers."

"I can't stay right now, Boit." Dreg dropped the coins on the counter, grabbed his bag, and walked backward out of the shop. He didn't want any of those douses to know where to locate him. Ever. "I'll find you another time and we can have a brew together. Are you still lurking around the…?"

"Inmate's Outpost, yeah," Boit said.

He was probably still lobbing rotten fruit at prisoners in the Bag while he was there too.

"Right, well, I'll stop by the next time I take the Pipe uptown." Dreg pushed the door open with his ass and left.

The burgeoning morning seemed too cold after encountering his old comrade. Dreg pulled up his hood and crossed his arms around the warm bag of biscuits. He'd wanted out of there in a way he couldn't quite explain. It was like the last time he'd joggled Jova.

He'd wanted her gone so badly, he'd barely enjoyed the sex. After he'd left the Tribe, being around anyone from that life felt off-beam.

The closer Dreg came to the contract house, the faster his pace. He almost ran down the alley and spiral stair, even made his way through the red room in a flash. Luugrar was just shuffling out of the doorway behind his desk when Dreg stepped inside, catching a rare glimpse into the manager's private world. Past Ochai's office, he saw only an ancient cabinet, a painting of birds in the sunshine, and an open washroom before Luugrar closed and locked the door.

"I didn't expect to see you so early today." The fuzzy-haired karju settled into his chair and fiddled with the mass of papers that always rested there. "I *did* expect to see you this early about eight or nine mornings ago."

We decided to stay on the *Ipesia*," Dreg said. "We figured it would be less sketchy than disappearing after the yacht sank."

"I'm sure you would have preferred getting back here to update your house manager rather than loitering around that zootie."

Dreg laughed.

The steel door behind him opened and in strolled Muddler, fresh from his own time aboard Marthoth's barge. Tall, blonde, and almost as attractive as Rift's Duke, he was the only other Toh in the Dockhaven house close to Dreg's age.

"Dreg!" Muddler clapped him on the back. "How was your jig on the *Ipesia*? Your first alone with Rift, right?"

Before Dreg could reply, Luugrar cut him off.

"Bup, bup, bup. You two sit." The contract house manager rose and gestured toward the small, dirty room full of too-tiny tables. "I'll bring tea and you can tell us both about the jig. I hear you lost a Dobencourt in the process."

SYLANDAIR

Syl checked the peep before opening his door. Though no one else had attempted to fulfill the contract on his life, he'd uncovered no new information as to its purchaser's identity. His expected breakfast guest, Mintryl Marthoth, stood alone on the landing, slightly sweaty from hauling his daunting frame up the many flights to the penthouse. Syl tucked his recently purchased Enaga holdout into the pocket of his slate-blue flannel coat.

"Mister Marthoth." Syl swung open the door and stepped back, waving the robust karju inside. "I am pleased you were able to join me on this chill morning."

The shipper stepped in and marched directly to the parlor. "Your message was intriguing, if overly cryptic." Marthoth removed his red overcoat and tossed it on the back of one of the white sofas.

Syl tugged the bell pull to alert Sviroosa his guest had arrived. "If you would not mind pouring your own drink," he indicated the cellarette, "I will retrieve the items I alluded to. My domestic will arrive shortly with a morsel plate."

Marthoth agreed and strode over to investigate the liquor cabinet.

Syl slipped into his office, where Schmalch still worked at packing the crate destined for Wuukuster. From his wall safe, Syl retrieved the two ledgers Aliara had liberated from Flark's penthouse. Marthoth's business diary, however, Syl kept. He strode into the parlor and presented the two books to his guest.

His brow crooked, Marthoth took the ledgers. "You either saved these from the *Lessee* as it was sinking, or you had a hand in the disappearances from Flark's penthouse." He tapped a ledger with a thick finger, calloused despite his wealth. "I hadn't expected you would arrange for the elimination of both Flark and Karna."

The news of Flark's death and the unsettling emptiness of his penthouse had circulated while they'd been aboard the *Ipesia*. According to Schmalch, no one had mourned for the old bung— several had, in fact, celebrated—but there were continued vigils at street shrines for those he'd killed in the Yinago Tower implosion as well as a rather elaborate service at the Pukatown piers for Marthoth's accountant. Syl was sorry the bookkeeper had to die in the process of retrieving the mask, but Daisy had insisted. Karna would have made a fine asset to someone with fewer secrets.

"The contract was not mine," Syl said, "though I was owed a favor by the recipient."

"Do I owe you a favor now?"

Syl half-shrugged. "That is, of course, up to you, Mister Marthoth. We each live by our own principles. Should I ask you for a favor, you will decide if you choose to fulfill it or not. It does not matter if I claim it is owed."

Marthoth smiled. "I like you Duke Imythedralin. I didn't expect to."

"The sentiment is mutual."

"Will you tell me how you knew these had…" Marthoth frowned, searching for a word that didn't make him look foolish. "…been misplaced?"

"Flark was fond of gloating when tippled. That last evening on his yacht, he enumerated the many ways he had outwitted his peers, including the Mayor, Daisy, me…and you." As he spoke, Syl rose and crossed to the cellarette, refilling his glass and raising the bottle to Marthoth.

The big man's frown flattened, and he nodded.

"Flark shared with all of us his brilliance in planning the raids on your vessels to discredit you and drive your fees down." Syl returned to his seat. "During that loutishness I learned that you should find some of the items he took at his penthouse. Sadly, I am told many pieces have already been lost to the undermarket."

The shipper grunted.

Syl topped off Marthoth's drink. "Forgive my presumption, but I have already spoken to Daisy on your behalf. She awaits an invitation to negotiate the return of your property in her family's possession."

"I'll be sure to schedule something when I return to my office," Marthoth said, emptying his drink in a grand quaff. "Fill my glass and let's discuss your transport needs for Isay."

When their deals were done and Marthoth sent on his way, the mask still waited in the office, a tantalizing reward after so much effort. Syl approached it slowly, tingling with excitement beyond the thrill of having circumvented Nihal Savesti. Only a handful of Voshar death masks had been found. *He* possessed the only one with its gland still intact.

Syl unknotted the twine and peeled back the flaps. Inside lay a poured-platinum face caught in the deepest sleep. The long eyes and lipless mouth made the orbed nose seem farcical, like a joke amongst harsh truths. Shallow quills projected from the cheeks and chin, some sharp enough to cut, others broken and cracked. It was a face that might spring to life at any moment, yet it was nothing but cold, hard platinum made priceless by the demise of the civilization that spawned it.

Syl blinked.

He was in a cloud, pungent and verdant, as though flora and fauna prospered just out of sight.

A figure he'd not seen in decades emerged from the mist. Her skin was blue, her eyes as black as his mate's, her arms split into pairs at the elbows. She stroked his face with her many-knuckled fingers, more intimate than any kiss. She traced a finger under his chin and blew in his face, her breath as sweet and cold as any winter morning.

Syl blinked.

He was back in his office, shadowboxed mask in his hands. Seeing Omatha again felt like returning to a home he'd never had, but the abruptness of the experience rattled Syl. The last time he'd seen the Duin, a dose of Portent had been required.

Syl's gaze shifted to *Pink Sister's Last Grace* on the room's back wall. Three bottles of that drug waited in the safe behind the painting.

IDRA

With a final thrust and an enthusiastic groan, Grehv flopped onto the bed, relieving Idra of his almost-suffocating weight. The former raider wasn't so much fat, but he was karju, half again Idra's size, and what wasn't muscle was becoming his marriage belly.

Idra rolled onto her back and cleaned herself with the sheet, studying the fabric of the canopy above. It was the nicest thing available to look at in this cellar. Grehv with his hairy back, ruddy face, and waning head of dark-brown hair wasn't all that pleasant to behold, and the earthen walls around them only reminded her of how low she'd sunk.

Grehv's connection to the Yenderot had proven useful and profitable on many occasions; Flark had hardly been the first client she'd brought to him. His value was worth her effort once or twice a month, but she'd grown weary of the setting. Grehv's idea of using the old tunnel beneath his wife's estate had seemed brilliant when the only thing they'd been doing was exchanging information about Pitta and her plans, sometimes swapping an item or two. The awkward climb up the hidden cliffside stair had been worth the adventure. When she'd run out of coin though, Grehv suggested a change in currency, and using the tunnel became far less thrilling. With him heaving on top of her, Idra could no longer delude herself that she was an early-Silver Era socialite hiding from a water riot, waiting for nightfall so she could escape into Lover's Sound.

Idra sighed. At least Grehv had moved a bed of sorts into a side chamber. It was one Pitta had been about to pass down to the help, stained, scored, and creaking with every movement, but it was better than being pressed between his sweaty bulk and the dirt wall.

Despite all the indignities, though, Idra really did enjoy reeving Pitta's husband quite literally beneath the windless Councilor's expensively shod feet.

"Pitta'll be gone in a few quarterns," Grehv said. "She's taking Handsome and Lurtair with her. We can use the house."

Idra rolled to face him. "Why? Where is she off to?"

"Ukur-Tilen. I think she's having that face fixed again." He sat up and picked at a toenail. "I told her some associates from my Norian venture were coming to town then, so she gave me a reprieve of sorts. I'm stuck with the imps, but Mara'll take care of them." He chuckled unpleasantly, like one of her old booth customers about to do something stupid.

"How long will Pitta be gone?" she asked.

"Well, me and the children'll be following along in few quarterns, so more'n a month. Until then…" He flicked toenail pickings onto the dirt floor and reached for her.

Idra swung off the bed and tugged on her clothes. "I have to discuss my Pukatown rally with Frung." She pulled on her boots. "Send a farspeaker when you know more about our arrangements for the Reapers Festival."

Grehv grabbed her around the waist and tugged her back onto the bed. "Just one more go. I'll make it fast."

She pulled away and stood facing him, hands on her hips. "You *have* talked to the Yenderot about the Reapers Festival, haven't you?"

He gave up any pretense of playfulness and flopped onto the bed. "Yeah, I've talked to Bikhark. He's sent the Harir a message."

"Good," Idra said. "What did he say?"

"Bikhark says the Harir's edgy about the whole election—your odds have improved, which might help—so he wants to see the plans before he agrees to the jig. And Bikhark can't take those plans back to the Refuge until the jig for your friend is done."

"W-what?"

"Huh? Bikhark told the Harir via farspeaker," Grehv said as though talking to an infant. "The Harir's interested, but Bikhark can't give him your diagrams and maps and all until he goes back to the Refuge of Kajasa. Right? And he can't go back until he's done the last raid for your friend. You catch?"

"Flark? You mean they're still doing Flark's last raid?"

"Yeah. I think this one's called the *Pohlit*."

Idra shook her head. "You didn't tell them the buyer was dead?" Grehv shrugged.

"So, who's receiving the boodle?"

"It's up to you, Idra. It goes through you."

Idra's eyelids fluttered. She was about to receive a whole shipment of Voshar antiquities fresh from the Tehtaemanian desert. As she had, Imythedralin and Daisy would assume the last raid had been cancelled. No one would challenge her ownership of the pieces, provided she didn't flaunt them.

"I'll see to it the deserving party receives everything." Idra pinched back a smile. "Contact me with news about the *Pohlit* or if the Harir gives you an answer about the Reapers Festival."

"Why should I?" He slid off the bed and pressed himself against her, soiling her outfit. "One more round and I guarantee you'll be the first one to know about the slightest whisper."

"When we have the run of the house, Grehv, I'll joggle you in every one of your wife's beds." Idra touched his nose with her fingertip. "But right now, I have to leave. I am still the Mayor, remember?"

ALIARA

Aliara was so pleased to be away from the flotilla of cavorting and debauchery that she almost skipped downstairs to breakfast. She'd even lingered in their bed after Syl rose, burrowing into the familiar sheets to watch the sun slowly rise over the sea. She'd missed the routine rhythms of life and the ease of regular clothes. The simplicity of a catsuit had never felt better.

Syl was in his office, eyes hard on the painting that hid his wall safe, familiar stone-inlaid aelde shadowbox in his hands. Had she known for certain Syl owned box 3443, Aliara could have saved Schmalch a trip to the Big Island. Even after Daisy revealed herself as the Toh's client, Aliara had still suspected Syl's involvement. At the very least, she guessed he had facilitated the contract. He'd been at war with Flark for months, but his more traditional methods had been tapped out, and Syl did not take well to being scaled. In Aliara's experience, no one stole from him without injury to their life or livelihood.

She slipped into his office, averting her eyes from the mask. Aliara had successfully avoided considering the one-eyed woman and her words since they'd returned home, though she'd been unable to eject the scene from her dreams.

Aliara put a hand on Syl's shoulder. He started and looked around as though woken.

"Oh, Pet. I didn't hear you." He set down the shadowbox,

coughed, and flipped over a stack of papers beside it. "An amazing piece. You have my gratitude for retrieving it."

"Are you keeping it?" She pointed to the mask.

"For the time being, yes. As you know, it's—"

"Where?"

"While I would like to hang it in here, I fear this piece is not for display. I intend to keep it in the bedroom safe."

Aliara shook her head. "Not if you want me in there too."

He frowned at her. "You usually enjoy odd pieces."

"I don't want it here."

He stroked hands down her arms. "It contains the only known viable bit of voshari spark. It must be kept from of Nihal's grasp."

The memory of Savesti carrying out fratricide in their parlor while Aliara slept above made her uncomfortable. She shuddered and glanced at the mask. Syl and his office disappeared, replaced by that bland room with the one-eyed woman.

"You're dead now," the woman said. "Do you want not to be?"

Aliara stumbled, bumping into Syl's desk as the world came back into focus. "Put it away," she hissed.

"Apologies, Pet." Syl crossed to the painting of Opoli's destruction. He swung it away, opened the safe, and deposited the mask inside. "It will not harry you again."

With a kiss and a muttered affection, she slipped out of the penthouse, taking her time strolling through Dockhaven's mid-morning bustle. Dreg had arrived at the contract house before her. He was busy regaling the gathered Toh with the story of being used for target practice.

"The boy loves his own voice," Luugrar said, gesturing toward Dreg. "Third time I've heard it."

Muddler, Bruclydian, and Bararre sat at the table with Dreg, laughing, ooing, and ahhing at just the right points. Dreg looked happier than a well-fed cat. Aliara didn't think she'd ever seen him genuinely smile before.

Luugrar dug in his drawer and produced a black leather bag, her payout clinking inside. Aliara took it, crossed to the table, and tossed the silver to Dreg.

"Double your price for the night, right?" she said, recalling Syl's promise after Daisy had shot the boy.

Dreg looked inside and smirked with pleasure. "Yeah, that's what your Duke said." He tucked the pouch into an interior pocket. "Grat."

"Sit down, Rift," Muddler said. "I want to hear your version of this jig because I *know* half of what this douse is telling us has to be a lie."

"In a bit," Aliara said. She dragged a chair back to Luugrar's desk with her.

"I was hoping you'd do something like that," the house manager said. "Making him a target, I mean, not giving him more coin. I don't know where he hordes it all. The boy needs to get past being a cocksure goon or take a hit that makes him think twice about sticking with this career. How'd he do?"

"Better than expected," Aliara said. She ticked points off on her fingers. "Nearly gutted by a gich , shot in the chest by a tippled toff, almost drowned by a dying propulsor."

Luugrar covered his mouth to hide the laugh.

"He did his part, albeit with plenty of griping. I'd work with him again."

The smile turned serious and pleased. "Good to know." Luugrar shifted his cheaters to the top of his head. "Did the Mayor really shoot Flark in the head?"

"Yes."

"Too bad for her a Dobencourt died in the process. I'd wager her odds would go up drastically if the voters knew how she'd dealt with Flark." He chuckled. "The Mayor."

"That's when I knew I was going to die," Dreg announced. "You should have seen how shaky Flark was with that pistol. At the very least, I thought he was going to shatter my hand."

Muddler, one eyebrow cocked, looked over to Aliara, who nodded.

"And the Mayor," Dreg continued, shaking his head, "who knew when she'd last held a buzzer?"

"Someday he'll realize there's a good chance this job'll make him dead whether he wants it to or not," Luugrar muttered.

"You're dead now." The winged woman, patch nailed over her eye, rose to the surface. Aliara closed her eyes, hoping the image would disappear. Instead, details like the berry-stain curls and the cup in her hand emerged. Aliara squeezed her eyes tighter. No, the hand *was* the cup. "Do you want not to be?"

"I want to live," Aliara murmured.

"Don't we all?" Luugrar asked.

Aliara opened her eyes.

He was watching her curiously. "Or is that your way of telling me you're quitting?"

"What do you know about Voshar death masks?"

EPILOGUE: **SYLANDAIR**

2086 INBAR 17

The clashing intervals of Burseer's *Midday Dream* moaned from the wheelharp, prickling in Syl's lower lug. He had not been fond of the instrument in his days as Orono's pupil, and over the years his appreciation had not improved. Nonetheless, Pitta Dobencourt had requested he play the ponderous device at her party. Though Syl had suggested a few other instruments, she had been stuck on the wheelharp. As he could find no tactful way to decline, Syl and the barrel-shaped contraption were now situated in the center of the mansion's atrium floor. Through the skylight, Dadeyah's nearly full face bathed him in green light. On the shadowed second story balcony, partygoers leaned on the balustrade and chatted with one another in subdued tones. Others milled in and out of the gallery, snatching morsels and caba from passing waitstaff. All of them knew the price of being obstreperous during one of Pitta's functions: ejection and exile from the heights of Dockhaven society.

Syl had not been invited to one of Pitta's parties until he had accepted control of the desalinization plant as part of Orono's bequest. A Vazztain duke slumming in the Rabbles had been one thing, easy for the Founding Families to ignore. One who owned the means to their drinking water was entirely another matter.

Pitta had shown up on Syl's doorstep only two days after the plant's transfer of authority was complete, pleasantly threatening him should he raise the city's rates. When he'd taken her on a tour of the run-down complex, including those sections left to ruin for decades, she'd been forced to agree that a moderate increase was justified, but only if he was willing to sign assurances regarding the repair or removal of the neglected towers. In addition, she had added the caveat that all would be void should he fail to also restore the Promenade, a one-time gathering place outside the plant used for concerts, picnics, and all manner of pleasant social outings. The breathtaking cliffside setting overlooking Lover's Sound had been spoiled far too long by Orono's shenanigans.

Syl adjusted position on the stool, working *Midday Dream* toward its crescendo. The song's torpid build had lulled his audience, subtly reaching an atonal peak that left everyone in the room on edge without understanding why. He doubted this was a piece Pitta had in mind when she had told him to be "whimsically mysterious" with his selections.

He enjoyed watching his audience's demeanor change as the song crept on, each chord progressively altered. One of the city councilors was scratching at the back of her neck. A man Syl had not yet met scowled at a planter of wispy white crane flowers while his companion chattered without drawing breath. A group that had just been laughing together was growing sullen. Across the room, Idra was picking at the ruching of her high collar.

Syl had forgotten how enjoyable performing music could be.

The piece reached its climax with a discordant caterwaul before veering into a brief and melodious end that tipped everyone back toward contentment. Burseer could not sing worth a plop and his face was difficult to look at, but he was a brilliant composer.

Syl rose, straightened his trousers and jacket, and bowed to Kaalyn, the minikin musician who was to be his replacement. She and her new velarin—the instrument had been replaced by Marthoth after being so shamefully destroyed aboard the *Ipesia*—hurried into the green moonlight and commenced a far more harmonious piece.

Syl snatched a glass of caba from a passing server's tray, two morsels from another as he strolled through the room. Every one of the Founding Families was represented among the guests, as were many of Dockhaven's more affluent capitalists. Idra and Daisy, fast friends since the yacht episode, stood chatting beside a glass case that held a mammoth printing press, early Reconstruction Era. Mintryl Marthoth lounged by one of the atrium's fireplaces, leaning so far over Lady Orilausko that the woman and her tight smile were nearly lost in his shadow.

Orilausko waved at Syl, and Marthoth looked up from his enjoyment of her cleavage to do the same. Syl returned the gesture, gave Her Ladyship a small bow, and strolled toward the Dobencourt's gallery, a two-story chamber dedicated to Pitta's most prized antiquities. He had just reached the door when a shadow slid into step with him.

"I didn't think you'd ever finish that terrible piece," Isnarin said, following Syl into the gallery. "You played it perfectly, of course, but Burseer? Do you dislike all these people so much?"

"Isnarin," Syl smiled. "I did not realize you and Pitta were friendly."

"Is anyone actually friendly with Pitta?" Isnarin asked, tipping his caba glass at the Councilor, who stood on the room's second-tier balcony, monopolizing conversation with her favored guests. "Grehv asked me. I've been pestering him for an invitation for months now, but I didn't find the right key until Marthoth's celebration."

The burly ex-raider was holding court by the grand fireplace, no doubt entertaining a group of Nesters with tales of life as a Yenderot. Though Syl could see the appeal of Grehv's roguish affability, he sometimes wondered if Pitta had married the man merely to entertain guests at her parties.

When Idra and Daisy joined the klatch, Grehv put a hand on the Mayor's back. She slapped it away like it was covered in maggots. Given their typically genial relationship, Syl attributed her abrupt dislike to the repelled raid on the *Pohlit* a few days previous. Whether she was annoyed because the Yenderot had not been called off or because the effort had failed, Syl couldn't be sure.

"Maybe *this* tidbit will be the right key to earn me an invitation to one your salons." Isnarin leaned closer and lowered his voice. "The contract on you came from the Dominion."

Syl stiffened. "Which duchy?"

"You won't like it." Isnarin smiled and waved casually at a woman across the room.

"Isay," Syl said.

"Correct."

Syl's jaw tightened. "Who?"

"Chella's kept her lips tight. The only reason she shared that much was that she finds it amusing." Isnarin raised hands in supplication when Syl snarled. "Her, not me."

Syl finished his caba, dropped the empty on a passing server's tray, and snatched a fresh glass. "What else?"

"No one reliable has accepted the contract…yet."

"Forgive the intrusion," a mild, male voice said.

Syl and Isnarin separated.

A sharp-faced man, smallish with dark-purple eyes and a tightly reserved demeanor, approached them. "Might I borrow Isnarin?"

"Certainly, Mister…"

The man looked like he had sucked citrus fruit. "Menelow."

Syl knew at least a dozen Menelows in Dockhaven alone, but he could not recall this face. Nonetheless, he smiled. "Of course, Mister Menelow. Apologies. My memory fails me on occasion."

Menelow released a quiet grumble and tugged Isnarin's sleeve.

"I'll be looking for that invitation," Isnarin said over his shoulder. He winked at Syl. "I prefer resin sculptors and poets."

Syl watched them go. There were many potential enemies in the Dominion of Chiva'vastezz. Few of Isay's lords and ladies had been thrilled to learn a phao had been appointed as their duke. As he strolled through the Dobencourt's two-story gallery, he considered the most vocal among the courtiers as well as those whom he'd given the greatest motives, the Empress herself included.

Books, maps, and historical documents lined the walls of the ground floor of Pitta's gallery. Most were bound, though a few shelves held baskets of loose and rolled pages. The artifacts were kept on the second story, Pitta's newest Voshar acquisitions prominently displayed. A handful of guests funneled along the narrow balcony circling the octagonal room.

Syl had been in this gallery only once before, and then his hostess had rushed his enjoyment of the collection. This evening Pitta flitted between her visitors, chatting and flaunting, occasionally selecting an object from the wall to display and discuss. He hoped she remained busy with others for a piece while he enjoyed the relics sans her unwanted guidance.

"You cannot imagine how glad I am to escape that man."

A dainty grey arm looped through Syl's, and he looked down into the near-flawless face of Lady Orilausko, so well-groomed she looked like a doll no child was allowed to enjoy. Her black hair was knotted at the nape of her neck, mouth a perfect bow of rich grey, and the elegant vines of ink marking her as a one-time Seer brazenly displayed on her exposed arms, neck, and upper back. She had once disclosed the meaning of a handful of the pictograms woven into the vines, but Syl had long-since forgotten them.

"Marthoth's been badgering me all evening. He desperately wants to hire me to assist him in…" Her little grey tongue darted out, moistening her lips. "He wants me to influence Pitta into revealing information. He thinks her new acquisitions were cargo aboard the *Fayrill* and the *Nimomyne*. Thus far, she's kept mum on the subject. I tried to persuade Mintryl otherwise, but he's so convinced that even my skills do nothing to dissuade him. He is not a man I relish disappointing, but I have no intention of joining him."

Syl nodded, leading her toward the staircase. "Pitta is not to be crossed."

"Don't I know it." She climbed alongside him. "I once arrived wearing the same color dress as her, and she spent the next month doing everything in her power to slow business at the Caba Club."

"Did she?"

"Quite effectively. The Club was closed for a whole quartern while city engineers examined its structural stability."

Syl followed Orilausko onto the balcony. The artifacts housed there were lit with individual spotlights, the spaces in between disappearing into darkness, making the ancient items appear to float. Unlike most collectors, who chose decorative antiques, Pitta preferred the more practical trappings of daily life. It was possibly the most interesting facet of her personality.

"I told Marthoth I'd promised to view Pitta's relics with you." Orilausko giggled, a more pleasant melody than anything Syl had played this evening. "He says I'm to consider his rather generous offer while we do so. No matter how much coin he offers, I can't help him. I don't understand why Mintryl is so convinced he can change that by increasing the amount."

"It is the instrument he understands." Syl crouched to study the set of Innovation Era dental tools.

"Goodness, those look horrifying." Without pausing to breathe, Orilausko switched subjects. "Has Isay remained free of raiders since that first attack?"

His crouch unbalanced by surprise, Syl rose and sipped his caba, gathering his wits. The woman had a gift for unnerving non sequiturs. "They have not returned."

"How much damage did they do?" she asked. "Oh! Look at that set of pie tins—Pitta's added those since I was last here."

"The raiders stole most of this season's seed, though I've replaced it. Lives were lost, but fewer than I would have anticipated. The worst sting was that they absconded with my harbor flag." Syl chuckled at his own folly.

Orilausko studied him. "That seems awfully personal. Have you done anything to gam off the...? What were they Suul? Yenderot? Surely not Bankal so far west."

"Commander Ortan has deemed them Suul."

"You're dubious."

"I am suspicious of every pearl that falls from that man's maw."

She slapped his arm playfully. "He's the commander of *your* guard. If you don't trust him, replace him. Behead him if he won't go away. It's your right as Duke."

Syl made a noncommittal noise. Having not been raised in the Dominion of Chiva'vastezz, he found the custom impractical. Bringing an enemy to the block made a fabulous show—during his first session of court Syl had seen his own predecessor decapitated— but to his mind, a beheading was messy and removed the subject's potential future usefulness. He preferred to reserve such tactics for hopeless individuals like Flark.

"Speaking of executions, I heard Duchess Vernuu has lost yet another of her husbands," Orilausko said.

"Poison again?"

"So my resource tells me. Vernuu was out of Vinex when he died. Again."

"She is a clever one."

"Anyone who marries or even courts her should keep a sniffer on hand at all times."

Syl chuckled. He paused by Pitta's newest display. Arranged on shelves and hanging from walls were more Voshar originals than Syl had previously seen in one place. A bone-handled saber caught his eye. Carved details highlighted with colorful enamel, it would almost perfectly fit his hand.

"Though Marthoth insists they're all pieces from the *Nimomyne*, even he isn't foolish enough to challenge the Dobencourts' rights of ownership." Orilausko nodded to a belt, hand-beaded in black and brilliant red. "I have a dress that would look divine with. The torque as well." She indicated a silver band broad enough to fit a karju bicep.

"Not for the neck, but cuffs worn on their upper legs," said the cultured voice of Councilor Pitta Dobencourt. "I believe the rhochrot sometimes wear similar—if notably larger—decoration."

"I've seen them before," Syl said, "but never in such good condition."

"Astonishing, isn't it?" Pitta leaned over to brush ears with Orilausko. Today, her suit was entirely cichlid-yellow. Even the shoes matched. "Have you heard? They're diving for Gasole? That will be my next conquest." She smiled as though the entirety of the discovery were hers.

Syl doubted Pitta had an agent inside the dive as he did. Haus was stationed there, waiting and working in the middle of the Castling Sea. Should the researchers locate the drowned city and its lost terminus, he would be there, ready to protect any find from Nihal Savesti.

"They're not really searching for Gasole, though, are they?" Orilausko asked.

"Yes, yes, the lost terminus." Pitta dismissed it with a flick of her wrist. "If they locate that, they can't help but find the city. The project is a cooperative venture between Queen's College and the Mucha Colleges. Both are always happy to accept my supportive funding in exchange for a few considerations." Bored by the subject, Pitta retrieved a bronze bowl from the display. "Have you seen this one? I'm particularly fond of it."

"It's lovely," Orilausko said.

"May I hold it?" Syl asked, passing his caba to Orilausko.

Pitta's face revealed her lengthy internal debate before she offered it to him. "Be gentle. The tone is superb. Dropping it would…"

"Seriously diminish its value, yes," Syl said. "I will use all due caution."

He raised the bowl to eye level and adjusted position for better light. Etched into the delicate metal, four-legged voshari chased a thick-tailed lizard, all of them inlaid with copper. Black serendibite chips replaced each creature's eyes. Flecks of red and green enamel clung to the surface in a familiar pattern. The bowl appeared identical to the one Aliara had pilfered from Flark's home, the one he'd sent to Wuuk's for authentication a few days past. Syl turned it on end, studying the sequence of circles on its base. He could not be certain this historiated bowl was identical to his, but it certainly appeared so.

"They are all unique, correct?" he asked Pitta.

"Yes. The scholars say making the bowl was a rite of passage. Supposedly each one portrays a critical episode from the maker's life." Another flip of her hand and the subject was dismissed. She tapped the bone-handled blade Syl had admired earlier. "This saber, though, is exclusively for dueling. Each voshari had their own. Maybe more than one. They did all have four hands, after all."

"Excuse my churlishness, Pitta," Syl said, still studying the bowl nestled in his palm. "You have had this authenticated?"

She nodded, though her perfectly coiffed white-blonde hair did not move. "By Master Kuruun herself. I offered to cover some of her losses aboard the *Ipesia,* and in exchange she agreed to authenticate my items before returning to Ukur-Tilen."

"Would you mind if I played it?"

Pitta's painted mouth puckered and shifted across her face. "I suppose not. I haven't heard it played since I acquired it, and you *are* a musician."

Syl dipped two fingers into his caba and ran them gently around the narrow lip of the bowl. A sweet, rich tone built, rising and falling with each twitch of his hand. Fundamentally, the note was identical to the one produced by his bowl, yet this one possessed an additional third and fourth overtone. Syl knew what his authenticator would say: Someone was forging artifacts.

Wordlessly, Syl returned the bowl to Pitta, who launched into a history of a set of boots, their toe boxes unusually wide. Orilausko patted his arm, her eyes turned down with concern. Syl smiled and shook his head. Pitta never faltered in her recitation.

Syl had no doubt the death mask stowed in his safe was authentic. It had shown him Omatha. Forgeries would hardly exhibit such mystical effects. But was there already a counterfeit mask in circulation? If not, might there be? For sufficient coin, a forger talented enough to reproduce the delicate and detailed bowl might be persuaded to copy such a singular piece.

"Duke Imythedralin?" Pitta asked.

Syl shook his head and refreshed his smile. "Apologies, Pitta. I was considering a lovely gift for a friend."

Gratitude for reading

If you enjoyed *They Eat Their Own*, **please leave us a review**. Your efforts do so much to help indie authors and keep us writing.

Visit ismae.com and sign up for our email list and enjoy bonus Ismae short fiction and concept art.

ACKNOWLEDGEMENTS

Our gratitude to everyone who helped us out in one way or another on this project: Eric Williams, Christopher Bennem & Lisa Moore (and Glen Hollow FLX), Todd Nelson, Corrie Jagger, Michael B. Fee, The Fenter Tribe, David & Jackie Boston, George Culbreth, Sam Cooke, and Steve Caldwell. You've kept us inspired and moving forward during a very chaotic year.

Our love and gratitude to our families, who have supported us through this and so much more: Will and Ellen King, Roland and Diane Swanson, Jeffrey and Sarah Swanson.

www.ingramcontent.com/pod-product-compliance
Lightning Source LLC
Chambersburg PA
CBHW031646100726
47898CB00006B/2003